K.G. LEWIS

This book is dedicated to Melissa.
Your insight will be sorely missed.

CONTENTS

MR. MERRY MAW'S HOUSE OF MADNESS

I reached into my pocket and withdrew a slightly crumbled carnival ticket.

"Alright, Chase," I said to my ten-year-old son, "It looks like you've only got one ticket left." I held it out to him.

Chase was staying with me for the weekend like he did every weekend. That was the custody agreement I had with his mother, my ex-wife.

"I don't think there's anything I can ride for one ticket," Chase said, taking the offered ticket and looking around at all the rides in the area where we were.

"We can walk around the fairgrounds one more time," I said, "But if you don't find anything to use that ticket on, it's time to go."

"Okay," Chase agreed.

We walked around for a few minutes, passing several thrill rides, all of which had long lines of kids waiting to ride them. I was glad Chase didn't have enough tickets for any of them otherwise I'd be stuck at the fair for another hour while he waited in line for his opportunity to ride.

"How come all of these rides are so expensive?" Chase asked as we passed one called the Cyclops. He watched the ride's pendulum swing a bunch of screaming kids back and forth, higher and higher into the air with each pass.

The ride cost 4 tickets. None of the thrill rides were cheaper than that.

"Because they're popular," I replied, "They know they can charge more for them and people will pay it."

"That's a ripoff," he realized, "That means you can only ride 5 rides for $20. It would've been cheaper to go to Six Flags. We could've ridden as many rides as we wanted."

Chase loved going to Six Flags. I did not. It was a two-hour drive to get there, and he'd want to stay from opening to close. That was a bit much for me, which is why I usually only took him there for his birthday.

We continued walking for a few more minutes until I saw a sign for a ride that said it only cost 1 ticket.

"What about that one?" I pointed at the ride that featured a bunch of boats going around in a circle, bumping up and down as they went.

"That's a baby ride," Chase sneered.

"I think that's the only kind of ride here that costs one ticket," I said.

Knowing his time to find a ride to spend the ticket on was running out, Chase scanned the collection of carnival rides and booths in our immediate vicinity.

"What about that one?" he suddenly declared, pointing at something in the distance.

Before I could figure out what Chase was pointing at, he hurried off across the fairgrounds, weaving around people as he raced to get to whatever carnival attraction he'd seen.

"Wait for me," I called out, trying to get him to slow down, but he just kept on hurrying through the crowd until he'd arrived at his destination.

When I caught up to him, he was standing in front of a dimly lit funhouse called Mr. Merry Maw's House of Madness.

"That only costs one ticket," he pointed at the garishly dressed clown who was holding a sign that showed the number one with the word ticket beneath it.

The clown was standing next to the entrance of the attraction, which was an enormous cartoonish clown head with its mouth wide open and tongue sticking out.

When the clown saw Chase pointing in his direction, he waved his hand and beckoned for him to enter the ride.

"Are you sure you want to go in there?" I asked, "It looks kind of scary."

I was afraid the attraction might have something inside of it that would frighten him. He was easily scared and I didn't want him to have nightmares. His mother would never let me hear the end of it if that happened.

"It doesn't look scary to me," Chase said, looking at me like I had said something stupid.

"Okay then, if you're sure, go ahead," I replied, "I'll wait for you out here." I wasn't going to press the issue with him. I was ready to leave and thought the sooner he went in, the sooner he'd be out.

Chase ran over to the entrance and handed the clown his ticket. Before he walked up the tongue and into the mouth of the enormous clown head, he turned back and waved at me with a big smile on his face. I waved back and then stood there watching him until he disappeared inside the funhouse.

Since I didn't know how long he was going to be inside, I decided to wait for him on a nearby bench.

I can't wait to get home, I thought, easing myself down onto the bench.

We'd been at the fair for over four hours and must've walked back and forth across the midway a dozen times. I was tired and looking forward to taking a nice hot shower.

I looked away from Mr. Merry Maw's House of Madness for only a moment while I checked the time on my phone. When I looked back up, I was shocked to find that the funhouse was no longer there. The place where it stood was now an empty lot filled with carnival trash.

What the hell!

I shot to my feet and looked around, wondering if I had somehow gotten turned around, but I hadn't. I was certain that Mr. Merry Maw's House of Madness was sitting between the funnel cake truck and the ring toss booth, and both of those things were still where they were supposed to be.

I hurried over to the funnel cake truck and stood at the window.

"Excuse me," I said to the woman taking orders.

"What can I get you, Hun?" she asked with a thick Southern accent.

"The funhouse that was next to you," I asked, "Where did it go?"

She looked over at the empty lot and then back at me, eyeing me like I was a crazy person.

"What funhouse would that be?" she replied.

"The one with the big clown head that was here two minutes ago," I gestured at the empty lot beside her truck, "You had to have seen it," I insisted.

"I think you might be confused, Hun," she said, "That lot's been empty since I got here, and the only funhouse that I know about is the one on the other side of the fairgrounds." She pointed off into the distance behind me.

"I'm not confused," I said, raising my voice in frustration, "It was right there." I jabbed my finger in the direction of the lot.

"I don't know what to tell you." She turned her back to me, letting me know that the conversation was over.

Seeing that his coworker was annoyed with me, the burly man that was in the back of the truck making the funnel cakes turned and glared at me. "Is there a problem?" he asked. The question was directed at the woman, but he was looking at me.

"No," I said, "No problem." I could feel his eyes boring into the back of my head as I turned and walked away.

I stopped in the center of the empty lot, looking around for any sign the funhouse was there but all I saw were weeds and trash. From what I could tell, it looked like nothing had been in the lot for quite some time. If something had been there, the weeds and trash would have been flattened into the ground.

This doesn't make any sense.

I walked over to the ring toss booth that was on the opposite side of the empty lot from the funnel cake truck.

"Ready to play a game?" the carnival employee manning the booth asked while twirling one of the rings around his finger, "One dollar gets you 3 rings…"

"I don't want to play," I snapped at him a little more forcefully than I had intended.

The smile dropped from the young man's face.

"I'm sorry," I apologized, "I'm looking for my son and was hoping you might've seen him."

I described Chase to the carnival worker and then ended by saying, "The last time I saw him, he was walking into the funhouse that was set up next to you." I jerked my thumb over my shoulder at the empty lot.

"I think you might've gotten turned around," the young man replied, "The funhouse is on the other side of the fairgrounds." He pointed behind me, just like the lady in the funnel truck had.

I knew the funhouse they were talking about and that's not the one Chase had gone into. He had gone into one that looked like a giant clown's head and was called Mr. Merry Maw's House of Madness, the one across the fairgrounds was designed to look like a haunted house and was simply called The Fun House.

Not knowing what else to do, I started asking people who were walking by if they'd seen my son or the funhouse. Nobody had seen either, which made me more frantic in my search.

"Is there something I can help you with, sir?"

I turned around and found a uniformed police officer standing behind me. His hands resting on his service belt.

"Yeah," I replied, "I'm looking for my son."

The officer proceeded to ask me all the questions you'd expect to be asked in that situation. How old is your son? What was he wearing? Where did you last see him?

I answered all the officer's questions, leaving out the part about Chase going into Mr. Merry Maw's House of Madness. Since nobody else but me had seen the funhouse, I figured if I mentioned it, the officer would think I was crazy. Instead, I told him that I went to sit on a bench while my son was looking for something to spend his last ticket on and that when I looked back, he was gone.

The officer escorted me to the front of the fairgrounds while he reported my missing son to the other officers on duty.

"Do you have a picture of him you can send us?" one of the officers asked while holding up his phone.

"Yeah," I said, pulling out my own phone and opening the photo app. I'd taken several photos of him while we were at the carnival to share with his mother.

"That's weird," I muttered to myself when I saw that all the pictures I'd taken of Chase were missing. "I'm sorry. I thought I had one, but I guess I don't," I apologized to the officer as I scrolled through all the photos saved on my phone.

"If you can track one down it'd be mighty helpful," the officer replied.

"I'll see what I can do."

When the officers dispersed to start searching for my son, I tried to go with them, but they told me to stay at the entrance in case Chase came looking for me.

***

"Is there any chance your son could've found his way home on his own?" the original officer I talked to asked.

The carnival had closed thirty minutes earlier without them being able to find any sign of Chase.

"It's possible," I said, "But I don't see why he'd walk all the way home without me." It was a ridiculous idea, but I wasn't going to insult the cop by telling him that.

"Kids can surprise you sometimes," was his reply.

"Chase would never do something like that," I insisted.

"Be that as it may, there's nothing else you can do here," he said, "My advice is for you to go home and wait and see if he shows up there. Maybe call a few of his friends to see if any of them have seen him. In the meantime, we'll keep searching the area…If he turns up, you'll be the first to know."

"Okay," I reluctantly agreed before walking across the parking lot to my car.

On the drive home, I started rehearsing how I was going to tell Chase's mother that our son had vanished right before my eyes.

When I finally did call her, the conversation was far stranger than anything I'd imagined.

"Are you on drugs?" she asked, "We don't have a son."

I was floored by her comment. I'd told her that I took Chase to the carnival and that I'd lost him, and that was her reply.

"Seriously?" that was the only way I could think to respond.

"I think I'd remember pushing another living being out of my body," she said.

"You really don't remember him?" I couldn't believe that.

"I think you might want to go to the doctor and get your head checked," she suggested, "And stop calling me, we're divorced." She hung up the phone after that.

After talking to her, I walked across the house and went into Chase's room. The room was completely empty.

What the hell is going on?

***

The next morning, after trying to get some sleep and failing miserably, I called in to work and told them I was sick so I could take the day off and drive over to the fairgrounds.

When I pulled into the parking lot, I expected the police to still be there looking for my son, but there was nobody there.

Where did they go?

I parked and took out the card the officer had given me the previous night and called the number on it.

"I was just about to call you, Mr. Howell," the officer said.

"Did you find him?" I asked, fearing the worst but hoping for the best.

"You and I know both know there's nobody to find," the officer said.

"We do?"

"You don't have a son, Mr. Howell," he continued, "We have video footage of you arriving at the carnival alone as well as video of you walking the midway by yourself."

"You do?" That was a surprise to me. Chase was by my side the entire night.

"I don't know what your deal is, Mr. Howell, but I'm going to give you some friendly advice," the officer said, "Get some help. Seriously, because I'm going to arrest you if anything like this happens again."

I didn't know how to respond to that, so I remained silent.

"Do you understand, Mr. Howell?" the officer asked.

"Yes," I answered, "I understand."

"Good." He hung up the phone.

What am I supposed to do now?

I stared across the parking lot at the carnival, watching the workers go about their business, getting everything ready for the crowds of people that would show up in a few hours.

Where are you, Chase?

I don't care what anyone else said or what kind of evidence they had. My son was real. If nobody else was going to help me find him, I would just have to find him on my own.

I saw Chase hand his ticket to the clown and walk into Mr. Merry Maw's House of Madness. Since that was the last time I saw him, that was where I needed to start my search.

I have to find that funhouse.

I didn't know how I was going to do that. I just knew that if I found it, I'd find Chase.

***

While sitting there in the parking, I called my boss and told him I had an emergency come up and I needed to take the rest of the week off. He reluctantly agreed.

From that day on, I went to the carnival and wandered the midway from the time it opened to the time it closed, hoping the funhouse would reappear in one of the empty lots, but it never did.

When the carnival started packing up to travel to its next destination, I quit my job and decided to follow it. So, that's what I did, month after month until I blew through what little money I had left.

The funhouse never returned, but I still had hope that it might one day reappear.

Broke and unable to afford to follow the carnival any longer, I did the only thing I could: I got a job with them as a maintenance man.

It worked out well for me since all I had to do was help set things up, help tear them down, and fix anything that broke down. That gave me lots of free time to keep my eye out for the funhouse should it reappear.

***

"Has it been a year already?" I stood at the end of the familiar fairgrounds, watching the carnival trucks pull into position so we could start unloading them.

It felt strange being back in my hometown where everything started.

"Hey, Montgomery!" the owner of the carnival yelled as he approached me, "Are you planning on working or are you just going to stand there all day?"

I hadn't realized how long I'd been staring until I heard him call out my name.

"Sorry," I apologized, "It just feels weird being back here."

That was the truth. Coming home had caused a bunch of re-pressed feelings to resurface. Even though I'd only been gone for a year, it felt much longer.

"You from around here?" the carnival owner asked.

"I am," I nodded.

"Got any friends or family in the area?" he asked, "I could comp you some tickets to give them."

"Nobody I'd want to talk to," I replied, thinking about my ex-wife and how the only friends I had were the ones I made while I was married to her and they stopped talking to me after the divorce.

"I know the feeling," he smiled at me, "Come find me if you change your mind," he added before turning and walking away.

"Do you think I can have the night off?" I called out before he'd gotten too far away.

Mr. Merry Maw's House of Madness had disappeared on the carnival's opening night the previous year. Maybe it would return on opening night this year. If it were remotely possible it could, I didn't want to risk missing it by being stuck somewhere else on the fairgrounds. It was wishful thinking on my part, but it was that kind of thought that kept me from giving up hope.

The carnival owner turned around and looked at me with his hands on hips, "It's opening night," he said, "I need all hands on deck. You know if this shit is going to break down it usually does so on the first night or two." He swept his arm, indicating all the rides that were being unloaded.

"I understand," I said. I was disappointed, but he was right.

"The best I can do is put you on standby," he offered.

"That works," I said.

Being on standby meant I wouldn't be the first maintenance man called to troubleshoot any problems that arose. I would only be needed if the other maintenance man was busy. If we were lucky, everything would go smoothly, and we'd have a perfect opening night without any problems, which would essentially give me the night off I'd asked for. It didn't happen very often, but it did happen, so I was hopeful.

I went to work helping to set up the rides, double and triple checking everything, even on the rides I didn't set up, to reduce the likelihood of problems later that night.

****

It was eight o'clock when I approached the bench that I'd sat on the night Chase entered Mr. Merry Maw's House of Madness. As I sat down, I noticed that my hands were trembling.

"This is it," I mumbled to myself.

I had decided that it was time to stop searching for my son. A year was long enough. If Chase didn't show up, I was going to have to face the reality that he was never coming back.

The empty lot was still there, but it was no longer flanked by the funnel cake truck and the ring toss booth. This time there was a lemonade stand to the right of it and a merry-go-round to the left.

I sat there for two hours watching the merry-go-round spin round and round, thinking about how much Chase used to love riding rides like that when he was little. He preferred the ones that had more than just horses, so he could pretend that he was riding an ostrich or a tiger, or whatever odd animal was available.

I got so lost in the memory that I drifted off to sleep.

Someone nudged me, disrupting the memory turned dream I was having about Chase.

I opened my eyes and turned my head to see who had woken me up. I was not expecting it to be a clown. And it wasn't just any clown. It was the clown who was standing outside Mr. Merry Maw's House of Madness the night Chase disappeared.

The clown smiled at me.

"Did you enjoy the experience?" he asked.

"What?" I was confused by his question. I had no idea what experience he was talking about.

He gestured across the walkway at the funhouse that had reappeared, filling up the empty lot. "Did you enjoy the experience?" he repeated.

Before I could figure out what he was talking about, I heard a familiar voice call out.

"Can I get a corn dog before we go?" Chase asked as he jogged up to me, "I'm really hungry."

"Chase?" I jumped up from the bench and grabbed him, wanting to make sure he was real.

He looked up at me, confused.

"You okay, Dad?" he asked.

"I am now." I pulled him into a hug as my eyes teared up.

That's when I noticed that the carnival had changed while I was asleep. Everything had reverted to how it was the night Chase went into the funhouse.

The Clown!

His question suddenly made sense to me.

All of the things that had happened to me since Chase had gone into the funhouse were products of the attraction. The entire year I spent searching for him, everything I lost, that was the experience the clown was referring to. I was the one who was really trapped inside Mr. Merry Maw's House of Madness.

When I looked back at the bench, searching for the clown, I wasn't surprised to see that he was no longer sitting there. It's a good thing he wasn't, as mad as I was at having been put through that hellish experience, I probably would've strangled him if he were.

"So?" Chased asked, "Can I get that corn dog?"

"You can get whatever you want," I smiled at him, "But if you ever want to come back to the carnival, you're going to have to ask your mother to take you."

MEET THE PARENTS

Fletcher pressed the doorbell and stepped back, straightening his clothing before correcting his posture so that he was standing up straight. He was supposed to be meeting Julie's parents and wanted to make a good impression.

When Julie answered the door instead of one of her parents, he relaxed a little.

"Did you find the place okay?" she asked.

"I did," he replied, "And I'm sorry that I'm late. I wasn't expecting all those twists and turns getting up here. I had to drive a lot slower than I'd anticipated." He was referring to the winding roads that weaved through the hills on the way to her house.

Fletcher assumed he'd be able to get to the house by 8 p.m. but had arrived fifteen minutes later than that.

"It's okay," Julie said, "With it being your first time out here, I figured you wouldn't make it on time." She stepped back and held the door open so he could enter the house.

"Wow!" he said as Julie closed the door behind him.

He was looking around the spacious foyer and admiring all of the expensive-looking antiques on display. "This place looks like a museum."

"My parents treat it like a museum," Julie sighed, recalling what it was like growing up in a house full of expensive one-of-a-kind decorations.

"Where are they? I'm looking forward to meeting them." Fletcher was surprised her parents hadn't already shown up to greet him.

"Really?" Julie sounded surprised, "I figured you'd be nervous considering they haven't liked a single man I've brought home." A fact she'd already warned Fletcher about.

"What's there to be nervous about? I'm not like those other guys," Fletcher smiled, "Honesty, it doesn't matter if they like me or not. It won't change how I feel about you." Fletcher leaned forward and planted a kiss on Julie's lips.

"It matters to me though," she pulled away, "I really want them to like you."

"I know." He took her hand in his, "I'll do my best to make a good impression."

"You better," she asserted, pulling him through a set of double doors and into a large sitting room filled with vintage furniture and a fireplace large enough for a person to stand in.

Above the fireplace was a large portrait of a middle-aged man and woman. The man was standing behind and slightly off to the side of the woman with his arm around her waist. They were both smiling.

"Is that your parents?" Fletcher pointed at the couple in the painting.

"That's them," Julie confirmed.

"They don't look that scary," Fletcher joked.

"That's because you don't know them," she warned, "Looks can be deceiving."

He couldn't tell if Julie was being sarcastic or not, so he kept his mouth shut. He was doing his best to remain positive, while she was doing her best to make him feel nervous.

"I'm going to go get something to drink," she gestured toward the door, "Do you want anything?"

"I'll have whatever you're having," he replied as he walked over to the couch and sat down.

Once Julie left the room, Fletcher pulled his phone out of his pocket and opened the messenger app. He had one unread message from Tina.

Tina was the other girl he was seeing.

Tina: Where are you???

Shit! Fletcher thought.

When Julie asked him to come over, he'd forgotten that he already made plans to see Tina. He'd been juggling the two girls for months and this was the first time he'd made a scheduling mistake like that.

He quickly typed out a reply.

Fletcher: Sorry something came up

When he saw the ellipsis indicating that Tina was writing a response. He sent her another text before she could finish.

Fletcher: Can't talk right now I will explain later

He added a kissy face emoji before sending it to her.

A minute later, Tina replied.

Tina: You better!!!

Fletcher: I will

Just as soon as I think of a believable excuse.

"What happened?" Julie snapped.

She was standing in the doorway, holding two cans of soda, one in each hand. What concerned Fletcher was the scowl on her face. She was clearly mad about something, but he had no idea why.

"Nothing," Fletcher replied, feigning innocence. "I was just sitting here, messing around on my phone, waiting for you to get back." He wiggled the device before sliding it back into his pocket.

Did Julie see me texting Tina? he worried. He didn't see how she could've, though. He was already done by the time she'd returned.

"Well, something happened," Julie insisted.

"I-I-I was just sitting here," Fletcher stammered, "I don't know what else to tell you?"

Julie walked over to the couch and set the sodas on the nearest table. "You can start by telling me why my parents look so upset!" She jabbed her finger toward the painting above the fireplace."

"What?" He looked up at the painting, confused. What Julie had said didn't make any sense. "I haven't seen…" He was about to say he hadn't seen her parents, but he couldn't finish what he was going to say when he noticed that the painting of her parents had changed.

Julie's mother and father were no longer smiling. They were now standing side by side with their arms folded across their chests, looking directly at Fletcher with scowls on their faces.

This has to be some kind of joke, he thought.

"How'd you do that?" he pointed at the painting, a smirk pulling at the corner of his lip. "Is it some sort of computer screen?" He'd seen something similar at a theme park haunted house.

"This isn't a joke," Julie snapped at him, "They are not happy with you." She looked up at the painting again as she spoke. "Oh shit," she hissed suddenly, noticing the painting had changed again.

Fletcher followed Julie's gaze, taking note of the knife that was now clutched in her father's hand.

"You need to leave right now." Julie pulled Fletcher off the couch by his arm and started pushing him towards the door.

"This is fucked up," Fletcher huffed, finally getting annoyed. "This isn't funny."

"I already told you this isn't a joke," Julie insisted, "Now leave before you get hurt." She pushed him toward the door again to emphasize her point.

Fletcher shrugged away from her before she could push him again.

"I'm going," he spat at her, "And once I'm gone, we're through, you crazy bitch."

He meant it. He didn't have the time or patience to put up with a psycho.

Julie looked back at the painting and saw that her father was no longer pictured in it. "Well, you're not going fast enough," she said to him.

Fletcher stormed over to the front door, threw it open door, and stepped out onto the porch. But he wasn't content enough to let her have the last word. He whirled around and yelled, "Fuck you and your crazy ass family too."

Those were the last words he ever said because it wasn't Julie that was standing behind him in the doorway. It was her father, looking exactly like he did in the painting. Fletcher didn't make a sound as the knife plunged into his chest.

He fell backward with a stupid look of surprise on his face.

***

"I really thought you were the one," Julie said later as she was dragging Fletcher's body across the yard to bury it in the garden with the bodies of the other men her parents hadn't approved of.

SURVEILLANCE

My phone began to rhythmically chime and buzz, startling me awake. I picked it up from the nightstand and had to wait for my eyes to adjust to the brightness of the screen before I could figure out why it was making all that racket.

Two words, written in flashing red letters, scrolled across the screen of my phone: INTRUDER ALERT, INTRUDER ALERT, INTRUDER ALERT…

The phone continued to vibrate and chime in my hand.

I jumped out of bed.

This is really happening!

"What's going on?" my wife, Elodie, mumbled from the other side of the bed.

The phone had woken her up too.

"Someone's trying to break into the house." I whispered while showing her the message flashing on the screen of my phone.

"What?" She propped herself up on her elbow and stared at me, "Why aren't you calling the police?"

"We signed a contract, remember?"

Shortly after we moved into the neighborhood, Elodie and I were approached by a new home security company asking us if we'd be willing to help them test one of their new security systems. If we did, they'd pay us $100,000 and we only had to use the system for a year.

It seemed like easy money, so we agreed.

"If we want that money…" As I spoke, I opened the drawer in my nightstand, searching for the card the security company had given us, "…we have to follow the protocols they gave us."

Once I found the laminated card, I pulled it out and examined it. On the back of it was the company's logo, Chimera Systems, along with their phone number. On the front was a magnetic strip with the following instructions: In the event of an intruder alert, proceed to the safe room.

Below that was a series of numbers: 3733366

"Let's go," I said to Elodie, carrying the card over to the swipe pad that had been mounted on the bedroom wall. "This better work," I said as I slid the card through the pad.

I said that because the first time I tried to use the card, which was the day after they'd installed the system, it didn't work. When I contacted Chimera Systems customer support line, I was told that the swipe pad only works when there is an active *Intruder Alert*.

I argued with them about how stupid that was, and they responded by reminding me that I had signed a contract to abide by the system's parameters and that if I no longer wished to do that, they would gladly remove it and find somebody else that would.

Not wanting to lose out on that $100,000 payday, I quickly shut my mouth.

There was a little red light on the swipe pad. As soon as I swiped the card through it, there was a beep, and then the light turned green. As soon as that happened, the door to the safe room, which was made to look like part of the bedroom wall, popped open.

After the door swung open, a signal must've been sent to my phone because it stopped broadcasting the intruder alert.

The absence of the alarm made the room eerily quiet all of a sudden.

I motioned for Elodie to enter the safe room before me and then followed her, shutting the door behind me.

I was assured by the security company that the likely hood of an intruder finding the hidden door was slim, but if they did, there was little they could do to open it.

"What's all this?" Elodie motioned at the bank of monitors on the wall of the safe room. Each one showing a live video feed of a different room in our home. "Did you know they put cameras in the house?"

"No, I didn't," I replied.

And I wasn't concerned about that at the moment. I was more concerned with the three men I saw pictured in the bottom right screen.

"That's the basement, right?" I pointed at the monitor.

"Looks like it," Elodie agreed.

The three men must have come in through the bulkhead door on the side of the house.

"What's up with that guy?" Elodie leaned in close to the monitor showing the basement.

Two of the three guys were on the basement stairs, making their way up to the kitchen while the third guy was just standing there in the corner of the room staring up at the camera with a smirk on his face.

"There's something different about him." I leaned in next to her so I could see better.

"It looks like he's wearing a robe," Elodie said.

She wasn't referring to a bathrobe, she was talking about the kind of robe monks would wear.

The two guys, who had made their way into the kitchen, were wearing hoodies and jeans.

My phone rang, causing Elodie to jump back and yelp.

"Jesus Christ," she hissed, "That scared the shit out of me."

"It's the security company." I showed her the caller ID displaying the identity.

"Answer it," Elodie urged.

"Hello," I said, after swiping my finger across the screen to accept the call.

"Hello, Mr. Hale. My name is Brian, I'm a support agent with Chimera Systems. I'm calling you because your intruder alert system has been activated. Since this is the first time that has happened, I'm going to walk you through the operation of your system, but first I need to ask you a couple of questions."

"Okay," I replied.

"Are the intruders still in the house?" Brian asked.

I looked at the monitors and watched as the two men left the kitchen and entered the living room.

"Yes, they are."

"How many intruders are there?"

"Three. Two in the living room and one down in the basement." I looked at the basement monitor briefly to see if the third man was still standing there staring at the camera. He was.

"The thing in your basement is not an intruder," Brian revealed.

Thing? What thing?

"The robed figure you're seeing is your security system," he clarified.

I didn't know how to respond to that.

"Are you still there, Mr. Hale?" Brian asked.

"Yeah, I'm here." Still confused about the comment Brian had made about the figure, I asked for clarification, "How can he be the security system?"

"I'm afraid I can't give you any more details than I already have," Brian apologized, "The rest is proprietary information."

Proprietary information?

I wanted to know who that person was and what they were doing in my house. I opened my mouth to protest, but Brian stopped me before I could get a word out.

"I know you have a lot of questions, Mr. Hale," Brian said, "But you signed a contract. If you don't want to be in breach of that contract, we need to proceed with the activation of your system."

I took a deep breath and exhaled. "Fine."

"Is there anyone else in the house besides the intruders?" Brian asked.

"Just my wife and I."

"Is she in the safe room with you?"

"Yes."

"Any pets?"

"We don't have any pets."

"Then we are ready to proceed to the next step," Brian declared. "Do you see the tablet?"

"I see it." There was a narrow desk pushed up against the wall beneath the monitors. Lying on it, plugged in and charging, was a tablet.

"On the card you used to access the safe room is a seven-digit code," he said, "Use that code to unlock the tablet." As he waited for me to comply, he added, "If you can't get the tablet to work, I can show you how to access the system with your smart phone."

I tapped the screen of the tablet, waking it up, and then did as he instructed.

"It's unlocked," I declared when I was done.

"On the upper lefthand corner of the screen should be a system status icon," Brian explained, "The icon should show that the surveillance system is active."

"It does," I said.

"I need you to toggle the status so that it is inactive," he said.

"Won't that turn off the cameras?"

"It will," Brian agreed, "And then your security system will be armed."

"That doesn't make any sense," I scoffed, "Shouldn't we keep the cameras on so we can keep track of the people who broke in."

"This system isn't like the ones you're familiar with," Brain replied, "It's something new and unique. That's why we asked you to be part of our test group."

"Just turn off the cameras," Elodie snapped at me. She'd gotten tired of listening to the exchange between Brian and me.

I tapped the corner of the screen. The status indicator for the surveillance system now said inactive. As soon as I'd done that, all the monitors on the wall went black.

"What now?" I asked Brian.

"Now, we wait," he replied.

A few moments later, we heard someone run into the room and slam the door shut.

"They're in our bedroom," Elodie whispered.

Something suddenly banged against the wall, startling the two of us.

"Please don't hurt me," we heard the muffled voice of a man pleading with someone.

There was no reply.

"I'll leave," he continued, "I…" the rest of what he was going to say became one long choking gasp and then there was silence.

Elodie and I looked at each other.

"Mr. Hale?" Brian's voice sounded far away, "Mr. Hale?"

I looked down at the phone.

"Mr. Hale?" he repeated.

I lifted the phone to my ear, "I'm here."

"I just got the all-clear notification," he announced, "You may turn the cameras back on," he said.

I reached out with a shaky hand and tapped the screen toggling the surveillance status button from inactive to active.

The monitors came back online.

Elodie yelped and pointed at one of the screens, "He's in our bedroom," she said.

The two of us stared at the monitor and watched as the robed figure turned to face the camera.

"The intruders are gone," Brian declared, "You can leave the safe room now."

"We're not going anywhere with that…that *thing* out there." That's what Brian had called it, a thing, not a man.

"You're perfectly safe," Brian insisted, "The security system cannot harm you as long as the surveillance system is active." When I didn't respond, he said, "It's been in your house for the past 6 months and nothing has happened to you. You have my assurance. No harm will come to you or your wife."

"What is it?" I didn't like not knowing what it was.

"We've been over this, Mr. Hale," Brian sounded exasperated, "I can't divulge that information. What I can tell you is that tomorrow morning a representative from Chimera Systems will be stopping by your home with a check for $100,000."

"But it hasn't been a year yet," I countered.

"You didn't read the fine print, did you?" Brian chided me, "The terms for your contract were for 1 year or until your system was activated. Since the system was just activated, you've fulfilled the terms of the contract."

"Really?" I thought it was a trick of some kind.

"Really," he agreed, "And if you'd like, we can remove the system from your home if it makes you uncomfortable. Just keep in mind that the non-disclosure agreement you signed means you are barred from ever discussing the system with anyone outside of the company."

"I'm okay with that," I said, having already made up my mind to get rid of the system ASAP.

"Is it safe to go out?" Elodie asked, having only been able to listen to my side of the conversation.

"He said it's safe as long as the surveillance system is on," I nodded toward the monitors.

"Well then, let's go," she urged, "I'm starting to feel claustrophobic in here."

"Are you sure it's okay to leave the safe room?" I asked Brian while looking at the robed figure on the monitor.

"I'm positive," he answered quickly, "If you like, I can stay on line with you while you check for yourself."

"How would I do that?"

"You said the security system is in your bedroom, right?" he asked, "Open the safe room door and take a look around. If you can't see the system, then you're in clear."

I walked over to the safe room door and eased it open far enough to peek out. The bedroom was completely empty.

Where'd the intruder go?

Something happened to him while he was in our room, Elodie and I heard it, but I didn't see any evidence that he was ever in the room.

I stepped back and looked at the monitors, checking all the camera feeds. The intruders were nowhere to be found.

Maybe they left.

"What happened to them?" I asked Brian.

He knew who I was referring to. "They're gone, that's all I can tell you and that's all you need to know."

"What if they come back?"

"They won't. I guarantee it."

I had a million questions I wanted to ask him, but I knew he wasn't going to answer any of them in any meaningful way, so I kept them to myself.

"If there's nothing else that I can do to help you, I'm going to let you go now," Brian said, "Should you find that you need further assistance, you can reach us at the number on the front of your access card." He hung up before I could respond.

I took a step out into the bedroom and waited to see if anything would happen. When nothing did, I took another step, and then another until I was standing in the middle of the room.

"It's okay," I called out to Elodie, "You can come out now." When she didn't appear in the doorway, I called out again. There was still no response from her.

"Elodie?" I started to walk towards the safe room door only to have it slammed in my face.

"Open the door, Elodie!" I yelled while slapping the wall with the flat of my hand.

Why'd she lock me out?

I got the answer to my question when I heard something hiss the word, "Intruder," behind me.

I whirled around and found myself face to face with the robed figure.

***

The representative from Chimera Systems pulled a check out of his briefcase and slid it across the table toward Elodie.

"$150,000?" She was surprised to see the amount. She was only expecting a check for $100,000.

"The extra $50,000 is a bonus from our quality control team for bringing to light a flaw in our system." The representative closed his briefcase.

"We're all done here," a technician stepped into the room and spoke to the representative.

After what Mrs. Hale had done to her husband, the executives of Chimera Systems had decided to pull the plug on the current testing cycle so that a resident recognition program could be installed in the surveillance system, preventing it from being disabled if one of the residents was outside of the saferoom.

The representative stood, picking up his briefcase in the process, "We'll show ourselves out," he said.

"That's it?" Elodie asked as she got to her feet.

She had expected some sort of punishment for what she'd done to her husband. Not a reward.

"That's it," the representative confirmed, "Providing you stick to the script." He pointed at the document on the table in front of her, inside which was a detailed story concocted by Chimera System's loss prevention team explaining the disappearance of her husband.

Elodie picked up the check and smiled.

WE ALL SCREAM FOR ICE CREAM

I was at the opposite end of the street when I heard the familiar jingle of the ice cream truck playing in the distance.

"It's early!" Andy, the friend I was playing with, jumped to his feet, and turned around, trying to see where the truck was.

"Maybe it's a different ice cream truck." That was wishful thinking on my part.

"You know it's not a different truck," Andy said, "There's only one ice cream truck that ever comes down this street."

"What should we do?" I asked.

"Run," he said.

Before I could reply, Andy was sprinting across the street, making a beeline for his house.

"Wait for me," I called out, trying to catch up to him.

He ignored me and kept running. I did my best to catch up to him, but he was too fast.

"Sorry, dude," Andy said, slamming the front door in my face.

I tried to open it, but it was locked.

I wasn't mad at him. If we were playing closer to my house, I would've done the same thing to him.

Standing on Andy's porch, I looked up the street toward my house, wondering if I had enough time to make it home before Max, the driver of the ice cream truck, saw me.

I didn't.

The truck was already turning onto our street. If I tried to run home now, Max would definitely see me. The only thing I could do was hide. The question was, where?

I scanned my surroundings.

There was only one place I could reach without being seen and that was the dense row of hydrangea bushes that lined the front of Mrs. Barnes' house.

I dashed across the yard and crawled under the low-hanging branches until I was in the thickest part of the bushes that bordered the house. When I couldn't crawl any further, I sat with back against the brick wall and drew my knees up to my chest, trying to make myself look as small as possible.

I couldn't see the ice cream truck from my hiding place, but I could hear it. The joyful music grew louder and louder until I knew the truck was on the street right in front of Mrs. Barnes' house.

Being that close to it gave me goosebumps.

As I sat there and shivered, the memory of what we did to Max flashed through my mind.

***

It happened three years earlier.

Max was what my dad referred to as an intellectually challenged individual. Everyone else in the neighborhood called him a retard, including me.

The truth was, he wasn't really retarded, he was just a little slow at learning certain things. If any of us had taken the time to get to know him, we'd have learned that he was quite knowledgeable about the subjects he was interested in, of which birdwatching was his favorite.

Max's dad owned a fleet of trucks that delivered ice cream to neighborhoods throughout the city. Once Max was old enough, his dad trained him how to drive one of the trucks and let him deliver ice cream to our neighborhood.

Unlike the other drivers who spent the entire day driving from neighborhood to neighborhood, Max only delivered ice cream to our neighborhood. His dad didn't trust him enough to give him a full route, so he put him in the smallest neighborhood that was closest to the company's distribution center.

He delivered ice cream to our neighborhood for two years until the day my friends and I put a stop to it.

"Did you get it?" Clint asked, reaching his hand out to me.

I handed him the jar. "I couldn't find a dragonfly," I said.

That was a lie. I'd found plenty of them, I just couldn't catch any of them. They were too fast.

Clint held the jar up and looked at the huge carpenter bee that was buzzing around inside of it.

"This is much better than a dragonfly," he smiled.

Carpenter bees are slow, which made it easy to catch the one I'd given to him.

Clint had concocted a plan to get us all free ice cream. My part in his plan required me to catch a dragonfly but, as I said, I was unable to catch one and caught the bee instead.

In the distance, we could hear Max's Ice Cream truck entering the neighborhood.

"Everybody ready?" Clint asked, looking from me to Andy to Joseph.

We nodded.

Clint handed the jar with the bee in it to Joseph. "Wait for my signal," he said.

"We don't have to do this." Joseph was starting to have second thoughts. "I have enough money to buy ice cream for all of us." His parents always gave him extra money to buy ice cream for those of us who couldn't afford it.

"You're not pussing out on me, are you?" Clint took a step toward Joseph.

"No," Joseph stepped back, "I'll do it." He was just trying to placate Clint.

Joseph had already decided he was going to pay Max for whatever Clint stole and if he didn't have enough money on him, he'd pay the rest next time Max came through the neighborhood.

"You better," Clint pointed a finger at Joseph, "You're not going to bail on me, are you?" He moved his finger so that it was pointing at Andy.

"No," Andy quickly shook his head.

"Alright then," Clint smiled, "Let's do this."

The four of us waited on the sidewalk until Max saw us and pulled over to the curb.

"Hey guys," Max waved after opening the side panel of his truck, "What can I get you?"

"Do it," Clint hissed at Joseph before approaching the ice cream truck, "Keep watch," he whispered to me.

Reluctantly, Joseph walked around the back of the truck. When he made it to the passenger side, he opened the door as quietly as he could. Once it was open far enough, he unscrewed the lid of the jar and released the bee into the truck. Before he closed the door, he reached into his pocket, pulled out the ten-dollar bill his mother had given him, and laid it on the seat.

"Sorry, Max," Joseph said as he walked back to the other side of the truck to join us.

"Hmm," Clint said, pretending to look at all the available flavors of ice cream listed on the side of the truck, "Everything looks so good. What would you recommend, Max?"

Max smiled, "I recommend the chocolate banana pop." He liked talking about all the different flavors, "It's my favorite. The orange cream is really good too."

Behind Max, the large bee had begun flying around the front of the truck, bumping against the windshield as it tried to escape.

"Get ready," Clint whispered to Andy. To Max, he said, "Do you hear that?"

"Hear what?" Max asked.

"That buzzing sound," Clint said, "It sounds like you've got a bug in there."

A few weeks earlier, a dragonfly had gotten into Max's truck. Max was so freaked out by the insect that he ran out of the back of the truck, leaving it unattended. Clint was hoping to recreate that scenario, thinking it would give him the perfect opportunity to steal as much ice cream from Max's truck as he wanted.

"A bug?" Max echoed Clint's words, the smile dropping from his face.

"Yep," Clint confirmed, "And it sounds like a big one, doesn't it, Devon?"

When I didn't answer, Clint jabbed his elbow into my side, prodding me to say something.

"Uh… yeah," I said, clutching my side, "A big one."

Having no luck escaping through the windshield, the unhappy bee changed direction and flew toward the center of the truck where Max was standing.

It was at that time that Max hesitantly turned around to look for the bug we had mentioned and came face to face with the large bee. If Max had just stayed frozen in place, the bee would have flown around his head and out the side of the track. But that's not what he did. Freaked out by the sight of the bee in his face, Max swatted the bee.

Agitated by the sudden assault, the bee latched onto Max's palm and stung him.

That's when Clint's simple plan to steal ice cream became a nightmare for us.

Within seconds, Max's hand began to swell. Shortly after that, he began to wheeze and gasp for air while clutching at his throat.

"What's wrong with him?" Clint asked.

"I think he got stung," I said.

"He must be allergic to bees," Joseph said, "We need to get help." He turned and started running toward his house to get his parents.

"This is your fault," Clint pointed his finger at me.

"My fault?" I snapped back, "This was your stupid idea." I pointed back at him.

"What's going on?" Andy returned to the side of the truck after hearing us yelling at each other.

Clint looked from me to Andy and then into the truck at Max whose face was now grotesquely swollen. Without another word, he turned around and took off running.

Not wanting to be stuck there when Joseph's parents arrived, I started running too.

Not sure about what was going on, Andy followed me. The two of us ran until we'd made it to the swing set in my backyard. Once there, I explained to Andy what had happened.

We found out later, after the paramedics had left, that Max had gone into anaphylactic shock and died. His parents never knew he was allergic to bees since that was the first time he'd ever been stung.

***

The sound of the music didn't recede. It continued to blare from the speakers, letting me know that the ice cream truck had stopped right in front of my hiding place.

He knows where I am.

I crawled to the edge of the bushes and peered through the leaves. The truck was parked at the curb. Behind the wheel was Max. His body was hideously discolored and bloated, looking the same way he did the day he died.

He must have sensed my eyes on him because he turned and looked directly at me, lifting his swollen hand, and waving at me.

I scurried back into the bushes and hugged my legs, burying my head in my knees.

When I heard the door of the ice cream truck open, I knew he was coming for me the same way he came for Clint the previous year, and Joseph the year before that. Both boys were never seen or heard from again.

"My dad gave me a new delivery route," Max said, his voice sounded wet and phlegmy, "He told me that all I had to do was come back here, pick you up, and bring you back to the distribution center so he could give you some ice cream."

I could hear the branches parting as he pushed his way into the hydrangea bush to get ahold of me.

"Joseph and Clint got to eat ice cream," he continued, "They ate so much ice cream they burst." Max chuckled.

He stopped and loomed over me when he reached my hiding place.

"Don't you want some ice cream, Devon?" he asked.

PILLOW TALK

I held the keycard up to the magnetic lock until it clicked and the light on top of it changed from red to green.

Before opening the door, I happened to look down the hall and caught one of the hotel maids staring at me. I smiled at her and nodded my head in greeting. She quickly turned away and busied herself with something on her cart.

That was rude, I thought as I walked into the room and tossed my suitcase on the closest of the two beds.

The Grand Edmon was not the hotel I expected to be staying at. I was only there because the Hilton I'd originally made my reservation at was overbooked and the Edmon was the only place that had any availability left. From the outdated appearance of the room, I could tell why.

At least it's cheap.

The nightly rate was about half what I would've had to pay if I'd stayed at the Hilton. Plus, I only needed the room to sleep in. I would be spending most of my time at the office of the company I was auditing.

Tired from driving all day, I decided to take a shower and go to bed early. I had to meet with the company's accounting staff in the morning to explain the reasons for the audit and I wanted to make sure I got enough sleep because those meetings could get tense.

***

I wasn't asleep for very long before I was awoken by the sound of a woman sobbing.

I looked over at the alarm clock on the table between the beds. It was 2:33 a.m.

I sat up and listened, trying to figure out where the sound was coming from, but it stopped as soon as I sat up. Whoever it was must've been sobbing really loudly, because it sounded like they were in the room with me.

Half asleep, I stumbled into the bathroom to empty my bladder before returning to the bed where I waited to see if the sobbing would start up again. When it didn't, I closed my eyes and tried to go back to sleep, hoping I wouldn't be awoken again.

Right as I started to drift off, I heard a feminine voice whisper in my ear.

"Help me," it said.

I jumped up and whirled around, expecting to see a woman lying on the bed next to me but there was nobody there.

It was just a dream, I sighed, taking a few deep breaths to calm my racing heart.

Hearing the woman sobbing must've triggered my overactive imagination, causing me to have some sort of auditory hallucination as I fell asleep.

I returned to bed and, despite being startled, was thankfully able to fall asleep quickly. But I did not sleep well. Thoughts about the sobbing girl stuck with me, causing me to dream about her.

In the dream, she appeared as a young woman with long brown hair who was in her late teens or early twenties. She was lying on one of the hotel beds and appeared to be drugged. I tried to talk to her, but I don't think she could hear me. All she could do was lay there and mutter "Help me," over and over again.

That went on until the alarm woke me up.

***

The meeting about the audit that morning went worse than I expected, but it was my fault. I was tired and found it hard to focus as my thoughts kept drifting back to the girl in my dream. More than once I had to ask someone to repeat themselves, which made them question my abilities as an auditor and that, in turn, made me more curt with people than I normally am.

When the meeting was over, I did my best to put the dream behind me by immersing myself in the company's financial data. It worked. By that evening, the dream was a distant memory due in large part to all the questionable accounting practices I had found. If the company couldn't answer for them, someone was going to get fired or worse, possibly end up in jail for fraud.

Because of everything I had found, I ended up taking some work back to my hotel room. Before I knew it, it was close to midnight.

"I think that's enough for one day." I saved my work and then shut down the laptop.

Exhausted, I went straight to bed.

As soon as my head hit the pillow, the voice of the girl from my dream whispered in my ear.

"Please help me," she begged.

I immediately got up and searched the bed for some sort of speaker, thinking that someone must be playing a prank on me, but I couldn't find anything.

What the hell is going on?

I put the bed back in order and then laid down again, intending to get the answer to that question. As soon as my head hit the pillow the girl spoke to me again.

"Don't leave," she said, "I can only talk to you when you're lying on this pillow."

I took a deep breath and exhaled, resisting the urge to get up.

"Why this pillow?" I asked.

When I searched the bed, I felt through the stuffing of the pillow, feeling for anything that shouldn't be there. Just because I didn't find anything didn't mean there wasn't anything there. I decided to play along and see what happened.

"Because I died on it," was her reply.

"So…you're a ghost?" As I said that, I reached over and grabbed my cell phone off the nightstand where it was charging.

"That's as good a term as any, I suppose," she said, "But I can see that you don't believe me."

While she was talking, I was searching on my phone for ways to find hidden electronic devices. Supposedly there was an app that allowed you to use your phone as a detector. I was about to open the app store and download it when she made her comment about not believing her.

So, you can see me and hear me.

I looked up at the light fixture on the ceiling, thinking about how that would be a perfect place to hide a camera.

I can do more than that, the girl's voice was suddenly inside my head, *I can also hear your thoughts.*

Creeped out, I jumped out of bed.

"How did you do that?" I was staring at the pillow like it was going to respond.

"Why are you doing this to me?" I stood there for a few moments, but the girl never responded.

I can only talk to you while you're lying on this pillow.

That's what she'd said to me earlier. If that were true, it explained why she wasn't answering me.

Not wanting to think that I was going crazy, I clung to the hope that this would turn out to be some sort of elaborate hoax. With that in mind, I downloaded the hidden device detector app and used it to search the room. Much to my dismay, the detector only detected the obvious electronic devices in the room, it didn't find anything else.

I sighed in frustration, hoax or not, the only way I was going to get answers was to talk to the girl.

"What's your name?" I asked as soon as I laid my head on the pillow again.

"Sylvia Price," the girl answered.

When she replied, I tried to see if I could pinpoint where her voice was coming from, but I couldn't tell. Her voice seemed to be coming from everywhere. No matter which direction I turned my head, the volume of her voice always sounded the same.

"I see you still don't believe me," Sylvia said.

I scoffed at her comment, "If you were lying here and the spirit of a dead girl started talking to you through a hotel pillow would you believe it?"

"Probably not," she agreed, "Not without some kind of proof."

Proof? That sounded like a good idea.

"Can you prove you are who you say you are?" I asked.

There were several moments of silence before she replied.

"Close your eyes," Sylvia instructed.

"Why?"

"I want to show you something," she explained, "And you won't be able to see it as well if you keep your eyes open."

That made sense so I closed my eyes. A moment later, an image formed in my mind. It showed three young women posing for a picture in what appeared to be a bedroom.

"I'm…," Sylvia started to tell me which of the three girls she was, but I interrupted her because I already knew which one was her.

"The one in the middle," I finished for her.

I knew because I'd dreamed about the same girl the previous night.

I sat up and broke the connection between Sylvia and me. Now that I knew her name, what she looked like, and potentially what happened to her, I figured I could use that information to try to make sense of what was happening.

Was she really a ghost? Was someone fucking with me? Or was I just losing my mind?

I opened the internet browser on my phone and entered the name Sylvia Price into the search bar. Several links appeared, the first of which was for a newspaper article with the following headline:

TEEN FOUND DEAD IN LOCAL HOTEL

I clicked on the article and the first thing I saw was a yearbook photo of Sylvia. I scrolled down and quickly scanned the short article. According to what I read, Sylvia's body had been found by one of the maids when she'd entered the room to clean it for the day.

Maybe it was the same made I saw when I entered my room. That would explain the way she reacted.

There wasn't any information about how Sylvia died. It just talked about who she was and then ended with a plea asking for anyone who might have information about what happened to her to come forward.

The article was dated three years ago.

This is really happening.

After reading a few more articles, I was convinced that I was actually talking to the disembodied spirit of a dead girl through the pillow she'd died on. Which was preferable to thinking that I was crazy.

"What do want from me?" That was the first thing I said when I laid my head back down on the pillow.

I wasn't stupid. I knew Sylvia was trying to gain my trust because she wanted something from me.

"I want you to help me punish the person who killed me," she replied.

"Punish them how?" I was more than willing to help bring her killer to justice if I could, but I wasn't going to be a vigilante on her behalf.

"Don't worry, I'm not asking you to kill anyone," she said, reading my thoughts, "I just need you to take me to them."

"Take you to them?" I pictured myself showing up at some stranger's house holding Sylvia's pillow.

"You don't know me," I said to the stranger, "But I think you know Sylvia." In my mind, I held up the hotel pillow for the stranger to see.

"It won't be that simple," Sylvia said, interrupting my thoughts, "You'd have to get the pillow into their house without them knowing."

"So…you want me to break in."

"You wouldn't have to break anything," she explained, "I can get you in and out of the house without anyone knowing you were there."

Her assurance wasn't enough to make me comfortable with the idea of sneaking into someone's house. Especially the house of a killer.

"Isn't there some other way we can go about this?" I asked, "One that doesn't involve breaking the law."

"I've had three years to think about this," Sylvia was starting to sound annoyed, "There is no other way."

"What if I went to the police and told them what happened?" I suggested, "Then they'd know who killed you and can build a case against them."

"With what evidence?" was her reply, "If there was anything linking him to my murder, don't you think the police would've already found it?"

She had a point.

"What if I took you to the police? Then you could tell them yourself."

"And what happens if they can't hear me?" she asked.

"Why wouldn't they be able to hear you?" I figured if I could hear her anyone could.

"I've been stuck in this room for three years," Sylvia explained, "And during that time hundreds of people have slept on this pillow. Out of all of them, only you and one other person have been able to hear me."

After hearing her revelation, another scene played out in my mind. This time it involved me carrying the pillow into the police station.

"You need to listen to this," I said to an imaginary officer, holding the hotel pillow up to his face.

"I'm sorry," I apologized, "But I don't think I can help you. If I got caught breaking into someone's house, that would be the end of my career, and I'm not willing to risk that."

Before Sylvia could respond, I left the bed and walked over to the other one, intending to sleep on it instead. I felt like a jerk for doing that, but I didn't think there was anything else to discuss at that point. Plus, it was late, and I needed to get some rest before another long day of auditing.

***

Work sucked. Lack of sleep, coupled with the fact that I couldn't stop thinking about Sylvia made for a very unproductive day. I ended up leaving early and going to a coffee shop around the corner from the hotel. It was there that I took the time to process everything Sylvia had told me. I felt bad about the way I left things with her and still wanted to help. I just couldn't help the way she wanted me to.

I decided I would talk to her when I got back to the hotel and try to convince her that letting me tell the police what happened was the right thing to do. Anonymously, of course. I didn't want to have to explain to anyone how I came to know what happened to Sylvia.

"I'm sorry about last night," was the first thing I said after I returned to the hotel room and laid my head on her pillow.

She didn't reply so I said, "This has all been a little overwhelming and I needed some time to think things through."

"I understand," Sylvia finally replied, "It's not every day that the spirit of a dead girl talks to you through a hotel pillow."

"I want to help you, I do," I insisted, "Let me transcribe your story and send a copy to the police. That way they'll know who was responsible for your death even if they can't prove it. I can even send a copy to your parents or the press if you want."

"That's not good enough," Sylvia sighed.

"Well, it's the best I can do," I said.

"That's where you're wrong," she said. Even though I couldn't see her, I could tell that she was smiling.

***

I don't remember anything after that point until I 'woke up' handcuffed to a metal table in an interrogation room.

"Hello?" I called out, turning to face the two-way mirror that took up most of the wall to my left, "Anybody there?"

I'd seen enough police dramas to know that someone was probably on the other side of that mirror watching me.

Turns out I was right.

A detective entered the room a few moments later.

"Are you finally ready to talk, Mr. Yates?" The detective slammed the manilla folder he was holding onto the table before taking a seat across from me.

"Where am I?"

The detective narrowed his eyes, "Seriously?" he scoffed.

"Seriously," I replied, "I have no idea where I am, how I got here, or even what day it is."

"Maybe this will help jog your memory." The detective opened the folder and pulled out some photos, tossing them across the table at me.

When I saw that they were crime scene photos of a young man's mutilated body I quickly looked away from them.

"That's why you're here," the detective jabbed his finger in my direction as he growled at me, "You did that."

I shook my head, "That's not possible."

The detective pulled out some more photos and showed them to me, "The evidence we found in your hotel room says otherwise."

One photo showed a bloody palm print on the outside surface of my hotel room door, another showed a bloody knife lying in the bathroom sink. The last photo showed a pile of bloody clothing lying on the floor of the hotel room.

"Sylvia," I whispered the name.

She must've done something to me. That would explain why I blacked out and can't remember anything that happened after I talked to her.

"That's where you're wrong?" her words echoed in my mind.

"Sylvia Price?" the detective asked.

"Yeah," I answered.

"How do you know Sylvia?" the detective leaned forward, eager to hear my response.

"This is going to sound insane," I said, "But I swear to you it's the truth." After I said that, I started explaining to him about how I ended up at the hotel and started talking to Sylvia through the pillow she'd died on.

I could tell from the look on the detective's face that he didn't believe me.

"I'm not crazy," I insisted.

"I don't know anything about that, Mr. Yates, I'm not a psychiatrist," the detective said, "What I do know is that you're full of shit. I know that because Sylvia Price wasn't murdered. She committed suicide."

"What?" I was shocked to hear that, "The papers said…"

The detective held up a hand to silence me, "The papers wanted to sensationalize the story," he said, "It was true that her death was treated as suspicious in the early stages of the investigation but we were eventually able to conclude without a shadow of a doubt that she took her own life."

"Suicide?"

"Yep," the detective confirmed, "She and her boyfriend had decided to run away together but he got cold feet and returned home after a few days. She refused to return with him and chose to end her life instead of going back to the abusive home she'd fled."

"Why wasn't that information ever released to the public?" I asked.

"The family asked us not to, so we didn't."

I was feeling so confused, "If she killed herself, why did she tell me she was murdered?"

"Is this the guy she said murdered her?" the detective asked. He gestured at one of the crime scene photos of the young man's body.

Instead of looking at the photo, I said, "She never told me who murdered her. She just told me she wanted me to help her punish them."

The detective collected the photos.

"Who was he?" I asked as the detective put the photos back into the folder.

"You really don't know?" he replied.

I shook my head.

"He was Sylvia's ex-boyfriend," the detective said, "The one that abandoned her."

GOOD TO THE LAST DROP

"Have a seat," the technician gestured at the padded chair in the corner of the room, "And please fill this out," she handed me a clipboard with a form on it.

On my way to grab lunch, I had walked past a pop-up blood donation location, and, on a whim, decided to go in and donate blood before returning to the office.

I filled out the form and handed it back to her.

"Are you left or right-handed?" the technician asked as she pulled a pair of latex gloves out of a box and started putting them on.

"Left," I replied.

The technician reached out and took my right hand, turning it over in the process so that my palm was facing up. With her free hand, she grabbed a lancet and used it on my index finger. When a bead of blood welled up on my finger, she grabbed a small card from her workstation and held my finger over it, letting a few drops of blood fall on it.

"What's that for?" I asked. There was writing of some kind on the card, but I couldn't make out what it said.

The technician set the card on the counter behind her, "It's a blood typing test," she said.

"Oh," I said, "I could've saved you the trouble and told you my blood type."

"I still would've had to do the test to verify your type," she said, "It's company policy." When she was done speaking, she turned her back to me to finish the process of typing my blood.

"Are you the only one here?" I asked, trying to make conversation. There were several workstations, but she was the only technician I'd seen.

"I'm the only one up here," she replied without turning around, "Everyone else works downstairs. If it gets busy, I can call for help and they'll send somebody up. But it never gets busy."

"I take it donating blood isn't very popular then," I remarked.

"Not really," she turned to face me, "You're the first person that's come in all day."

"Seriously?" I was surprised to hear that, especially considering that it was almost 1 p.m.

"It's like that most days," she revealed, "But it's okay, we get enough donations to meet our quotas."

On the counter behind the technician was a display full of colored cards. She grabbed a green card and held it out to me.

"You're all set," she smiled, "Just give this card to the technician downstairs and they'll take it from here."

"Oh," I stood up and took the card, "I assumed you did everything right here."

"We only do the blood typing up here," she explained, "All of the donations are handled downstairs." She gestured at the stairwell.

I don't know why, but at that moment I hesitated and considered leaving. Something about going down into the basement made me feel uncomfortable. I pulled out my phone and made a show of checking the time.

"It's okay if you've changed your mind about donating," she said, picking up on my indecision, "You wouldn't be the first person to leave and you certainly won't be the last."

"Sorry," I handed the card back to her, "I didn't realize what time it was. I really have to get back to the office," I lied. I still had about 30 minutes remaining on my lunch break.

"No worries," she smiled, "We'll be here until the end of the week if you change your mind and want to come back."

That's not going to happen, I thought to myself. But to her, I said, "Maybe. I might be able to stop by Friday afternoon."

Not wanting to linger in the awkward situation any longer, I quickly headed for the exit.

"See you Friday," she called out as I left.

I just smiled and nodded my head while thinking, *No you won't.* I wasn't even scheduled to work that Friday. I would be miles away in my apartment, enjoying my day off.

In my rush to leave, I accidentally collided with an older gentleman who was in the process of entering the building.

"Sorry," I apologized.

"No harm done," he replied and then added, "Did you donate?" he nodded toward the technician who had her back to us as she tidied up her workstation.

"I was going to," I said, "But I don't have the time right now. I need to get back to the office. Maybe another time," I lied again.

"I donate whenever I can," the man said, "Which, at my age, isn't as often as I'd like."

"I don't do it as often as I should." That was the truth and saying it out loud made me feel a little bit guilty about leaving.

"You're doing it," the man replied, "That's all that matters."

I wasn't doing it, and that made me feel like shit.

"You best be going," the man said a moment later, "I don't want to be the reason you're late returning to work," he smiled.

"Right," I returned the smile, "Sorry again for running into you."

He waved off the apology, "It was nothing."

I stood there and watched the man enter the building, second-guessing my decision to leave.

Should I go back inside and donate? I debated.

Not unless you want them to know you were lying, I replied to myself.

I could come back on Friday. Turning the lie into the truth.

Maybe.

I turned and started walking back to the office.

***

By the time I had returned home to my apartment that evening, my trip to the donation center had become a distant memory. I didn't think about it again until Thursday evening when I turned on the news.

"If you have any information about Mr. Sherman's whereabouts," the news anchor said, "You are urged to call the number on your screen."

Also on the screen was a picture of the missing man. He looked a little bit younger than when I saw him two days earlier, but I recognized him immediately. It was the elderly guy I had run into as I was leaving the blood donation site.

A moment later, the news anchor moved on to the next story.

Wanting to know more about the missing man, I pulled out my phone and began scanning articles, looking for details about when and under what circumstances he'd gone missing. From what I could tell, he'd disappeared shortly after I'd seen him, making me one of the last people to see him.

You should call, the voice of reason spoke up in my mind.

As I scrolled through my phone, searching for the number to call the tip line, I saw a headline that said: MISSING MAN FOUND. Beneath that was a time stamp that said the article had just been posted seconds ago.

I clicked the link that took me to the article.

My heart sank when I read that the old man's body had been found in the morgue of a local hospital. There was no explanation about how he ended up there. I tried searching again to see if any other news agency had reported additional information about the man, but none of them had.

"That sucks," I sighed.

He seemed like a decent guy. Thinking about him made me wonder what had happened to him.

Did he die because he donated blood, I mused, He was old. Maybe it was too much for him.

Maybe I should still call, I thought.

Telling them about my encounter with the man at the blood donation site might help them piece together what happened to him before he died. I felt like that was the least I could do.

I scrolled back through the articles on my phone until I found the one that had the number for the tip line, but before I could tap on it and initiate the call, there was a knock at my door.

I glanced at the time. It was 11:36 p.m. I wasn't expecting anybody, and nobody I knew would drop by my apartment that late, not without notifying me first.

I got up and approached the door, thinking whoever it was must have the wrong apartment.

When I looked through the peephole, I was surprised to see the technician from the blood donation place standing on my doorstep. I thought it was an awfully strange coincidence that she showed up right then.

I cracked the door open and looked at her, "What're you doing here?" I asked.

"Hi," she flicked her hand in greeting and gave a weak smile, "Sorry for showing up unannounced like this. I was hoping I could talk you into coming back to the facility and donating blood."

"Right now," I gawped, "It's almost midnight."

"I wouldn't be here if it weren't urgent," she insisted, "You have a very rare blood type, and we have found ourselves with a bit of a supply shortage."

"How did you find me?" I didn't care why she was there. It was rude to just show up the way she had.

"With this." She pulled a folded-up piece of paper from her back pocket and handed it to me. It was the form she'd handed me when I was originally going to donate blood. I'd forgotten that I'd filled it out.

"You could've called," I replied. My phone number was listed with my address on the form.

"I could've," she agreed, "But I didn't think I'd be able to convince you to come back over the phone, so I came here instead. I figured I'd have better luck talking to you in person."

"Well, I'm sorry to say you've wasted your time," I snapped, "I have no intention of donating blood at your facility." Especially after learning that the old man who'd gone there after me wound up in the morgue.

I started to close the door, but she jammed her foot in the gap, stopping me.

"I'm afraid I'm going to have to insist." She shoved her shoulder against the door.

The unexpected move caused me to stumble back, allowing her to force her way into my apartment where she used the door to pin me to the wall.

"What the fuck is wrong with you?" I yelled at her, struggling to slide out from behind the door.

"There's nothing wrong with me." She suddenly had a syringe in her hand, "I'm just doing my job."

Before I could free myself, she jabbed the syringe into my thigh and then backed away.

I kicked the door shut and then reached out to grab hold of her, but she easily sidestepped my attempt.

"What did you do to me?" I slurred the words as I suddenly found it difficult to move.

"It's just a little sedative," she replied.

Now that I was no longer a threat, she stepped in close and helped guide me to a sitting position on the floor before I fell on my face.

Unable to do anything but watch, I sat there as she pulled out a cell phone and called someone.

"He's all ready for you," she said to the person on the other end of the line.

My vision started to blur but I was still able to see the two men who entered my apartment a few minutes later. Both were dressed like paramedics. They lifted me off the floor and carried me onto a stretcher they had waiting just outside my door. Out on the street, I could see an ambulance waiting.

HELP!

I tried to cry out to my neighbors who had come outside to see what all the commotion was about, but I couldn't get the words out of my mouth. All I could do was lay there as they loaded me into the back of the ambulance.

The last thing I remember before blacking out was the technician climbing into the ambulance with me and slamming the doors shut.

***

When I awoke, I found myself strapped to a procedure chair in a brightly lit room, wearing nothing but my boxer shorts.

The walls and floor were stark white, and the air smelled like antiseptic.

"Where am I?" I grunted as I tried to free myself from the leather straps holding me down. "Why are you doing this?" The memory of being taken from my apartment felt like a bad dream. I could only remember bits and pieces of what happened.

The technician from the blood donation site stepped into the room.

"YOU!" I snarled, "You're the one who did this to me!" Upon seeing her, the gaps in my memory were filled in. She'd drugged me after she showed up at my apartment and I refused to donate blood.

I renewed my struggles to free myself.

"Good morning, Mr. Morton," the technician said as she approached the chair.

"You can't do this to me!" I snapped.

"Actually, we can," she replied, "You willingly came into our donation site with the intent of donating. Once I typed your blood and established your nutritional value, you became our property."

"What?" I scoffed, "That's crazy. I'm nobody's property."

"I'm afraid you are." She produced the form I had filled out, "You consented to it when you signed this." She waved the paper in my face. "You really should've read the fine print before you signed."

"There's no way this is legal." I insisted, "I want to speak to a lawyer."

She laughed, "If the world operated the way you think it did, it wouldn't be legal," she agreed, "Unfortunately for you, that world is an illusion. The one we really live in is governed by a race of beings older than time itself. To them, we're just cattle. Allowed to roam free and do as we please, providing we abide by a few simple rules."

"You're insane." She had to be if she believed what she was telling me.

"If I were insane," she said, "I wouldn't be allowed to work here." She began checking my straps to make sure they were secure. "In fact," she fixed her eyes on mine, "I'm probably more sane than you are."

"I doubt that," I laughed.

"All employees who work here have to undergo a strict psychological evaluation to ensure we have the mental fortitude to do what needs to be done," she explained, "And that evaluation is administered by psychiatrists working for the CIA."

"Bullshit."

"It doesn't matter if you believe me or not." She stepped away from the chair and started to leave the room, "You're about to find out for yourself."

Before she could move out of sight, I called out to her, "Is this what you did to that old man?" Whatever they did to him, I assumed they were going to do to me.

She turned in the doorway to face me.

"Not quite," she said, "He was scheduled to be assimilated like you are, but he had a weak heart and died before the Great Old One, that's what we call the beings we work for, could start the process. They can't assimilate you if you're dead." She took a deep breath and exhaled before continuing, "As you can probably guess, the Great Old One wasn't happy about being denied its meal, so it gave us 48 hours to find a replacement or it was going to assimilate the staff. We couldn't let that happen, so that's why you're here."

I just stared at her, dumbfounded, thinking she was absolutely nuts. But my opinion quickly changed when I heard a loud squelching sound out in the hall. It sounded like something heavy was flopping its way through a muddy swamp. As the sound got closer, a horrid stench began wafting into the room. It smelled like rotten fish and sewage.

"I know its little consolation," the technician said, "But your sacrifice is appreciated. Without it, the world we know wouldn't be able to exist." When she was done talking, she stepped aside to let the formless mass of the Great Old One ooze its way into the room.

THE PLAYGROUND

"It's this way, Paige," Declan said. He'd veered from the sidewalk to approach the line of trees while I'd kept walking, not realizing he was no longer beside me.

"You didn't say anything about going into the woods," I stopped and stood where I was with my hands on my hips.

"If that's a problem, we can find something else to do," he offered.

After a week of begging, Declan finally promised to show me where the infamous playground was. When he agreed, I didn't think I'd have to follow him out into the middle of the woods to see it.

"It's not a problem," I said, "I just thought it would be someplace more accessible."

The playground was an urban legend in the town of Salt Creek. The locals spoke of it in hushed whispers and wouldn't discuss it with anyone they considered an outsider. Since my family had just moved to the town a little over a month ago, we were considered outsiders.

I first heard about the playground when I started classes at Salt Creek High two weeks ago. A couple of boys who sat behind me in my third-period English class were talking about it. I couldn't make out most of what they were saying, which is why I got the wrong impression and thought that the playground was some sort of secret hangout where the local teens went to drink and smoke.

When I tried to ask the boys about it, they essentially told me to fuck off.

I didn't become friends with Declan until a week after that happened. The first time I asked him about the playground, he told me I was better off not knowing. That was not an answer I was willing to accept. After continuously pestering him about it, he eventually told me this ridiculous story about how the playground was cursed. When I told him I thought his story was bullshit, he laughed and said, *"You'll see."*

That was I how ended up following Declan into the woods behind the high school.

"Watch your step," Declan warned, pointing at a long, thin piece of broken concrete barely visible under the layer of dead leaves lying on top of it.

We'd been walking for about ten minutes before he pointed it out. If he hadn't, I would've tripped over it.

"What the hell is that doing out here?" I asked as I stepped over it.

"This used to be the parking lot for the Salt Creek community park," Declan gestured at the surrounding area, "Before they moved it across town."

As soon as he said that I realized that the concrete piece I'd almost tripped over was a parking block. When I looked around, I saw several more of them sticking out of the ground.

"The baseball field used to be over there." Declan pointed through the trees at the rusty skeleton of a bleacher that had collapsed in upon itself. "The basketball courts were over there." He moved his finger to the left a little where a pole jutted out of the ground.

"They moved the entire park because of the playground?" I scoffed.

"They did," Declan confirmed, "About fifty years ago."

"Because they thought it was cursed?" I couldn't stop myself from sounding sarcastic.

"Maybe you should wait until you see it before you decide if it is real or not," Declan replied.

"Real or not," I said, "It sounds like a lot of trouble to go through for a playground. Why didn't they just tear it down, or call a priest to exorcise it?"

"They did," Declan replied, "Or so I heard," he clarified since everything he'd heard about the park was second-hand knowledge. He wasn't alive when it was in active use and was just retelling me all the stories he'd been told.

"Seriously?" My comment about the exorcism was meant to be a joke.

"They tried a bunch of different things," Declan said, "They even hired a couple of psychics."

"Psychics?" The story surrounding the playground was getting more and more ridiculous.

"Yep," Declan said, "They were the first ones to suggest the playground was cursed."

"How does a playground become cursed?" The idea sounded absurd to me.

"By being built on cursed land," Declan explained, "At least that's how the psychics explained it according to my grandfather. They said the playground had become tainted by whatever was affecting the ground beneath it."

"And everyone believed them?"

"They must have," there was a hint of irritation in Declan's tone when he responded, "Otherwise the park would still be open and we wouldn't be walking through the woods, right?"

"Sorry," I apologized after realizing I was starting to annoy Declan, "I'll shut up." He'd only brought me out there to see the playground because I'd pestered him, and he was only repeating what he'd been told about it. "At least until I see it," I smiled as I warned him that I'd likely have more to say once I saw the playground.

"I'm sure you'll have plenty to say once you see it," he smiled back. "Come on, it's just over that rise," Declan pointed before walking in the direction he'd indicated.

***

"That's it?" I said as we approached the playground. That was all I could think to say when I saw it.

"Not what you were expecting, was it?" Declan had a smirk on his face.

"Is this some kind of a joke?" There's no way the playground I was looking at was built fifty years ago. All the equipment looked brand new. Even the rubber surfacing that covered the ground looked like it had never been stepped on.

"There's no joke," Declan insisted, "This is the playground."

"Why does it look like it's been cleaned?" I asked.

The area around us was surrounded by trees. Dead leaves and branches littered the ground everywhere you looked, everywhere except for the playground. There wasn't a single leaf or stick anywhere in the circular area that the playground sat upon.

"That's the way it always looks," Declan replied.

The playground consisted of six swings, three spring riders, 2 slides, 2 teeter-totters, a merry-go-round, and a set of monkey bars shaped like a dome.

"Somebody has to be taking care of it for it to look this good," I said as I stepped onto the rubber matting near the monkey bars.

"I don't think you should be messing around in there," Declan warned. He was standing about ten feet away from the edge of the playground and wouldn't come any closer.

I ignored him and climbed through the monkey bars so that I could stand under the dome.

"Help me, I'm trapped," I joked, grabbing the bars like I was a prisoner.

"That's not funny," Declan shifted nervously, "You shouldn't joke like that."

"Oh, come on," I scoffed, "There's no way this park is cursed, look at it." I spread my arms, "It's too nice looking. I bet someone in town is just fucking with everyone."

"If that were true," Declan challenged, "How do you explain all of the accidents that have happened here?"

"It's a playground," I replied, "Kids are bound to get hurt. Especially with all this metal around." Everything in the playground was made of metal except for the seats of the swings.

"Do you know who Joey Peterson is?" Declan asked.

I had to think about it for a moment, but I eventually put a face to the name, "Yeah," I said, "The kid with the scar."

Joey Peterson sat at the table in front of me in my science class. That's how I knew about the scar he had that curved behind his ear. It was nasty looking and hard to miss.

"The swings did that to him," Declan said, "He got lucky he didn't lose his ear."

"Did you see it happen?" I countered, "Or is that what he told everyone?"

"I saw it," Declan revealed, "Kevin and I dared him to come out here and sit on one of the swings. We told him we'd give him our lunch money for a week if he did it."

I could tell from the far-away look in his eyes that he was reliving the memory in his mind.

"There was so much blood," he whispered.

"Accidents happen," was my reply as I climbed to the top of the monkey bars and sat down. I still didn't believe the playground was cursed.

"I think we should go," Declan declared.

"But we just got here," I complained, "Plus, it's pretty nice out here." There was a quiet peacefulness to the area.

"You wouldn't think that if you knew you were sitting above a mass grave," Declan said.

"A what?" I wasn't sure I had heard him correctly.

"My grandfather was on the crew that helped build the park. He told me they found twelve bodies buried here." He pointed at the playground.

"Bullshit," I spat the word out, "You're just trying to scare me." Even though I thought Declan was lying, the idea that there may be bodies buried under the playground gave me the creeps.

"I've seen the pictures," Declan said, "The foreman had the crew rebury the bodies and paid them to keep their mouths shut, but not before my grandfather managed to get a few photos."

"Why would they cover the bodies up instead of calling the police?" I asked. That didn't make sense to me. That many bodies in one place was something that should be investigated.

"Because of how old they were." Declan explained, "The foreman was afraid the state would come in and find that the site had some sort of historical significance and would shut the project down."

"How old were they?" I asked.

"I don't know," Declan shrugged, "But my grandfather made it sound like they'd been buried there for hundreds of years."

If what he was saying was true, the bodies likely belonged to the first European settlers in the area, which would have been a big deal if it had been reported to the authorities.

"You can't tell anyone I told you about the bodies," Declan pointed his finger at me, "My grandfather only told me after he'd heard about what happened to Joey. He said I needed to have more respect for the place."

"I won't say anything," I promised, "I don't think anyone would believe me if I did."

"Can we leave now?" Declan practically begged, "This place gives me the creeps."

"I suppose," I said.

As soon I'd finished speaking, I felt myself slip. I had no idea how it happened. One moment I was sitting on top of the monkey bars and the next I was falling. It was almost like the bar I was sitting on had rotated, causing me to slide forward.

The fall happened so suddenly that I didn't have time to react. When I fell, I hit my upper lip and nose on one of the bars. The taste of blood quickly filled my mouth as I hit the ground.

"PAIGE!" Declan yelled.

"I'm okay," I tried to say, but my upper lip had already started swelling, so it came out sounding unintelligible.

I could hear Declan running across the playground toward me. I looked up just in time to see the end of one of the teeter-totters lift off the ground far enough to catch him in the shin as he tried to jump over it in his haste to get to me.

I did not just see the teeter-totter move on its own. My befuddled mind tried to make sense of what had just happened. But that is exactly what I saw.

Declan tumbled forward, cracking his head against the large metal bar the two teeter totters were sitting upon.

"Declan?" I mumbled as I forced myself to my hands and knees and started crawling towards him.

He wasn't moving.

I kept calling his name as I crawled out of the monkey bars and pulled myself to my feet.

"Get up, Declan." I begged before having to turn my head and spit out the blood that had been collecting in my mouth, "I'm ready to go now."

I stumbled over to where he was lying on the ground and nudged him with my shoe, but got no response.

"Declan?" I started to get down on my knees so I could check on him, but I ended up having to jump back and roll out of the way as the second teeter-totter started to descend toward me.

If I hadn't seen it move out of the corner of my eye it would've knocked me upside the head.

This is not happening, I kept repeating to myself as I backed out of the playground, keeping my distance from all the equipment.

"I'm going to go get help," I yelled at Declan before I stumbled out of the woods, hoping he was just unconscious.

I returned to the park thirty minutes later with a Salt Creek Deputy and two paramedics, but when we got there, Declan was nowhere to be found.

"He was right there," I insisted, pointing at the space between the teeter-totters, "Lying on the ground."

As I was looking at the teeter-totters, I realized that there were now three of them instead of two like there were when I was there earlier.

"There's too many," I blurted out.

"Too many what?" the officer replied.

"Too many teeter-totters," I pointed at them.

"If you say so," the officer said with a patronizing tone to his voice. He motioned for the paramedics to come and get me, "I think you might've hit your head harder than you realize. I think you should ride with them to the clinic and get checked out."

"What about Declan?" I asked.

"He doesn't seem to be here any longer," the deputy said, "The way I see it, that's a good thing," he added, "He probably went home." After that, the deputy led us out of the woods.

That all happened a week ago and nobody has seen Declan since he took me to the playground, and I don't think anyone ever will. I think he's become a part of the playground. I know how insane that must sound, but how else can you explain the appearance of the third teeter-totter?

WHAT DREAMS ARE MADE OF

The officer at the barricade lifted his hand, signaling for me to stop as I walked down the wide hallway of the indoor storage facility.

"This area is closed, ma'am, you'll have to come back later," he said.

"Medical examiner," I replied, flashing my identification card.

He examined it for a moment before lifting the police tape and motioning for me to walk under it.

"Storage unit fifty-four sixty-six," he said as I ducked under the tape, "It's around the corner to the left," he pointed with his free hand.

"Dr. Holland," Detective Bennet raised a hand in greeting when he saw me come around the corner, "Thanks for coming," he added when I got a little closer.

The detective was standing next to an open storage unit. Lying on the ground, sticking partially out of it, was the body of an elderly man.

"What've you got for me?" I asked as I walked up and stood over the body.

"The deceased man's name is Herman Chambers, age 89. According to surveillance footage," Detective Bennet pointed to the security camera at the end of the hall, "He collapsed around 8:45 last night and wasn't found until 6 am this morning."

From what the detective just told me, it seemed likely that the man had died from a heart attack or a stroke. And if that was the case, I shouldn't have been called to the scene.

"Sounds like he died from natural causes," I said, "I'm not sure I need to be here to tell you that."

"He's not the reason I called you," Detective Bennet walked into the storage unit, "These are," he gestured at the large wooden crates sitting on the concrete floor. There were six of them spread out across the unit, the closest one was lying next to the body.

"He was carrying this one when he collapsed," Detective Bennet knelt next to the crate near the body of the elderly man and lifted the lid. Inside of it was the head of a human male packed in what appeared to be a very fine-grained sand, leaving only the face visible. "There are arms in those two crates over there, legs in those two by the door, and a torso in that big one right behind you." He pointed at each of the crates as he mentioned them.

I knelt next to him and peered into the crate, but I couldn't see much because of all the sand.

"I thought you'd like to see how we found them before we sent them to your office," Detective Bennet said.

"Definitely," I replied while getting to my feet, "I appreciate that."

I walked over to the next closest crate, the one he said the torso was in, and pointed at it. "May I?" I asked.

"Go ahead," Detective Bennet said, "The forensic techs have already processed them."

Before I opened the crate, I noticed that there was an overseas shipping label stuck to the side of it, with the port of origin listed as Durban Harbor. I wasn't a geography expert, but I knew enough to know that port was located somewhere in South Africa.

"Did all of the crates come from the same place?" I asked.

"Nope," Detective Bennet answered, "They all came from different places and were shipped at different times."

"That means…"

Before I could complete my thought, Detective Bennet finished it for me, "We've got six crates potentially containing the body parts of six different individuals. Could be more, could be less. That's for you to determine, doc."

I eased open the crate and was surprised to find the torso of a woman, also packed in sand, with only the breasts and abdomen visible. After seeing the head, I assumed all the parts were going to be from men.

"Well," I said, returning the lid to the crate, "I can confirm that you have at least two bodies here."

"Hey, Doctor Holland!" someone interrupted us.

I turned around and found Amir standing out in the hallway next to the stretcher from his van. He worked for the medical examiner's office as a diener, someone who helps with the transportation and preparation of bodies in the morgue.

"Have they released the body yet?" he asked.

I looked over at Detective Bennet for the answer.

"He's all yours," the detective replied.

Detective Bennet and I stepped out of the storage unit to give Amir room to bag the body of the elderly man and place him on the stretcher.

"There isn't going to be enough room in the van for the crates too," I said as Amir wheeled the body past us.

"I can have one of the forensic techs drop them off when we're done here," Detective Bennet offered.

"Thanks, I appreciate that," I said, "I'll rearrange my schedule and get started on them as soon as they arrive. In the meantime, I'll see if I can find out what killed Mr. Chambers."

Before I left, I caught up to Amir and asked him to prep the body of the elderly man for me when he got back to the morgue.

****

"He's all set," Amir said, hooking his thumb over his shoulder towards the doors that led into the autopsy suite.

"Thank you, Amir," I said, heading towards my office.

"There is one thing I wanted to show you before you sit down," he said. I could tell from the tone of his voice that he'd rather show me whatever it was, sooner rather than later.

I stopped and turned to face him, "Lead the way."

He took me into the autopsy suite and over to a table where all of Mr. Chambers's belongings were laid out.

"While I was taking off his overcoat, I found that," he pointed at an old leather journal sitting at the far end of the table next to a wallet and a set of keys. "It was tucked into the lining. I figured the police might've missed it and that it might be important."

"Good catch," I said, "I'll call Detective Bennet and let him know when I get back to my office."

"Just doing my job," Amir replied humbly.

"Was there anything else?"

"No," he shook his head, "That was it."

Amir excused himself after that, while I decided to go ahead and start the autopsy of Mr. Chambers.

Normally, the first thing I did in the morning was try and get the day's paperwork out of the way, but I decided that could wait. I was eager to get a look at the body parts from the crates, but I couldn't do that until I'd finished the autopsy of the elderly man they were found with.

Two hours later, I held his bloody brain in my hands, the clear cause of his death. He'd had a massive brain aneurysm, which was obvious to me as soon as I'd removed the top of the skull. There was nothing suspicious about his death, which I'd already expected.

Based on what Detective Bennet had told me at the scene, it was my opinion that Mr. Chambers pushed himself a little too hard trying to carry that last crate into his storage unit, causing the already weakened blood vessel in his brain to burst.

His death wouldn't have been instantaneous, and likely occurred a few hours after the aneurysm ruptured. If someone had found him sooner, there's a slim chance he could've survived.

After I'd cleaned up and put Mr. Chambers's body in the freezer, I started to pack up his personal belongings, stopping when I got to the journal Amir had found.

It won't hurt anything to take a peek, I convinced myself.

***

I took the journal into my office and sat down at my desk before unwrapping the leather cord that was bound around it.

At the end of the cord was a small pendant in the shape of a four-petaled flower. I wasn't a horticulture expert, but I knew enough about flowers to know a poppy when I saw one, and I was certain that's what the pendant was supposed to represent.

Once I'd finished unwrapping the journal, I carefully laid it on the desk and opened it to the first page, sighing in disappointment when I saw that the writing inside of it was written in a language I didn't recognize.

I started flipping through the journal to see if there were any pages that I could read, but I couldn't find any. I did, however, find six photographs, each one paper clipped to a different page.

The photos showed close-ups of a peculiar-looking birthmark. A birthmark that looked strangely similar to the flower pendant hanging from the cord on the journal. And, as far as I could tell, the photos were not of the same person. I believed each one showed a similar birthmark possessed by a different individual.

The photos also varied in age. The one closest to the front of the journal was in black and white and looked like it might have been taken in the '50s, while the one on the last page was in color with a resolution that made it look like it was taken recently.

I didn't remove the pictures from the journal, but I did use my phone to take photos of them. I was pretty certain I'd be able to match them up to the body parts found in the storage shed.

When I was done with the journal, I wrapped the cord back around it and called Detective Bennet to let him know about it. He instructed me to give it to the forensic tech that should be dropping off the crates at any moment.

****

"Where do you want these?" Amir asked. He was holding one end of a crate while the forensic tech held the other.

"Put them on the floor in the freezer for now," I instructed.

When the two men were done unloading the crates, I stopped the forensic tech and held the journal out to him, which was now secured in an evidence bag.

"This is for Detective Bennet," I said.

The tech took the bag and left.

"Do you need me to prep the next autopsy for you?" Amir asked.

"Not yet," I replied, "I think I'd rather get started on the contents of those crates first."

"Which one do you want to start with?" he asked.

"Let's get x-rays of all of them and then I'll decide."

I wanted to see if there was anything else in the crates besides the expected body parts before I went digging around in them.

It took us an hour to finish the X-rays.

"Here's the last one," Amir said, handing me the X-ray film.

"Thanks." I took it and hung it on the illuminator with the other X-rays we'd taken. I was happy to see that there was nothing else in the crates with the body parts. "You can leave that one there," I gestured at the crate sitting on the table, "I'll start with it."

"In that case," Amir said, "Now would probably be a good time to take my lunch."

"Go ahead," I urged him, suddenly realizing that I hadn't eaten anything since the previous night, "Would you mind bringing me something back?"

I knew where he was going for lunch, the same place he always goes, a little sandwich shop around the corner.

Amir agreed to bring me back my usual, and I told him I'd pay for both of our lunches.

After he left, I reached into the crate and gently removed the severed arm from its bed of sand, and laid it on an empty table.

Of the six crates, the arm was in the one with the oldest shipping label on it. If the label was to be believed, the arm was shipped in August 1954 from Italy. I had my doubts about that, considering how intact the arm appeared to be.

My primary goal in examining the body parts that were found was identifying who they belonged to, and that wasn't going to be an easy task since all evidence pointed to these people being dismembered somewhere far away with their respective parts being shipped into the country. Regardless, it was still my responsibility to try.

During the external examination of the arm, I was not surprised to find a flower-shaped birthmark on the inside of the upper part of the arm. When I compared it to the photos I had taken of the journal, the birthmark matched up perfectly with the first photo I'd found inside it. The black and white one.

Based on the musculature of the arm, and the dense hair covering it, it was easy for me to conclude that the arm belonged to a man.

What I found most fascinating was how much care was taken in removing the arm. It was removed at the shoulder with the head of the humerus intact. Also of note, was how smooth the cut through the muscles was. The flesh wasn't ripped or torn as you'd normally see with dismemberments.

The last thing I noticed was an absence of blood around the area where the arm was cut free. That suggested to me that the blood was likely drained from the body before the arm was removed.

Whoever had removed the arm did so with expert precision, meaning they had plenty of time to do what needed to be done.

I was in the process of photographing the arm when Amir returned with our lunch.

***

"Have you fingerprinted it yet?" Amir asked as he wadded up the trash from his sandwich and walked it over to the trashcan in the corner of my office. He was referring to the arm I was in the process of examining when we stopped to eat lunch.

We decided to eat in my office because it was a lot more convenient than having to go to one of the designated breakrooms on the floor above us.

"Not yet," I replied, "That was next on my list along with plucking a few hairs for DNA analysis."

"I can do it for you while you finish," he offered, gesturing at my half-eaten sandwich. Amir was a much faster eater than I was.

"Thanks, I appreciate that," I said, "If it's not too much trouble, can you tag and bag it and put it in the freezer when you're done?"

"That's no trouble at all," he said before leaving the office.

After he left, I picked up the phone and called Detective Bennet again.

"How can I help you, doc?" he asked.

"I've started my examination of the body parts in the crates, and I wanted to know what you wanted me to do with the crates and the sand inside of them when I'm finished?" I needed to know if he wanted them back for evidence or if I should toss them.

"Unless something comes up during your examination to suggest they might be important in some way, you can go ahead and dispose of them. We've got plenty of pictures and samples and the crime scene techs have said they have no further use for them," he replied.

"Did you get the journal?"

"I did," he said, "But I won't know if it contains anything useful until I can find someone who can translate it. I had a tech take it over to the university to see if one of the foreign language professors could help us." After a brief pause, he said, "Was there anything else you needed, Dr. Holland?"

"Nope, that was all," I said, "I'll email you my report once I've finished the examinations."

"The sooner, the better," Detective Bennet sounded stressed out, "I've got the captain breathing down my neck to get our end of this thing wrapped up as quickly and quietly as possible before we hand it off to the feds. Speaking of which, I know I don't have to remind you to avoid talking to the press. Can your staff be trusted to do the same?"

"Of course," I couldn't keep myself from sounding irritated.

"Good." He hung up the phone after that.

Detective Bennet wasn't normally that gruff with me. Whenever he was, it meant that he was under a lot of pressure from his superiors to deliver results. To relieve him of some of that stress, I went ahead and wrote up the preliminary autopsy report for Mr. Chambers and sent it to him.

Shortly after I sent the report, Amir knocked on my office door and peeked his head inside, "I'm done with the arm," he said, "Which one do you want me to bring out next?"

"Let's take a look at the other arm," I said, pushing myself up from the desk and following him into the autopsy suite.

***

Other than being from a woman, the second arm was in the same condition as the first one. When I finished my examination, I stepped aside so Amir could fingerprint it and take a few hairs for DNA analysis.

"It's about that time," Amir said, glancing up at the clock on the wall when he returned from placing the second arm in the freezer.

"Not for me it isn't," I replied.

Our small-town morgue wasn't as busy as morgues in larger cities, and that allowed me to keep regular hours most days. Normally, Amir and I would finish whatever we were working on by four or five o'clock and then clean and prep the autopsy suite for the next morning. That wasn't going to happen this time. I needed to finish the examination of all five body parts and wasn't going to leave until I had.

"You can go." I didn't see the point in making Amir stay.

"No way, Doc," he replied, "If you're staying, I'm staying."

***

It took us until midnight to finish the examination process, concluding with the torso which was currently sitting on the table between Amir and me.

"I think we're done," I declared, "Now, I just have to write up my report."

"Do you want me to wheel this back into the freezer?" Amir asked, gesturing at the torso.

"You can leave it," I replied, "I'll put it away. You go on home."

"Are you sure?"

"I'm positive," I insisted. "You've been here long enough. Go on home." I nodded toward the exit.

"Alright, I'm going." He took off his latex gloves and tossed them in the trash before walking over to the sink to wash his hands. "See you in the morning," he said as he walked out of the autopsy suite.

Once Amir left, I decided it might be a good idea to bring out all of the parts and arrange them on the table, to see if I could discern anything new by comparing them to each other side by side. So far, the strange flower-shaped birthmark and the method of dismemberment, which remained a mystery to me, was the only thing they had in common.

I had already put all of the parts on the table, except for the head, which I was currently carrying out of the freezer when my phone began to ring. I quickly set the head down with the other parts, pulled off my gloves, and looked at my phone to see who was calling. It was Detective Bennet.

If he's calling me this late it must be important.

"Hello," I said, answering the phone.

"Sorry to disturb you so late, but I just got the first part of that journal translated and thought you'd want to hear what it said," he sounded dismayed.

"Of course," I agreed. If there was anything inside of it that explained the motives and methods behind Herman Chambers's motives for possessing the body parts, I wanted to hear it.

"What language was it written in?" That was the first thing I was curious about.

"Ancient Greek," Detective Bennet said, "According to his neighbors, Mr. Chambers was supposedly an expert on Greek mythology. I don't know how much of an expert he was, I haven't been able to corroborate that yet, but he certainly was obsessed with it, especially with something called Hypnos."

"Hypnos is the Greek god of Sleep," I explained to the detective.

Like many people, when I was younger, I was fascinated by the stories of the Ancient Greek and Roman gods and just fantasy in general, and did a lot of reading on the subject.

"Well, according to the journal, Mr. Chambers believed this…God, Hypnos, was real, and he'd been tasked with creating a new vessel for him so he could return. He claimed the god was sending him instructions through his dreams after he visited Greece back in the '50s."

"What kind of instructions?" I asked.

"What parts to look for and how to preserve them once he found them," Detective Bennet sounded disgusted when he answered.

"The birthmarks," I said.

"Yep," he agreed, "Chambers refers to them as 'poppy marks' in the journal. Whenever he had a dream, he would hire private investigators to track down the person he dreamed about. Once the person was found, a different person was hired to acquire the necessary body part from the person and ship it back to Mr. Chambers. The man was obviously insane. He thought by bringing the parts together, he'd bring a god back to life."

While I was talking to Detective Bennet, my back was to the autopsy table and the body parts laying on it. When he mentioned bringing the parts together, I turned around to look at them, shocked to find a fully formed body, comprised of the parts I'd laid out, sitting up with its legs dangling over the edge of the table.

When it saw me looking at it, it lifted its feminine arm and waved at me.

"I'm not so sure he was insane," I mumbled my reply.

WHISPERING WINDS

"How much?" I held up the table fan so the old guy behind the thrift store counter could see it.

The summer had just begun, and we'd already had several record-breaking days of heat. To better disperse the limited cool air put out by my window-mounted AC unit, I'd gone to the thrift store to look for a cheap fan.

"There should be a sticker on it somewhere," was his reply. He was busy sorting through a box of costume jewelry and couldn't be bothered to look up at me.

I turned the fan over in my hands looking for a price sticker, but I couldn't find one anywhere.

"It doesn't have one," I declared.

He finally stopped what he was doing and looked over at the fan in my hands, "Two bucks," he said.

That was cheaper than I thought he was going to say. The fan was clearly vintage and made out of metal. It was heavy and felt sturdy. I would've had no problem paying two or three times that price.

I walked over to the counter and set it down, "Do you mind if I give it a try?" I asked.

"There's an outlet on the wall over there," he pointed, "Knock yourself out."

"Thanks," I carried the fan over to the outlet and set it on the floor before plugging it in and flipping the switch to turn it on.

Please work.

I'd been to every thrift store in town, and that was the only fan I'd been able to find. If it didn't work, I'd have to buy a new one which was something I was trying to avoid, given the limited funds at my disposal.

I was relieved when the fan whirred to life.

Not wanting to give the man enough time to change his mind about the price, I quickly turned the fan off and wrapped the cord around the base after unplugging it. After carrying it over to the counter, I took two one-dollar bills and a quarter out of my wallet and set them next to the fan.

The man took the money without a word, rang me up, and then handed me my change along with a receipt.

"Do you want a box to put it in?" he asked.

"Nah, I'm good," I declined, picking up the fan and carrying it out of the thrift store.

***

When I returned home to my trailer, I set about finding the right spot to place the fan.

The AC unit was on the wall in the living room, closer to the front end of the trailer. It did a great job of keeping that area of the house cool but didn't help much with the master bedroom, which was on the opposite end of the trailer.

"This looks like a good spot," I muttered to myself after placing the fan on the counter in the kitchen.

The counter was near the AC unit, meaning if I angled the fan towards the hall that led to the master bedroom, it should help direct the cold air that way, thereby cooling the back half of the trailer more efficiently.

I was in the process of adjusting the fan when the front part of the metal guard came loose and fell off. I tried to catch it but only succeeded in knocking it onto the floor, cutting my finger on one of the blades in the process.

I hissed in pain as I felt the sting of the metal slicing through my skin.

A surprising amount of blood welled out of the cut, dripping down the fan blade and onto the counter.

I rushed over to the sink and rinsed my finger off.

"That doesn't look good," I muttered to myself after seeing how deep the cut was.

Most people would've gone to the hospital and gotten stitches for a cut like that, but I couldn't afford an ER visit so I had to take care of it myself. Instead of a bandage, I folded up a paper towel and wrapped it tightly around my finger. Then I used a piece of duct tape to hold it in place.

I was in the process of making sure the bandage was going to hold when there was a knock on the trailer door.

"Knock, knock," Eddie said as he opened the trailer door and stepped inside.

Eddie was my neighbor. He lived in the trailer next door and was one of those people who had no problem inviting himself into someone's home. He was the main reason I kept my door locked when I was home. Something I never did until he moved in. I must've forgotten to lock it when I carried the fan inside.

"Hey, Eddie," I said.

If he picked up on the lack of enthusiasm in my voice, he didn't show it.

"What happened?" he pointed at my injured finger.

"Cut it on the fan," I replied while picking up the guard and putting it back in place.

Eddie walked over to my fridge, opened it, and grabbed a soda.

"Do you mind?" he asked.

He knew I wouldn't say anything now that he already had it in his hands. If I did, he'd just promise to pay me back for it later. Which, of course, he never did. Accepting my silence as permission, he popped the top and took a drink.

"My folks had one like that," Eddie gestured at the fan with the can of soda, walking around the counter to stand opposite me.

By then, I'd reattached the guard and turned the fan on.

"My brother and I used to stand behind it and pretend we were Darth Vader." When he finished talking, he leaned forward and spoke into the fan, repeating a popular misquote from the *Empire Strikes Back* movie, "Puke," he said, intentionally making fun of the character's name, "I am your father." The sound of his voice wavered through the fan blades.

I turned the fan so it was blowing toward him and said, "Eddie, you are an idiot," into it, chiding him for his misuse of the famous movie line.

The fan thrummed as it projected my warbling voice in an unexpectedly deeper and sinister tone. Hearing it gave me chills.

Eddie didn't seem to notice, he just stood there with a slack-jawed look on his face.

"Eddie?"

He kept staring off into space, which was starting to concern me.

"Eddie?" I repeated.

He swiveled his head to look at me, "Who's Eddie?" he asked, speaking slowly.

"You are," I pointed at him.

"No, I'm not." He shook his head, "I'm Edward."

"You're joking, right?"

"No," he sounded very serious, "Why would I joke about my name?"

We stared at each other for a moment as I tried to determine if he was pulling my leg or not, but the glazed look in his eyes made me think he wasn't joking. There was something seriously off about him.

"My bad," I apologized.

What the hell is going on here?

Eddie lifted his can of soda to take a drink, but he didn't have the hole lined up properly with his lips and ended up dribbling some down his chin and onto the counter.

"Sorry," he said, wiping his mouth with the back of his hand before using the end of his shirt to wipe up the mess on the counter.

"Are you okay?"

"Yeah." He looked down at his wet shirt, "It'll dry. I didn't spill that much."

I wasn't asking about his accident with the soda, I was asking about how he was feeling in general because he was acting really weird. It was like he had suddenly been struck dumb.

He's become a real idiot.

The thought brought me back to what I'd said into the fan and the weird way my voice had sounded.

Did I do that to him?

I had declared that he was an idiot, and then he was. Did the fan transform my words into reality? It was an insane idea, but I couldn't come up with any other explanation for why Eddie was acting the way he was. He seemed fine otherwise.

Maybe I can undo it.

I leaned down and said, "Eddie, you are not an idiot," into the fan. Unlike the last time, though, my voice didn't have that weird intonation.

What did I do differently the first time?

"You're not an idiot either," Eddie said, thinking I was talking to him, "You're the smartest person I know."

"Thanks," I replied, lifting my hand to brush a stray lock of hair out of my eyes. The movement brought my bandaged finger into view.

Was it the cut?

The first time I had spoken into the fan I had just cut my finger on one of the blades. The injury must have somehow triggered the fan's effects.

If that's true, I thought, *Why didn't it do anything when Eddie spoke through it? He used the fan before I did.*

Then it dawned on me.

It didn't work for Eddie because Eddie didn't say anyone's name. He'd said 'Puke' instead of Luke. I said Eddie's name when I declared he was an idiot.

Now I needed to figure out what exactly I'd done to trigger the fan's effects.

Was it the blood or the cut? Or both? Only one way to find out.

I quickly popped the guard off of the fan and ran my thumb along the edge of one of the blades. It was very sharp and didn't require much pressure to slice through my skin.

"What're you doing?" Eddie asked, leaning close to the fan to watch me.

"Fixing you," I said, holding my thumb over the blade so a few drops fell upon it.

I put the guard back into place and turned on the fan, but before I could speak into it, Eddie ruined everything.

"Brian," Eddie said, "You're so crazy."

The fan distorted Eddie's voice the same way it did mine.

"What have you done, Eddie?" Those were the last words I remember speaking before I started having strange thoughts and ultimately blacked out.

✱✱✱

"Are you having those strange thoughts right now?" the detective sitting across from me asked.

I was handcuffed to a table in one of the precinct's interrogation rooms. I wasn't quite sure why I was there, but I assumed it had something to do with all of the horrible images flashing through my brain. Images that felt like shards of a memory.

"Yeah," I nodded, "But they're not as bad as they were at first."

"This is your friend Eddie, right?" He pulled out a photo, showing me a mug shot from one of the many times Eddie had been arrested.

"He's not really my friend," I clarified, "He's my neighbor, but yeah, that's him."

"And you claim this fan you bought at the thrift store, turned him into an idiot and made you crazy?" the detective said, summing up the story I'd just told him.

"I know how stupid it sounds, but it's true," I insisted, "If you go back to my trailer and get the fan, I can show you."

"It just so happens that we already have the fan here," the detective said.

He turned towards the large mirror and motioned at someone who couldn't be seen. A minute later, the door to the interrogation room opened, and another detective walked in carrying a covered box. He set the box on the table and then left.

The detective sitting across from me stood up, opened the box, and then pulled out a large evidence bag inside which was the fan, but it was in pieces and all of them were covered with blood.

"What happened to it?" I asked.

"You did, Mr. Arnold," the detective said, "Don't you remember?"

As I stared at the broken fan, the fragmented images in my mind started to coalesce into a coherent memory. In the memory, after Eddie had said I was crazy, I picked up the fan and beat him to death with it. I was still beating his head to a pulp with the remnants of it when the police arrived.

REVOLVING RACKS

"If you're good while we're in here," my mom pointed to the doors of the Days Past Vintage Clothing Store, "We can go across the street and have ice cream when we're done. Okay?"

My mom had a thing for old clothing, especially things from the 60s and 70s. Most of the stuff in her closet was bought from second-hand stores like the one we were standing in front of. She'd tried to dress me similarly, but it didn't last long. Once I started school, she realized she was torturing me by dressing me in a fashion that made the other kids single me out.

"Okay," I agreed.

She was trying to bribe me because I had a bad habit of getting restless and running around the stores we shopped at, playing amongst the racks of clothing. According to her, whenever I did that, I was embarrassing her.

My mom opened the door and motioned for me to walk inside.

"I mean it, Erica," she warned me as I walked past her into the store, "No horsing around."

"I won't," I insisted.

I had no intention of messing around. I really wanted some ice cream. However, based on past precedent, the chances of me behaving were slim. It wasn't for lack of trying, though. I always tried to behave. My mom just took so long looking at everything in the store that my patience always wore out well before she was ready to leave.

"Welcome in," the older lady behind the counter greeted us, "I love your shirt." She pointed at the *My Little Pony* t-shirt I was wearing.

"Thanks," I replied shyly while looking down at the cartoon characters printed on it, "It's my favorite."

Like all my clothes, the shirt was bought from a thrift store, so it was several years out of date. But I still loved it.

"Then I bet you'd probably like this too." She laid her arm on the counter so I could see the bracelet she was wearing. It had pink, purple, and white beads of various sizes and little charms of the six main characters from the *My Little Pony* cartoon series.

I nodded. I did like the bracelet very much.

"Which one is your favorite?" I knew she was asking about the characters depicted on the charms.

I pointed at the yellow Pegasus with the pink mane and tail, "Her."

"Fluttershy is my favorite too." The lady winked at me when she saw the surprised expression on my face.

My mom couldn't name the characters, so it was a surprise for me to hear this woman, who was at least twenty years older than her, name one of them.

The lady slipped the bracelet from her wrist and held it out to me, "I think you should have it."

I looked back at my mom who'd been silently watching the exchange between the lady and me.

"That's not necessary," my mom said.

My mom assumed the lady was trying to guilt trip her into buying something by giving me something for free. It was a tactic used by a lot of the secondhand stores we visited, but none of them had ever offered me anything as cool as that bracelet.

"It's no trouble," the lady insisted, "It's not something I can sell in the shop."

"Please, mom?" I asked with a hopeful look in my eyes.

Ever since my dad died, I didn't get a lot of presents. My mom couldn't really afford them outside of Christmas and my birthday, both of which were still months away.

"Fine," she sighed.

I took the bracelet and put it on my wrist, "Thank you!"

The lady smiled at me, "It was my pleasure."

As my mom and I walked away from the counter to start shopping, she leaned over and hissed at me, "You better behave or I'm going to make you give it back. Do you understand me?"

I nodded my head, terrified at the thought of losing the bracelet. In the few seconds I'd had it, it had become my most treasured possession.

I glanced back toward the lady at the counter, wondering if she'd overheard the exchange. From the sad way she was looking at me, I figured she must've heard.

****

"Psst."

I was sitting on a little stool at the back of the store, next to the racks of shoes, when I heard the sound. After looking around for a moment, I couldn't figure out where it was coming from.

"Over here."

I looked around again and saw an arm waving at me from a circular rack full of pants.

I got up and walked over to the rack.

The girl who was trying to get my attention stuck her head out and looked at me.

"What's your name?" she asked.

She looked to be about my age.

"Erica," I replied, "What's yours?"

"Lori," the girl replied.

Lori was doing what I would've been doing had my mom not threatened to take my bracelet away and promised me ice cream. There was a lot of fun to be had playing amongst the racks. It was hard to resist the allure of the hidden spaces behind the densely packed clothing.

"Is that the correct date?" Lori asked, pointing at the television that was mounted on the wall. It was turned to a news channel, and the date was listed along the bottom of the screen where various headlines of the day scrolled by.

"I guess it is," I shrugged. I had no reason to think it wasn't correct.

"Do you want to see something cool?" Lori asked enthusiastically.

I looked over at my mom, glad to see that she was too preoccupied with the large selection of shoes laid out before her to notice me.

"Sure," I agreed.

Lori reached out and grabbed my hand, pulling me into the rack with her.

"Whatever you do, don't let go of my hand, okay?" She had a serious tone in her voice.

"Okay," I tightened my grip on her hand as she led me out of the rack of clothing and into another.

"One more should do it," Lori declared, once again pulling me along as we left the confines of our current rack for a new one.

When we stopped, she parted the jackets hanging around us and nodded toward the wall where the TV was mounted, "Check it out," she said with a smile.

The flatscreen TV that had been there five minutes ago was gone. In its place was a much smaller and boxier-looking TV.

"Look at the date," Lori pointed at the screen where a different news channel was playing.

"June thirteenth nineteen-ninety-three," I read the date out loud. The day was right, but the year was wrong. "Nineteen-ninety-three was…" It took my eight-year-old brain a moment to do the math, "Thirty years ago."

"No, it wasn't," Lori declared, "Nineteen-ninety-three is right now."

I gave her a confused look.

"Go and have a look around," she urged. "You'll see."

I stepped out from the rack and walked toward the back of the store where I last saw my mom. She was nowhere to be seen. Worried, I spun around, looking for her. That's when I noticed that the store looked different.

"Can I help you with something?" the lady working behind the counter asked when she saw me looking around. She didn't look like the lady who had given me the bracelet. This new lady was much younger looking than her.

"I'm just looking for my mom," I replied.

The lady behind the counter also looked around. Not seeing anyone but me, she said, "I'm pretty sure your mom isn't here. I haven't seen anyone in the shop all morning besides the two of you."

"Do you believe me now?" Lori whispered from her place in the rack.

I didn't want to believe her, but I couldn't explain all of the things that had changed while we ran through the racks. There was one thing I could do to prove that I wasn't losing my mind.

"Excuse me?" I turned back to the lady behind the counter, "What's today's date?"

"June thirteenth, nineteen-ninety-three," the lady replied.

"Nineteen-ninety-three?"

Stunned, I just stood there, wondering how Lori had been able to bring me back in time thirty years.

"Are you okay?" the lady asked.

Lori darted out of the rack and grabbed my arm, pulling me into a different rack across the aisle, "Come on," she said, "We need to get out of here."

"Wait!" I heard the lady call out, but her voice sounded far away.

"We need to keep moving," Lori said, dragging me from one rack to the next.

"I want to go back," I said, meaning back to my time where my mom was.

"We will," Lori promised, "I just need to rest for a minute."

We had stopped in the middle of a rack of sweaters.

"How are you doing this?"

Lori shrugged, "I don't really know. I was just playing in the racks one day and suddenly found myself in the future."

"How'd you get back home?"

"I thought about going home and the path through the racks just sort of came to me," she gave me an apologetic look, knowing that she wasn't offering much of an explanation. "I can't explain it. I just think about where I want to go and follow the path I see. But I can only do it in this store," she pointed at the floor, "It doesn't work anywhere else. I've tried."

"Got you!" someone cried out, thrusting their arms between the sweaters and grabbing hold of me.

I fought against the person, struggling to free myself as they dragged me out of the rack. Lori tried to help me, but whoever had grabbed hold of me was stronger than the both of us combined.

The person who grabbed me was a middle-aged woman. Once she'd pulled me out of the rack, she turned me around to face her. That's when I saw the name tag pinned to her chest, telling me her name was Connie.

"Wait a minute," Connie said, momentarily stunned, "You're not her." She looked me over for a moment as she released her hold on me. "Have you seen a little blonde girl with pigtails? About your height and probably around your age," she asked.

She was talking about Lori.

I couldn't stop myself from flicking my eyes over to the rack where Lori was peeking at me between the sweaters. She was shaking her head and holding her index finger up to her lips, begging me not to say anything.

But I didn't have to say anything, Connie had followed my gaze and saw Lori.

"There you are, you little thief!" Connie blurted out, lunging for Lori.

Lori took off running out of the sweater rack and into a rack of dresses across the aisle. After that, I didn't see where she went, and neither did Connie.

She's gone.

I didn't know if she had gone into the future or the past. All that I did know was that she was no longer in the clothing shop.

****

"I tried the phone number you gave me, but it doesn't work," Connie said, "Is there another one I can try?"

I shook my head. I was pretty sure any phone number I gave her wouldn't work, since they all belonged to people I knew in the future.

After Lori got away, Connie took me into the store's office to talk to me. She snapped off a series of rapid-fire questions, which I did my best to answer.

"What's your name?"

"Erica."

"Where's your parents?"

I shrugged.

"Who's that girl you were with?"

"Lori."

"What's Lori's last name?"

I shrugged again.

"Do you know where she lives?"

I shook my head.

"Her phone number?"

I shook my head again.

"Is there anything you can tell me about her besides her name?"

"No...I just met her."

That's when Connie stopped giving me the third degree and softened her approach, offering to call my parents for me.

"If I can't get ahold of your family, I'm going to have to call the police," Connie said, "You can't be running around down here unsupervised."

Overwhelmed, I started crying.

Connie did her best to comfort me, but it was clear that she wasn't used to consoling children. The best she could do was hand me a tissue, put her hand on my back, and tell me everything was going to be okay.

When it became clear to her that she wasn't going to be able to get any useful information out of me, she picked up the phone and called the police.

I considered running out of the shop, but the more I thought about it, the more I realized that was a bad idea. If the little calendar on the corner of Connie's desk was correct, I was stuck in 1973. Once I was outside, I wouldn't know where to go. Nobody I knew would be alive.

That wasn't entirely true. My grandparents were alive, but I had no idea how to find them, or if they even lived in the area at that time. Plus, I doubt they'd believe me if I just showed up at their doorstep and said, *"Hi, I'm your granddaughter from the future. Can you help me get back home?"*

Lori was my only hope, but I wasn't sure she'd come back for me.

"I dropped my other bracelet," I lied, holding up my arm so she could see my empty wrist, "Can I go look for it?"

Connie sighed heavily, "I suppose," she said, "But you better hurry, the police will be here any minute."

She led me back onto the sales floor and stood close by, keeping an eye on me as I climbed into the center of the sweater rack Lori and I were in when we arrived.

"Lori," I whispered, "Are you there?"

When I didn't get a reply, I stepped out of the rack and into the one I saw her disappear into when Connie was chasing her.

"Lori?" I repeated.

She never responded.

"Did you find it?" Connie called out.

"Not yet."

I'll have to find my own way home. I decided. *If Lori could use the clothing racks to move through time. Maybe I could too.*

I closed my eyes and pictured my mom, standing in the shop, waiting for me back in 2023. Then I tried retracing the path Lori had taken, quickly moving from rack to rack, thinking about home the entire time.

After running in and out of a few racks, and seeing that nothing around me had changed, I gave up.

"No luck?" Connie said sympathetically, seeing me step out of the rack with my head hung low.

I shook my head, wiping away the fresh tears that rolled from my eyes. That was when the police arrived.

***

"Are you sure this is the address?" the officer driving the cop car said, "There's nothing here."

"I'm sure," I replied.

It just hasn't been built yet, I thought to myself.

After questioning me about who I was and failing to get ahold of my parents from the store, the two police officers who arrived decided to drive me home.

While we sat there on the side of the road, next to the vacant lot that would one day become the site of the apartment complex where I lived with my mom, the officer in the passenger seat used the car's radio to contact the police precinct to see if anyone had reported me missing yet. Of course, nobody had. And nobody would. Not in 1973.

Having no other choice, the police handed me off to a social services worker named Carol.

***

"Are you hungry, Erica?" That was the first thing Carol asked me after introducing herself.

I hadn't realized it until I thought about it, but I was starving.

She took me to a McDonald's restaurant, which made me feel a little bit better. There was something familiar about the place that made me feel like I wasn't stuck in 1973.

"What would you like?" Carol asked me when we reached the counter.

"A happy meal," I replied. That's what I always got when I went there with my mom.

"I'm not sure what that is," Carol said, "But I'm certain there's something up there that will make you happy." She gestured at the menu.

I scanned the available items, surprised to see no mention of a happy meal.

I guess they don't have them yet.

"I'll just have a cheeseburger and French fries."

When our food was ready, Carol let me pick the table we were going to sit at. While we ate, she asked me basic questions about myself, nothing too serious. I knew she was just trying to win me over before she started asking the difficult questions.

"Can I have some ice cream?" I asked when I was done with the rest of my food.

I had seen it listed on the menu and it made me think about what my mom had said about getting me ice cream if I was good. I thought I deserved it at that point.

"I'll tell you what," Carol leaned forward, "I'll get you an ice cream cone if you promise to tell me the truth."

"Okay," I agreed.

She got up and returned a few minutes later with the promised ice cream cone, along with a second for herself.

We ate our cones in silence and then Carol gathered up all of the trash and threw it away. When she returned, she sat down and said, "Alright, Erica, it's time to talk."

She pulled a notebook out of her purse and set it on the table. She flipped it open and turned it around so I could read what was written on the page before reaching back into her purse for a pen.

"This is the phone number and address you gave to the police," she tapped the page with the pen, "But we both know that's not your phone number or your address, is it?"

I didn't know how to respond to that.

"I want you to write down your real address and phone number," Carol set the pen down on the notebook, "Don't forget, you promised to tell me the truth if I got you that ice cream cone."

"That is my real address and phone number." I kept my eyes on the notebook, "They just don't exist yet," I mumbled.

"What do you mean, they don't exist yet?"

I took a deep breath and then told Carol everything that had happened to me since I woke up that morning, leaving nothing out. I rambled quite a bit and had to backtrack a couple of times, but I was pretty sure I didn't forget anything.

"That's the truth," I said when I had finished my story.

The way Carol looked at me made me feel like a bug under a magnifying glass.

"That's quite a story." It was clear from her tone that she didn't believe me, "Do you have any proof?"

"No," I dropped my head and looked down at the table. Doing that brought the cartoon characters on my shirt into my field of view. "I do have proof," I blurted out, getting to my feet and pulling on the hem of my t-shirt to straighten it out.

"I don't see how that's proof, Erica," Carol said.

"*My Little Pony* won't exist for decades," I insisted. At least the version I was familiar with wouldn't be.

"I don't have any way of verifying that," Carol had a sad look on her face.

I dropped back into my chair and pouted.

Nobody is ever going to believe me.

Before I'd finished that thought, I'd decided that the only way I was going to get back home was to return to the clothing store and wait for Lori to come back for me. She had to come back for me. She couldn't just leave me stranded there.

I got up and ran out of the McDonald's restaurant before Carol could react.

It took me a moment to orient myself once I was outside, but after I did, I knew exactly where I needed to go to get back to the shop.

Fifteen minutes later, I stood in front of the clothing shop, panting.

Please be here, Lori, I thought as I pushed the door open and walked inside.

I did my best to stay out of sight, running into the rack of dresses that was nearest to the door. From there, I moved from rack to rack until I made it to the sweater rack that Lori and I were in earlier when we'd arrived in 1973. Then I sat down and waited.

I was prepared to sit there as long as necessary, but I wasn't allowed to sit there that long.

About ten minutes after I arrived, Carol walked into the store. I watched from between the sweaters as she walked up to the counter and started talking to Connie. I couldn't hear what they were saying, but I knew they were talking about me. I also knew that I hadn't been as sneaky as I'd thought when Connie pointed at the rack that I was hiding in.

Carol walked over and stood next to the rack.

"I'm only trying to help you, Erica," she said softly.

"I know," I replied, "But I don't belong here. If you want to help me, let me stay here."

"You know I can't do that."

I pulled my legs up to my chest and wrapped my arms around them.

"I'll tell you what," Carol said, "If I promise to let you sit here until the store closes, will you promise to come with me if nothing happens?"

I thought about it for a moment. It sounded like a reasonable request. Mostly because I had convinced myself that Lori would come back for me.

"Okay," I agreed, "But you can't sit here with me."

I didn't think Lori would return if there were adults around.

"I won't," Carol smiled, "Connie said I could sit in her office, but first, I'm going to run over to the supermarket and pick us up some snacks. I'll be back soon. If you need anything while I'm gone, ask Connie." She gestured to where Connie was standing behind the counter, "She was nice enough to let us stay, so I expect you to be on your best behavior."

"Okay," I quickly agreed.

I wasn't planning on doing anything except sitting there and waiting for Lori to come back and take me home.

****

"I'm sorry," Carol apologized.

She was squatting on the floor next to the sweater rack while she talked to me.

"I know you thought your friend was going to show up, but it's time for you to accept that she's not coming."

Her words brought tears to my eyes. I was sure Lori would come back for me.

"It's time for us to go," Carol reached her hand out between the sweaters, "Connie needs to close up the shop."

I briefly considered asking if we could stay a little bit longer, but I knew Carol would say no. Plus, I doubted Lori would show up that late. She was probably already home in bed in whatever time she came from.

"Okay," I sniffled, taking Carol's hand and letting her help me out of the rack.

After we left the clothing shop, Carol drove me to a hospital. I didn't realize it was a mental hospital until we were locked inside.

"You'll only have to stay here for a couple of days," Carol promised before the nurse led me away.

They think I'm crazy!

From that moment on, I knew better than to talk about being from the future. I kept my mouth shut about it and decided to act like I couldn't remember anything. Whenever I was asked anything about myself, I just told the doctors and social workers that I couldn't remember anything other than my name. When they asked me why I made up that story about being from the future, I told them it was just a silly game me and Lori were playing while we were in the store.

The doctors diagnosed me with something called retrograde amnesia. An inability to remember things from my past. As long as they didn't treat me like a crazy person, I was fine with that.

They kept me locked up for a month before they transferred me to a group home for children. Since no next of kin could be found and nobody had come forward to claim me, I was considered a ward of the state. That meant Carol would act as my guardian in all legal matters until I turned 18.

The first few months at the group home were rough. The other kids weren't that nice, and everything around me felt so archaic. Back in 2023, I was used to being surrounded by all sorts of gadgets and gizmos to entertain myself. Without having that stuff in 1973, I grew bored easily. And when I got bored, I did stupid things, like running away.

I ran away from the home three times and, every time I did, I went back to the shop to look for Lori. And every time, Connie would let me stay for an hour or so before she called Carol and told her to come and get me.

After the third time I ran away, Carol had me transferred to a different group home, one that was several hours away from the shop. But that didn't stop me from trying one more time to get back there.

As time passed, I eventually gave up the idea of going home and started settling into a routine. After a few years of good behavior, I was placed in a foster home until I turned 18. The week after my 18th birthday, I packed up all my stuff and moved back to the town where the clothing shop was.

Carol was resistant to the idea, thinking it wouldn't be good for me to go back there, but I assured her I was fine. That would be the last time I saw her. A few weeks after helping me get settled, she passed away. The year was 1983.

That June, I returned to the clothing store. When I walked through the doors, Connie, who was in her 50s now recognized me immediately.

"You're a little big to be running through the clothing racks these days, aren't you?" she smiled.

I returned the smile, "I'm sorry about all of that."

She brushed aside the apology with a wave of her hand, and stepped out from behind the counter, "Come here," she motioned, wrapping her arms around me when I got close enough, "I'm just glad to see you're alright."

"Thanks."

"What brings you back here?"

"Well," I said, turning my head to look over at the help wanted sign in the window, "I was thinking I might apply for the job. If that's alright with you?"

"Seriously?" her smile grew, "You're hired." She walked over to the window and removed the sign.

***

I worked in the store for ten years, always keeping an eye out for Lori, but no longer hoping she'd take me back to 2023. During that time, I'd gotten married and had a couple of kids of my own and was content with my life and wouldn't change anything about it even if I could.

It was June 13th, 1993, when Lori reappeared in the shop. When I saw her, I was surprised to see she wasn't alone. I was also with her or, rather, my younger self was. Seeing the two of us step out of the clothing rack gave me a feeling of déjà vu.

"Can I help you with something?" I asked my younger self.

"I'm just looking for my mom," younger me replied.

The thought to tell her that her mom was back in 2023 and that she should turn around and go right back to her crossed my mind, but I couldn't bring myself to say it. I was happy with the way my life had turned out, and the thought of losing my two beautiful children made me hold my tongue. I didn't know what would happen if that version of me didn't end up in 1973 and I didn't want to risk it.

"I'm pretty sure your mom isn't here. I haven't seen anyone in the shop all morning besides the two of you," is what I said instead.

"Excuse me?" younger me asked, "What's today's date?"

"June thirteenth, nineteen-ninety-three," I replied, giving her the day's full date since I knew she really just wanted to know what year it was.

"Nineteen-ninety-three?" Younger me just stood there, stunned.

"Are you okay?" I asked.

Lori darted out of the rack and grabbed the arm of younger me, pulling her into a rack, saying something that I couldn't hear as they fled.

"Wait!" I called out, suddenly having second thoughts about letting them leave, but it was too late. They were already gone.

***

The last time I saw Lori was also the first time. It was June 13th, 2023. The day my mom and the younger version of me walked into the store for the first time. I was ready for them this time.

"Welcome in," I said when they walked into the shop, "I love your shirt." I pointed at the *My Little Pony* shirt younger me was wearing.

"Thanks," she replied, "It's my favorite."

"Then I bet you'd probably like this too." I laid my arm on the counter to show her the *My Little Pony* bracelet I was wearing. The one I had purchased just for this occasion.

Younger me nodded.

"Which one is your favorite?" I asked her.

She pointed at the yellow Pegasus with the pink mane and tail, "Her."

"Fluttershy is my favorite too." I winked at her before slipping the bracelet off my wrist, "I think you should have it."

Younger me looked back at our mom to make sure it was okay to take the bracelet.

"That's not necessary," our mom said.

"It's no trouble," I insisted, "It's not something I can sell in the shop."

Connie had passed away in the late '90s and left the store to me. Since that time, I had made a few changes to the business. The most notable one was changing the store's focus to vintage clothing, instead of just selling second-hand clothing.

"Please, mom?" younger me begged.

"Fine," our mom sighed.

Younger me took the bracelet and put it on her wrist, "Thank you!"

I smiled, "It was my pleasure."

A short while later, our mom rushed up to the counter in a panic, "Have you seen my daughter?" she blurted out.

"I have," I replied.

"Where?" she practically shouted at me, "Where is she?"

I dragged a chair out from behind the counter and set it near her, "I'll tell you," I said, "But I think you're going to want to sit down first."

THE BURP

"Look what I got," Dennis declared as he walked through the door of my apartment. In his hand was a paper bag that he was holding up like a trophy.

Printed on the side of the bag was the logo for a fast-food restaurant named Bruja Burger. I'd never heard of it before, but apparently, my roommates had, and it was a big deal to them.

"No way," Jasper said, taking the bag from Dennis and holding it in his hands like it was a priceless relic. "Where did you find them?"

"Down by the river," Dennis said, snatching the bag back from Jasper, "I decided to cut through the park on my way home and there it was, parked at the end of the road under the streetlight."

"There what was?" I asked, unable to follow along with the conversation.

"The Bruja Burger truck," Dennis answered.

"What's so great about some burgers from a food truck?" Dennis and Jasper were acting like they'd won the lottery or something.

"These are not just any burgers," Dennis dangled the bag in front of me, "They are Bruja Burgers," he said as if that were explanation enough.

"Leon's not from around here," Jasper said to Dennis, as he clapped his hand on my back, "He's never heard of Bruja Burger, have you?"

"Can't say that I have," I agreed with him.

I'd moved into town from out of state less than a year ago and had never heard anyone mention Bruja Burger until Dennis brought the bag into the apartment.

"Well then, you're in for a treat," Dennis grinned as he carried the bag over to the dining table.

If the burgers were as amazing as he was making them sound, why was this the first time I was hearing about them? I thought to myself as Jasper and I walked over to the table.

Dennis pulled one of the burgers out of the bag, looked at it, and then held it out to Jasper, "This one's yours," he said. He reached into the bag again and pulled out another burger, "This one's mine." He reached into the bag one last time and held the final burger out to me, "And this one's yours."

When I took the burger from his hand, I noticed that my name was written on the wrapping.

"What makes these burgers so special?" I asked as the three of us took our seats at the table.

Dennis and Jasper exchanged a look.

"Well," Jasper paused before he continued, "That's kind of hard to explain to someone who's not from around here."

"Try," I urged.

"Do you believe in ghosts?" Dennis blurted out, "Or life after death?"

"Uh…," I stuttered, confused by the sudden question, "No, not really…Do you?"

"100%," Dennis replied without hesitation.

"Me too," Jasper added.

"Where's this coming from?" I looked from Dennis to Jasper, "I thought we were talking about the burgers." I gestured at the wrapped bundle sitting on the table before me.

"We are talking about the burgers," Dennis said, "You wanted to know what made them so special and I needed to know what you believed before I answered you."

"Why does that matter?" I had no idea why that information was so important to him.

"If we were talking about normal burgers here, it wouldn't matter," Jasper answered, "But these aren't normal." He picked up his burger.

I unwrapped my burger and looked at it.

"It looks pretty normal to me," I said, lifting the bun and inspecting the toppings on it.

I was surprised to see that all my favorite things were there, as if I had special ordered the burger myself.

"You remembered," I said to Dennis.

"Remembered what?" he sounded confused.

"How I like my burgers," I replied, "Lettuce, pickles, onions, ketchup, and mustard," I gestured at the ingredients as I rattled them off. I assumed he'd customized them and that's why our names were written on them.

"That wasn't me," Dennis said, "The burgers come the way they come. You don't get to customize them."

He and Jasper unwrapped their burgers, both of which were also made just the way they liked them.

"So, you're saying they just happened to guess how each of us liked our burgers, and you had nothing to do with it," I replied.

"That's exactly what I'm saying," Dennis said.

"The Bruja Burger truck isn't a regular food truck," Jasper started to explain, "You don't place an order like normal. If you see the truck, your order is already waiting for you."

"Are they psychic?" I taunted, "Is that how they knew what we liked on our burgers and how they knew exactly where you were going to be so they could deliver them to you?"

The two of them sat there looking at me.

"I should've known this was going to be another one of your ridiculous fantasy stories about all the weird shit that goes on in this town," I sighed, "How about we just skip it this time and eat? I'm not in the mood to hear another one of your stupid fairy tales."

Jasper opened his mouth to say something but, Dennis stopped him with a shake of his head.

"It doesn't matter what you say," Dennis said to Jasper, "He's not going to believe us."

"Of course, I'm not going to believe you," I scoffed, "Why would I? Remember the story you told me about the guy who came into the ER with a stick growing out of his ass?" I pointed at Jasper, "Or the story you told me about the guy who bought a haunted TV that kept playing the same infomercial over and over again from the thrift store where your sister worked." I moved my finger so that it was pointing at Dennis. "Or the one about the college student who awakened some deer god up in the mountains." I moved my finger back and forth between the two of them, "I don't remember who told me that one."

"We didn't make those stories up," Jasper replied, "Those things really happened."

"Sure, they did," I smirked, before picking up my burger and taking a huge bite out of it.

"You'll see," Jasper replied softly.

"What'd you say?" I mumbled around a mouthful of food, not catching what he'd said.

"He said, you'll see," Dennis repeated what Jasper had said.

I ignored them and continued eating my burger. Dennis and Jasper just sat there watching me.

"Damn that was good," I said after I finished. It really was a good burger, perhaps the best I'd ever eaten, but I wasn't going to tell either of them that.

"If you don't want yours, I'll eat it," I pointed at Dennis's untouched burger.

"That would be a really bad idea," Jasper said.

"Why?" I snapped with a smile, "Will a stick start growing out of my ass?"

I tried to laugh but winced in pain instead as I felt a sharp pressure building inside my stomach.

"Here it comes," Dennis said.

He and Jasper leaned forward, watching me intently.

"What did you do to my burger?" I pointed my finger at Dennis while holding my stomach with my other hand.

"I didn't do anything to it," he replied, "If you had let us explain, you'd have known this would happen. It's all part of the process."

"What the hell are you talking about?" I squirmed in my seat as the pressure continued to build inside me, "What process?"

"Someone sent you a message from beyond the grave," Jasper explained, "The Bruja took that message and baked it into the burger and now that you've eaten it, the message is about to be delivered."

"Shut the fuck up," I spat at him. I couldn't believe he was trying to make a joke out of the discomfort I was feeling. "Can't you be serious for five minutes?"

"You'll see," was his reply.

I was getting tired of hearing him say that.

I stood up and was about to spew a torrent of expletives at him, but that's not what happened. Instead, I opened my mouth and belched. It was the longest and loudest belch that my body has ever produced. It scared the shit out of me. I felt like my soul was being expelled from my body.

Even more concerning were the words that echoed within the burp, spoken in a hollow, feminine voice.

As I burped out the words, Dennis and Jasper jumped up from the table and backed away from me.

"I'm calling the police," Dennis declared, pulling his phone out of his pocket as he and Jasper backed toward the front door of the apartment.

I couldn't do anything to stop them. All I could do was drop to my knees in exhaustion, the message I'd received via the burp replaying through my mind.

You can run, but you can't hide, they'll find my body eventually, along with the evidence you left behind.

If I had known that was what was going to happen when I ate the burger, I never would've eaten it.

VOWS

"What's that?" Layton asked, pointing at the sheet of paper in my hands.

Layton was my best friend and the best man at my wedding, which was due to start in less than an hour.

"Wedding vows," I replied, "Brianna's family is from Ireland and she asked me if we could honor one of their traditions during the ceremony."

"You must really like this girl if you're willing to stand up there and recite that gibberish," he clapped his hand on my back.

"It's not gibberish, it's Celtic," I explained, "And if I didn't like her, I wouldn't be marrying her."

Layton never missed an opportunity to give me grief about getting married ever since I told him that Brianna was the one who proposed to me. In his mind, women didn't propose to men unless they had some nefarious ulterior motive. I didn't have a problem with it.

Brianna and I had been dating for three years, the last of which we'd been living together. We had a lot in common and got along great. When she asked me to marry her, I didn't have to think about it, it was like we were already married. So, I said yes. Might as well make it official.

Layton caught me looking down at the engagement ring Brianna had given me. She and I had matching rings designed to look like Celtic knots tied around our fingers. They were family heirlooms passed down to her from her parents.

"That's so gay," he quipped.

"Whatever," I rolled my eyes at him, "You're just jealous no girl has ever liked you enough to propose to you."

***

While I was standing at the altar, waiting for Brianna to come down the aisle, I kept repeating the words I was supposed to say over and over again in my mind. This family tradition was important to her, and I didn't want to screw it up by mispronouncing one of the words.

You've got this, I thought, giving myself a little pep talk.

When the organist began to play, announcing the bride's arrival, I took a deep breath and turned to watch Brianna enter the chapel.

Even though Brianna's wedding dress lacked all of the flair normally seen on a traditional wedding dress, she looked stunning in it.

My mom originally scoffed at the idea of Brianna wearing something so simple on her wedding day, but she softened her stance after Brianna told her how the dress had belonged to her great-great-grandmother and had been worn by every bride in her family ever since.

Not wanting to insult Brianna's family heritage, my mom agreed that wearing the dress was the right thing to do, especially considering that Brianna's parents had died when she was a child and wouldn't be there to see her getting married.

When it came time to say our vows, the Celtic ones we'd added, I managed to recite them without missing a syllable. When I finished speaking, Brianna smiled at me. I could tell she was pleased that I had gotten it right without her needing to coach me. Which, if she had, would've been very embarrassing for me.

There was only one thing left to do to complete that part of the ceremony: the exchanging of rings. We both pulled our Celtic knot rings from our fingers and slid them onto each other's hands. I was surprised at how well the ring from Brianna's hand fit onto my much larger fingers, but I didn't get to dwell on it long because she unexpectedly stepped forward and kissed me.

"The ceremony is complete," she whispered after pulling away.

"Not quite," I whispered back, "We still have to say I do." I nodded over at the pastor, who was patiently waiting to complete his part of the wedding ceremony.

Sorry, Brianna mouthed to the pastor as she stepped back and took her place so he could proceed.

We finished the ceremony with both of us now wearing two sets of rings, the Celtic ones, and our traditional wedding bands. After we left the chapel, we went to the country club my parents had rented for the reception. Once that ended, we boarded a late-night flight for our honeymoon trip to Europe, another gift from my parents.

***

"I'm going to run into town and pick up a few things," Brianna said, picking up her purse and heading to the door of our hotel room.

It was the morning of our second day in the UK, the first stop of our two-week honeymoon tour of Europe. I had slept in while she had gotten up early.

"Give me a second to get dressed and I'll come with you," I swung my legs out of bed.

"You can't come." She walked over to the bed with a smile on her face, "You'll spoil the surprise." She leaned down and kissed me, and then rushed back to the door. "I won't be gone long," she declared before leaving.

Not knowing what else to do with myself while she was gone, I decided to take a shower.

It was while I was washing my hair that I suddenly felt very dizzy. I had to place my hand on the wall of the shower to steady myself while I waited for it to pass. But it didn't pass, it got worse.

The room started spinning, making me feel weak and sick to my stomach. It got so bad that I had to sit down on the floor of the stall to prevent myself from falling.

From there, things only got worse.

The dizziness eased, but it was replaced by a growing pain in my abdomen. It felt like someone was twisting my intestines into knots. I couldn't do anything but curl up on the floor, clutching my stomach.

That went on for about ten minutes before it suddenly stopped.

I slowly sat up and turned off the shower, thankful that the water temperature had remained tolerable during the entire ordeal.

What the hell was that?

I felt like I had been hit by a freight train. The only thing I could think of is that I must have eaten something bad the previous night when Brianna and I went out to dinner.

Keeping my back against the wall, I pushed myself up until I was standing. After waiting a moment to make sure I wasn't about to have another episode, I grabbed a towel and started to dry myself off. By the time I was finished, my strength had returned, and I was feeling much better.

While I was getting dressed, Brianna returned to the room carrying several shopping bags and a box of pastries.

"I hope you're hungry." She opened the box after dropping the shopping bags onto the floor.

"Those look delicious," I said, "But I'm not sure I should eat anything right now."

"How come?"

I told her about what happened to me while I was in the shower.

"You're fine," she smiled, "That was just separation sickness. It won't happen again as long as we stay together." She leaned over and kissed me, "Now, eat one of these, I guarantee you won't regret it." She thrust the box of pastries at me.

Separation sickness?

The idea that being separated from her was what caused me to become ill was ridiculous.

"Separation sickness?" I repeated out loud.

"Don't worry," she picked up a pastry and shoved it into my mouth, "It won't happen again as long as you stay close to me."

I took the pastry out of my mouth and set it back in the box, and then I took the box out of her hands and set it on the bed.

"How close?" I asked, wrapping my arms around her and pulling her towards me. "This close," I whispered in her ear as our bodies pressed together.

"Closer," she whispered back.

***

The rest of our honeymoon was uneventful. And by uneventful, I mean I didn't have another episode like I had in the shower. Everything else about it was amazing. When it was time to return home, we joked about leaving everything behind and just staying in Europe. Unfortunately, neither of us had the financial stability to make that dream a reality.

Life returned to normal for us over the next few weeks. Since we'd already been living together for a year, there was no awkwardness between us. We had our routines and easily went back to them as if nothing had changed.

Everything seemed fine until three months later when I was asked by my boss to deliver some documents to a client.

"I'll let you leave early if you do this for me," my boss said, trying to persuade me, "I'd do it myself, but I've got a meeting in fifteen minutes that's expected to run until the end of the day, and I'd rather not have to drop these off during rush hour." He raised the documents in his hand.

I looked at the clock. It was almost 2. The address I was supposed to deliver the documents to was about 15 miles from the office in the opposite direction from my apartment.

When my boss asked me to deliver the papers, I immediately opened the map app on my phone to see how bad the traffic was. The estimated travel time was 30 minutes.

That's not too bad. I could get there and home in about an hour.

I normally worked until 6 every day, so getting to leave early for once would be nice, especially considering that Brianna had the day off.

"Sure," I agreed, "I'll do it."

"Thanks, Eugene" my boss dropped the papers onto my desk, "You're a lifesaver."

I quickly closed out all of the programs I was using on my laptop, set my out-of-office notification, and then left to deliver the papers.

I got a few miles down the road before a feeling of dizziness came over me. A short while later, the stomach pains began.

Oh no, not this again.

The episode I had in the shower while on my honeymoon came rushing back to me.

Thinking I could power through it long enough to deliver the papers and then get back home, I kept driving.

That was a big mistake. The further I drove, the worse I felt, and my symptoms were quickly becoming more severe by the second. The pain eventually got so unbearable that I had to pull over.

I think I need to go to the hospital.

I pulled out my phone and quickly texted Brianna, letting her know what was happening and that I was going to go to the ER.

She responded by telling me that I didn't need to go to the ER, I just needed to turn around and drive back to the office. She insisted that I would feel instantly better once I did that.

Whether I was going to the hospital or the office didn't matter, I was going to have to turn around and start heading back the way I came since both locations were close to each other.

A few minutes later, my phone chimed. I looked down and saw that I had gotten a text from Brianna that said: Feel better yet?

Yes, I texted back. The truth was I did feel better. A lot better.

She replied by telling me to come and pick her up and that she would drive with me to deliver the papers and then we could go out and have an early dinner together.

***

"Don't you think I should go see a doctor?" I asked Brianna while we were waiting for our food to arrive.

"There's nothing wrong with you." She reached across the table and grabbed my hand, "I told you what happened the last time you felt that way."

Her words reminded me of the comment she'd made back in the hotel room when she'd referred to my condition as separation sickness.

It won't happen again as long as we stay together, she had said.

"I'm being serious." I pulled my hand away.

"So am I." Brianna held my gaze for a moment before she took a deep breath and sighed, "This is going to sound insane, but I promise you it's the truth and I swear that I only did it because I love you and didn't want to lose you."

I didn't know how to respond to that, so I remained silent.

"Remember the vows we said during the ceremony, the Celtic ones?" she asked.

"Yeah," I nodded, of course, I remembered them, I spent well over a month memorizing them so I wouldn't screw them up.

"They weren't vows. They were part of a binding ritual," she had a guilty look on her face, "The women in my family have been using it for centuries to keep their men from straying too far."

I couldn't stop myself from laughing. When I saw that she wasn't smiling, I stopped, "Wait…you're serious."

Brianna nodded her head. "The further apart we are, the worse you'll feel."

"That's insane."

"The same is true if you ever touch another woman." She kept her eyes on the table as she spoke.

That would explain the strange feeling of vertigo I got in the elevator a few weeks ago when my boss introduced me to our new payroll employee. When I shook her hand, I felt light-headed and a little dizzy, but I just assumed it was from the motion of the elevator.

"Why would you do something like that?" I didn't believe in magic, but I did have to accept the fact that something weird was going on between the two of us.

She looked up at me, "Because I love you and I didn't want to lose you," she repeated what she had said earlier.

I pushed my chair back and stood up.

"Where are you going?" she sounded worried.

"To the restroom," I said, "I need a moment to think."

My first thought upon hearing about the ritual was that Brianna was crazy. But the more I thought about it, the less I was convinced that was the case. I'd been with her for three years. If she were crazy, I think I would've picked up on it the way I had with some of my previous girlfriends.

She's not crazy, she just believes that magic is real.

I was staring at my reflection in the restroom mirror as I talked to myself.

Maybe magic is real. It would certainly explain what's happened to you.

Both sides of the conversation were playing out in my head.

If it is real, there's an easy way to prove it.

That's what I was going to do.

After I walked out of the restroom, I left the restaurant and went back to my car. Before I drove off, I sent Brianna a text telling her that I would be back in twenty minutes. She didn't respond.

As I drove, I kept track of how many miles I had driven before I started feeling bad. As soon as I started feeling the symptoms, I pulled over.

About 10 miles, I said to myself, looking at the odometer.

I turned around and drove in the opposite direction, starting my count when I passed the restaurant. Once again, when I started feeling the symptoms, I pulled over.

10 miles again.

By then, the twenty minutes had come and gone. Just to be sure, I decided to drive in another direction. Unsurprisingly, the results were the same, so I returned to the restaurant.

While I was gone, Brianna finished her dinner. My dinner sat across the table from her, getting cold.

"I can't believe it's real," I said, dropping into my chair. "I'm sorry I left like that," I apologized, "I needed to see it for myself."

"I figured that's what you were doing." She held up her phone, showing me that she had been watching my location on the Find My app.

I started picking at my cold food.

"What now?" Brianna asked.

"Is there a way to unbind us?" If there was a binding ritual, there had to be an unbinding one too, right?

"There is," she admitted, "But it will have the opposite effect on you."

"What does that mean?"

"It means the closer you get to me, the sicker you'll feel." She dropped her head before continuing, "We can do the ritual, if that's what you want. I won't try and talk you out of it."

That's not what I wanted. I didn't like that she had tricked me into performing the binding ritual, but I didn't want to spend the rest of my life without her. Everything else in our life was perfect.

"That's not what I want," I set my utensils down and reached across the table to grab one of her hands, "I want you."

Brianna's eyes watered up and then a tear rolled down her cheek.

"But I can do without the magic," I continued. "I realize there's nothing we can do about our current situation, but I want you to promise me that this is the end of it. No more rituals and no more secrets. Okay?"

"Okay," she agreed, wiping the tear from her cheek.

I released her hand and pushed my half-eaten plate of food to the side, "What do you say about getting some dessert? I think we've earned it."

****

Life went back to normal, at least as normal as it could be knowing that there was a ritual binding Brianna and me together. Now that I knew about it, it was easy to avoid its effects. It also helped that we lived in the heart of the city where everything we needed was just a short drive away, keeping me well within the ten-mile radius of Brianna that I had to maintain.

On our first wedding anniversary, Brianna surprised me by undergoing the same ritual she had me perform. I told her doing that was unnecessary, and I tried to talk her out of it but she insisted. Now, neither one of us can stray far from the other without becoming violently ill.

I remember the look on Brianna's face when I returned home after letting her experience the separation sickness for herself.

"I am so sorry." She placed her hand on my hips and pulled me close so she could kiss me, "That was horrible. I thought the ritual would just cause you to feel sick, like you had the flu or something. I didn't know it would be so painful." She stepped back and placed a hand on her stomach as she recalled the pain she'd felt.

Everything from that point on was perfect. I should've known it couldn't last.

On my 28th birthday, about six months after Brianna and I's first wedding anniversary, my best friend, Layton, showed up where I worked.

"What are you doing here?" I asked when I saw him leaning against my car in the parking garage.

"I came by to wish you a happy birthday," he said with a smirk.

I had seen that look on his face many, many times when we were roommates. It meant that he was up to something. Something that usually ended with one or both of us getting into some kind of trouble.

From behind me, I heard the shuffle of feet. Before I could turn around and see who it was, I was grabbed from behind. The giggles of the assailants as they bound my hands told me all I needed to know. I was pretty sure I recognized their voices as Callum and Spencer, friends of Layton and I, who were also groomsmen at my wedding.

"Come on, guys, this isn't funny," I said.

"Calm down," Layton said, "We just want to take you out and celebrate your birthday. We promise to have you back in time for your dinner reservation with your wife."

"Where are we going?" I asked as Callum and Spencer led me toward one of their cars and shoved me in the back seat. Once I was inside, they sat on opposite sides of me.

"Harrah's," Layton replied.

Harrah's?

That was the casino on the reservation just outside of town.

"We can't go there," I protested.

It was at least a thirty-mile drive from where we were.

"Sure, we can," Layton replied as he got into the driver's seat and started the car, "It'll be just like the old days before Brianna castrated you."

"I'm serious," I pled with them, "Bad things are going to happen if we go."

I couldn't tell them the truth about the ritual. I'd only sound insane.

"Gag him," Layton said.

"Please don't do this," I begged.

"You'll thank me for this later," Layton was looking at me through the rearview mirror with that stupid smirk on his face.

I started to protest again but was unable to get a word out before Callum shoved a tie into my mouth. Spencer then tied his tie around my head, keeping the gag in place.

"This is going to be a night to remember," Layton declared as he pulled out of the parking garage.

I continued to fight to free myself, but Callum and Spencer were much bigger than me and easily kept me contained. I continued to fight until the fight was taken out of me by the separation sickness.

When I doubled over in pain, Spencer and Callum showed genuine concern, but Layton made them believe it was all an act.

"Don't let him fool you," he said to them.

My thoughts turned to Brianna as I realized she must be feeling the same thing I was.

"He's faking it," Layton continued, pressing his foot down on the accelerator to avoid stopping at a yellow light. "You'll see."

Those were the last words I heard before the pain became too unbearable and I passed out.

CRONE LAKE

"Do you want to drive?" my dad asked, dangling the keys from his finger.

"Seriously?" I smiled.

"If you're going to take over for me, you need to get comfortable driving Big Betty." He tossed the keys to me.

Big Betty was the name he'd given to his tow truck. The vehicle my mom often referred to as his second wife because of how much time and money he'd invested keeping the old GMC running.

Since I'd turned 18 earlier that month, my dad decided it was time I got involved in the family business. He assumed I was going to take over the company when he retired the way he had for my grandfather. I didn't have the heart to tell him that I was planning on moving out and going to college once the summer was over.

I climbed into the truck and started her up.

"Where to?" I asked once my dad had sat down and buckled his seat belt.

"The festival grounds," he replied.

Every June, our small town of Foggy Mill has a week-long summer solstice celebration along the shores of Crone Lake. The most recent festival, which ended the previous night, was the town's bicentennial celebration. Last I'd heard, over 15,000 people had attended, breaking last year's record of 12,000. It's hard to imagine that it had survived that long and had grown as large as it had. I'd heard it said around town that without the festival, Foggy Mill would've gone bankrupt decades ago. I know my dad made a killing that week, towing the vehicles of tourists who couldn't be bothered to park in the designated parking lots or who'd had a bit too much to drink and found themselves spending the night in the drunk tank.

"How come you didn't want me to start working with you before the festival?" I asked as I pulled out of the driveway, "I could've helped."

"Festival week is crazy," he said, "There wasn't enough time to prepare you."

"You're just towing cars and taking them to the impound lot, right? How hard can that be?"

He turned his head and looked at me, "That's the easy part," he said, "Dealing with the drunk and angry vehicle owners, that's where things get crazy."

I hadn't thought about that.

"Let's get you comfortable with towing first and then I'll show you how to handle the people," he smiled, "By this time next year, you'll be a pro."

Only if I get trapped here, I thought to myself. I hoped to be long gone well before next year.

***

When I pulled into the festival parking lot, I was surprised to see several cop cars and an ambulance parked over near the boat ramp.

"Another drowning, do you think?" I asked my dad.

"I can't think of anything else it could be," he replied.

Crone Lake covered almost fifty square miles of countryside, making it a popular destination for people looking to spend a little time on the water. Most of those people know their way around the lake, but some don't, and that's when accidents happen. I can't think of a single year where there haven't been at least three drownings. Sadly, most of those incidents occurred during the week of the festival. I think that's because of the increased number of people visiting the lake at that time, but some claim it's because the lake is cursed.

"Pull up next to the sheriff," my dad pointed at the police truck.

Sheriff Tate had been the sheriff of Foggy Mill for as long as I could remember. The only thing I knew about him was that he and my dad had gone to high school together.

As I brought the truck to a stop next to the sheriff's truck, Sheriff Tate looked over at us, gave a quick wave of his hand, which my dad returned, and then started walking over to greet us.

"Morning, Seth," my dad said after rolling down his window. My dad was one of the few people in town that could get away with using the sheriff's first name.

"Morning, Gus," the sheriff replied, leaning down a little to look inside the truck, "Morning, Cole," he said to me, "I see your father finally had the good sense to put you to work.

"Morning, Sheriff," I replied, ignoring his other comment because I didn't know how to respond to it.

I desperately wanted to ask him what had happened, but I didn't want to seem nosy, so I kept my mouth shut. Thankfully, my dad didn't have that problem.

"How many this time?" my dad asked.

"Two," the sheriff replied, "Newlyweds. That's their car over there." He pointed across the front of the tow truck to a blue sedan parked several spaces away from us. Painted in large white letters on its rear window were the words JUST MARRIED.

"We'll take it to the impound lot," my dad said. A moment later he added, "Is that all you've got for us?"

"Doris claims she has another at one of her cabins," the sheriff said, "But we haven't finished our sweep of the lake so I can't confirm that yet."

"We can swing by after we drop off the car and talk to her," my dad suggested, "It's on the way back from the impound lot."

"Let me know if you find anything," Sheriff Tate said, "And I'll do the same. I've got to get back," he nodded toward the group of deputies and paramedics gathered on the shore of the lake. "It was nice seeing you, Cole." He gestured at me, "I look forward to working with you."

"Me too," I said.

"Alright," my dad declared after the sheriff had walked away, "Let's go hook up that car."

***

Hooking the car up to the tow truck wasn't as difficult as I had thought it would be. The most time-consuming part was trying to line up the wheel lift with the front wheels. Once I was able to do that, the rest was easy, thanks in large part to my dad being there to guide me through the process.

"Take it slow and easy until you get used to the car being back there," my dad said as I pulled out of the festival parking lot.

That's exactly what I did.

"You can speed up a little," my dad suggested when he noticed how slow I was going, "As long as you don't swerve or make any sharp turns, you'll be fine."

I did speed up a little, but it still took me twice as long to get to the impound lot as it should've, but I got there without incident.

When I pulled up to the lot, the deputy assigned to man the gate opened it without bothering to come out of the gatehouse.

"Pull up over there," my dad pointed to the corner of the lot, "There should be plenty of room for you to back the car into that spot."

It took me a few tries to keep the truck and the car we were towing straight, but I was eventually able to back into the indicated spot. After that, all I had to do was release the car and we were done.

"Not bad for your first time," my dad clapped his hand against my back.

The two of us were standing at the rear of the truck as I secured the tire lift back in its resting place.

"Is there anything else we need to do?" I asked him. "Any forms we need to fill out?"

"Not for this one," he replied, "Because it's tied to the accident victims Seth will handle the paperwork. If this were just a standard tow, you would have to fill out one of the towing forms and leave the carbon copy with the deputy in the gatehouse. The original copy goes into our files at home."

"Where do I get the forms?"

He popped open the side compartment in the bed of the truck where he kept his tools, "Right here." He pointed to a clipboard that was attached to the wall of the compartment with magnets. On the clipboard was a thick stack of forms. "It's pretty self-explanatory," he said, "Just fill out as much information as you can."

I picked up the clipboard, looked at the form to see what information it required, and then put it back.

"You ready to head on over to Doris's place?" my dad asked as he shut the compartment.

"I'm ready if you are," I replied.

Turned out my dad wasn't as ready as he thought he was. On our way back through town, he had me stop at the diner on Main Street so we could have breakfast.

***

When we arrived at Doris's, she came out of the office to greet us as soon as I pulled into the parking lot.

"Pull up to the curb and roll down your window," my dad instructed when he saw her.

Doris owned Crone Lake Cabins. A family-operated rental company that has 18 cabins spread out around the lake. If you wanted a place to stay that was on the lake, Crone Lake Cabins was your only option.

Outside investors have tried to get permission to build more rental properties, but the city council had always denied their petitions. My mom, who teaches English and History at Foggy Mills High, said they did that because the town charter has strict restrictions about who can own land around the lake.

"Well, what do we have here?" Doris smiled when she saw that I was the one driving the truck.

"Good morning, Mrs. Welch," I said to her.

"How do you like it so far?" she asked, referring to working the tow truck with my dad.

"It's okay," I said.

"Well, if you ever get tired of working with your old man," she gestured at my dad, "You can come work for me in the rental office."

"Thanks, I'll keep that in mind," I lied.

Thinking about being stuck in that small office with her all day sounded boring. If I had to stay in town, I'd rather drive the tow truck.

"Seth said you might have a pickup for us?" My dad wasted no time getting right to the point of our visit.

The smile vanished from Doris's face, "Number 10," she said, "She was supposed to check out this morning, but I haven't seen her. I tried calling, but she never answered and when I drove by earlier, her car was still parked out in front of the cabin."

"Have you tried knocking on the door?" There was a hint of sarcasm in my dad's tone.

"Not yet," she replied, "I was going to let the sheriff do that. In case she was," she paused and looked at me before looking over at my dad, "You know," she finished cryptically.

"He's pretty busy over at the festival grounds," my dad said, "Might be awhile before he can get over this way. If you want, Cole and I can go over and check it out for you."

"That's fine with me," Doris agreed, "Let me get you the spare key." She turned and walked back to her office.

"What was she talking about?" I asked my dad once Doris had walked away. "What does she think happened to the woman?"

"She thinks she might've drowned like the others," my dad said.

"Why didn't she just say that?"

My dad shrugged, "You'd have to ask her."

"Could it be because she thinks the lake is cursed?"

"Cursed?" my dad scoffed, "I can assure you that Doris does not think the lake is cursed. In fact, you won't find anybody in Foggy Mill who believes those stories," he stared intently at me for a moment, "You don't believe them, do you?"

"Of course not," I said quickly, "But there's a lot of people out there who do."

There are entire websites and social media groups dedicated to discussing The Curse of Crone Lake and none of them can agree upon what the curse is exactly. The only thing they can agree on is that the lake kills people. The most popular theory unsurprisingly involves witches. It is believed, but not supported by any historical facts according to my mom, that the townsfolk of Foggy Mill used to drown witches in the lake and that the spirits of those dead witches are still there, doing to others what was done to them.

"The only people who believe that crap are people who don't live here," my dad snapped, "If they did live here, they'd realize how blessed we all are."

This was the first time I'd actually mentioned the curse in front of my dad, and I regretted it. Normally, I'd talk to my mom about it since she was an expert on local history. Whenever I did, we'd have an engaging conversation where she would happily debunk whatever new theory I'd found on the internet. I thought my dad would respond similarly, instead of getting annoyed as he had.

I decided to keep my mouth shut on the subject. Thankfully, Doris emerged from the office a moment later, keeping the awkward silence between my dad and me from growing.

"Here you go," she reached across me to hand the key to my dad, "If she's still there, tell her she needs to pay for another night or get the hell out."

"I'll let her know," my dad replied, taking the keys. To me, he said, "Alight, let's go."

***

"Which way?" I asked as I was about to pull out of the parking lot. I had no idea where I was going. I'd never been out to one of Doris's cabins.

"Take a left and follow Lake Drive until you come to Willow Pass," my dad instructed, "The cabin is about a mile from the Chapman house."

The Chapmans were the first family to settle in Foggy Mill, making the Chapman house the oldest original structure in the area. When the last remaining Chapman died in the late 50s, he willed the house to the town with instructions to turn it into a museum.

The house is an impressive structure that takes up half of the island it was built upon. When I was little, I used to refer to it as the castle.

I drove like I was going to the Chapman House until my dad said, "Turn here," pointing at the wooden sign at the end of a gravel-lined drive. The sign featured the Crone Lake Cabins logo along with the number 10.

I turned down the drive and parked in front of the cabin, next to the pickup truck that was already there. Even though it was referred to as a cabin, it looked more like a regular lake house with a strong country aesthetic.

"Stay here," my dad said before getting out of the truck.

I sat there and watched him walk up to the front door and knock. When nobody answered, he knocked again. Before using the key Doris had given him, he walked entirely around the house, stopping to peek through the windows whenever he came to one. Once he completed his circuit, he motioned for me to join him on the porch.

"What's up?" I asked.

"There's nobody here," he said, "So we're going to go inside, collect any personal belongings we find, put them in that truck," he hooked his thumb over his shoulder, "And tow it to the impound lot."

"Okay," is all I said, even though I wanted to ask him if he thought the woman who was renting the place had drowned as Doris had hinted at.

"Wait here for a second," my dad said as he unlocked the door and stepped into the foyer, "Hello!" he called out, "Anybody home? We're with Crone Lake Cabin Rentals! You were supposed to check out this morning!"

He stopped and listened for a moment.

"It's clear," he declared, motioning for me to enter.

"I'll take the bedrooms, while you clean up out here," he gestured towards the living room and kitchen area, "Pack up anything that doesn't belong."

I checked the living room first. Besides a few empty soda cans, there wasn't anything else in the room to show that someone had been there.

I picked up the cans and tossed them into the trash on my way into the kitchen. When I did that, I got a view of the dining area, which wasn't visible to me while I was in the living room.

"What is all of this?" I said to myself, walking over to get a closer look at the stacks of books and papers that were spread out across the dining table.

In the center of it all was a map of Foggy Mill and Crone Lake with several small red circles drawn on it. As I examined the map, I was shocked to see that one of the circles was drawn around the area where my house was.

What the hell?

I picked up the top book from one of the stacks and read the title, trying to make sense of what this woman was doing in Foggy Mill and why she'd circled my house on the map.

Cursed Lake.

I put it back and quickly read the titles of the rest of the books on the stack. They were all about Crone Lake, Foggy Mill, and the Chapman family.

"Dad!" I called out, "You might want to come and look at this!"

He walked into the kitchen carrying two luggage bags, which he dropped on the floor before walking over to join me at the table.

"What is all of this?" I gestured at the stuff on the table.

He walked around the room, looking at everything but not touching anything.

"It's nothing," he suddenly said.

"If it's nothing, why is our house circled on the map?" I pointed my finger at it.

"It's not important," he said, the tone of his voice warning me not to question him further, "Take those bags out to the truck and start hitching it up." When he was done talking, he pulled his phone out of his pocket.

"Now," he snapped at me.

I brushed past him, grabbed the bags, and left the kitchen, but I did not leave the cabin. I opened the front door and set the bags on the porch, then closed it again while remaining in the entryway.

I stood there, listening, waiting to see who he was going to call.

"Hey, Seth," I heard him say, "We've got a problem." There was a moment of silence before he spoke again, saying, "The woman who's been staying at Doris's place knows something," there was another period of silence before he said, "Alright, I'll see you there."

When he was done talking, I heard him start to gather up the things that were on the table. That was my cue to leave.

A short while later, he stepped out of the cabin carrying two large file boxes, one stacked on top of the other. By then, I had backed the tow truck into position and was in the process of securing the truck's front tires to the lift.

"Where to now?" I waited until he put the boxes in the back of the pickup to ask.

"Home," my dad said.

"Why home?"

"To drop you off."

"Why're you dropping me off?"

I knew it was because he was going to meet the Sheriff somewhere, but I wanted to see what he would say.

"The person this stuff belongs to is dangerous," he gestured at the truck we were going to tow, "Until we know what happened to her, I'd feel better knowing you were at home with your mother."

"Dangerous how?"

"I don't have time to explain right," he said, dismissing my question, "I need to get this truck to the impound lot so Seth can look at it."

I knew better than to protest or push him any further. He'd already made up his mind and no matter what I said, he wasn't going to give me a straight answer.

"Fine," I said, walking around to the passenger side of the tow truck and climbing inside, "Let's go home."

As we drove away from the cabin, neither one of us said a word. We both just kept our eyes forward and our mouths shut. We drove that was for about a mile until a woman suddenly stepped out of the woods in front of us.

"Look out!" I yelled at my dad when I saw her rush out into the middle of the street from my side of the road. She was waving her arms in the air, trying to get us to stop.

As we raced toward her, I thought my dad was going to hit her because he was not slowing down. Not knowing what else to do, I grabbed the wheel and yanked it towards me, forcing the tow truck onto the shoulder where my dad had to slam on the brakes to avoid driving into the woods.

"What the hell is wrong with you," he snapped at me.

"What's wrong with me?" I spat back at him, "What the hell is wrong with you? You almost hit that woman."

Before he could reply, the woman started banging on his window, "That's my truck," she said. She did not look happy.

My dad rolled down his window and calmly addressed the woman, "Your car was on private property, and we were asked to tow it," he said, "If you want it back, you're going to have to pick it up from the impound lot once it's been processed."

"Actually," the woman reached behind her and pulled a sleek-looking pistol from the waistband of her jeans, "You're going to give it back to me right now." She pointed the pistol at my dad's head.

"Your name is Cole, right?"

It took me a moment to realize she was talking to me.

"Uh… ye… yeah," I stammered, surprised she knew my name.

"Hop out of the truck, Cole," she flicked the gun in my direction, "And release my truck."

I looked over at my dad, and without looking back at me he said, "Do it."

I slowly opened the door and got out, making my way to the back of the tow truck. I briefly considered running into the woods and trying to get help while I was out of her line of sight, but I was too scared to try. I was hoping that if I did what she wanted, nobody would get hurt and she would leave.

"It's free," I said once I'd released her truck.

The woman looked over at me.

As soon as she turned her head, my dad threw his door open, knocking it into the woman and sending her falling to the ground.

No!

I couldn't believe how stupid my dad was being.

"NO!" I yelled the word that time as I watched the woman recover from her fall and aim the pistol at my dad.

He'd only gotten one foot out of the truck before she fired.

My dad's head snapped back, and then he slumped to the ground.

The woman quickly got up and started walking towards me, pointing the pistol at my head.

"You're coming with me," she said.

I didn't hear her at first. I was in shock, staring at the lifeless body of my dad lying on the ground.

"Let's go," she jabbed me with the pistol, "Get in the truck." She pulled a set of keys out of her pocket and used the remote to unlock the doors to her truck.

I couldn't get my feet to move.

"Cole," she said softly, "I know you're in shock right now, but I need you to listen to me, okay?"

"Okay," I replied.

She walked around the front of the truck to the passenger side and pulled the door open, "Come on," she motioned for me to get in.

Afraid and unable to make sense of what was going on, I climbed into the truck as she told me.

Once I sat down, she shut the door and ran over to the driver's side, got in, and started the truck.

As we drove by the tow truck, I couldn't help but look at my dad's prone body lying on the side of the road.

"This isn't going to make a lot of sense to you right now," the woman said, "But that wasn't your father."

I looked at her like she was crazy. I didn't see how that was possible. I'd seen my birth certificate, both of my parents' names were on it.

"I'll explain everything once we get the hell out of Foggy Mill," she said.

I didn't care about what she had to say. She'd just killed my dad. There was no way she was going to be able to justify that.

***

We drove in silence for a couple of hours before the woman eventually pulled into the parking lot of a rundown-looking motel. The kind that looked like it would be run by someone like Norman Bates.

She got out of the truck and shut the door behind her, shoving the pistol into the waistband of her jeans before covering it with her shirt.

"I'm going to go get a room," she said, "You're welcome to stay with me if you like. If you do, I'll tell you everything I know about Foggy Mill and Crone Lake. Otherwise, you're free to go," she gestured down the road, "The nearest town is a few miles up that road."

"You're letting me go?" I asked.

"You were never a prisoner, Cole," she said, talking to me through the open window of the truck, "I just wanted to get you somewhere safe. Somewhere far away from Foggy Mill."

"Why?" the word came out with a lot more force than I intended, "And how do you know my name?"

"I can't give you a quick answer," she said, turning to walk towards the motel office, "If you really want to know, you'll have to stick around and listen to the whole story."

As soon as she walked into the office, I got out of the truck and started walking towards the road. When I passed the bed of the truck, I happened to glance inside and saw the boxes of stuff that my dad had collected from the cabin. Seeing the boxes reminded me of the map and the books and all the other weird stuff I had seen on the table in the cabin.

She knows something about Foggy Mill.

Or she's just crazy, I argued with myself.

If she's crazy, why'd she let me live? Why'd she say I could leave?

The longer I stood there, the easier it was to convince myself that I owed it to my dad to find out who the woman was and why she shot him.

"I'm glad you decided to stay," the woman said when she'd returned from the office and found me standing next to the truck, "Help me bring this stuff inside and I'll tell you everything I know."

***

There were two beds in the motel room. I sat on one while the woman used the other to lay out a bunch of items from the boxes we'd brought inside.

"I supposed I should start by introducing myself," the woman said, "My name is Gabrielle," she placed her hand on her chest, "And my story starts thirty years ago when my sister, Tina, and her boyfriend, disappeared."

As Gabrielle told her story, I learned that Tina wasn't really her sister. The two girls had been placed with the same foster family and had become so close that they started telling everyone they were sisters.

"This is her," Gabrielle said, lifting a photo from the bed and handing it to me.

Seeing the girl in the photo gave me a feeling of déjà vu. "She looks familiar," I said.

"She should," Gabrielle said, picking up a printout of a different picture and handing it to me.

"This is Andrea," I said, immediately recognizing the girl in the photo. In the picture, she was manning one of the refreshment booths at the summer solstice festival.

When I held the two photos side by side, the resemblance was incredible. But it couldn't possibly be the same person since the photos were obviously taken decades apart.

"What do you know about Andrea?" Gabrielle asked.

"Not much," I admitted, "She hasn't lived in Foggy Mill very long."

"When I first saw this photo," she tapped the printout, "I thought I was looking at a ghost."

"Where did you get it?"

"I found it online, on one of those travel sites where members can post pictures of their vacations. It was taken three years ago during the festival," she said, "As soon as I saw it, I went to Foggy Mill to find her."

"Did you find her?"

"I did," she replied, "And that's when all of this craziness started." She swept her hand over the bed, indicating all the books and papers she'd collected on Foggy Mill and its residents.

"When I saw Andrea I was convinced she was Tina. She looked identical to her from the placement of the moles on her cheek to the scar on the back of her hand. But there was no way she could be Tina. She was too young. If Tina were still alive, she'd be in her 40s like me."

"I left Foggy Mill feeling confused. How could this girl look exactly like Tina did on the day she disappeared? No matter how hard I tried, I couldn't let it go and that brought me back to Foggy Mills a few more times, where I eventually stumbled upon this."

She handed me another printout of a photo. Like the photo of Andrea, I recognized the person in it immediately.

"This is Dewey," I said.

"I knew him as Shawn."

Gabrielle handed me another old photo. In it, Tina had her arm wrapped around the shoulders of a young man who looked exactly like Dewey.

"Shawn was Tina's boyfriend," I said, stating the obvious.

"I thought it was one hell of a coincidence to find someone who looked like Tina. Then, when I saw that kid," she pointed at the printout of Dewey, "I figured I was going crazy or something really bizarre was going on in that town."

She reached behind her and picked up a book that looked like a photo album and held it out to me. I set the photos I was holding onto the bed next to me so I could take the book.

"What's this?" I asked.

"That's all the proof I collected to convince myself that I wasn't going crazy."

I set the photo album on my lap and opened it. Stuck on the first page were two things, a newspaper article about one of the drownings in Crone Lake and a photograph. Handwritten underneath both was a different year. Underneath the article was the year 1973 and underneath the photograph was the year 2003.

"It looks like the same person," I said, looking from the photo of the man in the newspaper article to the man in the photograph.

"Weird, right?" she said, "Keep going, it gets weirder."

I flipped through the next few pages and found more of the same thing.

"Stop right there," Gabrielle held her hand out as I was about to turn the page, "Look at this one," she tapped the open photo album with her index finger.

I read the article. Like the others, it was about another drowning in Crone Lake, but this one was different. It wasn't about a single person. It was about a family.

"They never found the son's body," Gabrielle said.

"Why is that weird?" I asked. There have been plenty of other bodies that hadn't been recovered from the lake. My dad told me it was because the lake was too deep in some places to search.

"It's weird because the day after that couple went missing, this little boy appeared," she pointed to the other page where there was a photograph of a kid, no more than two years old, playing in the front yard of a familiar-looking house. The kid looked very similar to the boy pictured in the news article.

"Wait a minute!" I said, suddenly realizing what I was looking at, "That's my house!"

"And that's you," Gabrielle pointed at the boy.

"No," my first impulse was to deny what she was implying, "There's no way that's me," I gestured at the news article.

"I didn't want to believe any of this stuff either," she said, "But the evidence is all right there." She flipped forward a couple of pages to another article about a young couple that had drowned. "Your parents are not who they say they are."

The couple in the article looked like my parents did when they were younger, but it couldn't be them because the article I was looking at was from the 1950s. They'd both be in their 90s if it were really them.

"In fact," she took a deep breath, then let it out with a sigh before revealing another ridiculous accusation, "They're not even human."

"What?" That was all I could think to say.

"Did you know that Crone Lake used to be known as Carogne Lake?" Gabrielle asked, changing the subject.

I shook my head.

"Carogne is a French word that means carrion," she explained, "Therefore Crone Lake was essentially once known as Carrion Lake. It was changed to Crone Lake in the early 1800s because Crone was much easier to say than Carogne."

"Why was it called Carrion Lake?" There was an idea already forming in the back of my mind about why, but I wanted her to say it.

"Because of all of the bodies that kept washing up upon its shores," she said, confirming my suspicions, "Something that's been happening every year, ever since that area was settled. Not a year has gone by without a body being found."

"People drown," I replied, finding myself parroting the explanation my parents always used.

"That's true," Gabrielle agreed, "People do drown, but why is it that many of the people who've drowned are missing their hearts?"

"What?" I found myself unable to say anything else again. Her story was getting weirder and weirder and harder to process.

"After I discovered all of those dead or missing people, suddenly living again in Foggy Mill, I started digging into the town's past and eventually started looking at its legends." She placed her hand on the stack of books sitting on the bed. All of them were about the curse of Crone Lake.

"Through these," she was talking about the books, "I was able to start piecing things together and eventually figure out what was going on. The final piece of the puzzle came to me by chance while I was researching the idea of witches and lake monsters, and the other absurd theories surrounding the curse of Crone Lake."

She reached behind her and picked up a book. She flipped it open to a page marked with a post-it note and turned it around to face me.

"Read the highlighted part," she instructed.

"The shapeshifter has been known by many names throughout history, including changeling, doppelganger, and skinwalker." I looked up at her.

"Keep reading," she urged.

"Despite minor regional differences, all these creatures have one thing in common. To take the form of someone, they must ingest a part of that person. For most of them, the heart seems to be the organ of choice."

She closed the book and set it aside.

"You know how crazy that sounds, right?" The idea that the town was full of shapeshifters was a bit much to accept.

"But it all fits," was her reply.

"You haven't explained my part in all of it," I said, "Where do I fit? Why would a bunch of shapeshifters kidnap me and raise me as their son?"

"They're not raising you," she said, "They're farming you. You and all the other kids they've taken over the years."

"Farming us?" I raised an eyebrow at the thought, "What does that even mean?"

I should have left when I had the chance. I was beginning to think the woman really was crazy and that staying there with her was a mistake.

"It means you were never going to leave Foggy Mill alive," she said, "As soon as your body was needed, they would've done to you what they've done to so many others."

"Kill me and eat my heart?" I scoffed at the idea.

"Maybe this will help convince you," she pulled out her phone, tapped the screen a couple of times, and then held it out to me, "Watch this."

I took her phone and watched the video that was playing on it. In it, the sheriff of Foggy Mill and the man I'd been calling dad, loaded what appeared to be a couple of bodies onto a boat and drove them out into the middle of the lake where they were unceremoniously dumped into the water.

"Still don't think he's a monster?" Gabrielle said, taking the phone from me.

I didn't know what to think. The only thing I was sure of was that my life was a lie.

"Your dad and the sheriff aren't the only ones involved with what's going on," Gabrielle started unfolding a map. The same map I had seen with all the circled locations on it, "All of the prominent members of the town are."

"Does anyone else know about this?" I asked.

"Not yet. I was waiting until I had some more substantial evidence before I went to the authorities," she said, "And now that I've got it," she indicated her phone and the video it contained, "I'm going straight to the FBI as soon as I leave here. You're welcome to come with me if you want. If not, I can drop you off wherever you like."

"I think I need some time to process all of this," I said.

"I understand," Gabrielle said softly, placing her hand on my knee, "I really do, and I'm sorry you had to find out about it like this."

We sat there in silence for a moment before Gabrielle stood up and declared that she was hungry.

"I haven't eaten anything since last night," she said, "There's a burger joint a couple of miles up the road. Do you want to go and grab something to eat?"

"I think I'd rather stay here if that's okay." I had a lot to think about and wouldn't mind getting to do that by myself.

Gabrielle walked over to the motel room door, "I'll bring you something back," she said, "While I'm gone, feel free to go through that stuff," she gestured at the collection of books and papers on the bed, "It might help you better understand what's really going on in Foggy Mill."

I didn't say anything as she opened the door and left.

***

While Gabrielle was gone, I did go through the stacks of information she'd compiled. One of the more interesting things I found was some notes she'd written, detailing how she believed the Foggy Mill coroner was removing the hearts of the drowning victims during their autopsies.

Apparently, she'd even gone so far as to bribe a funeral director the previous year, asking him to verify if all of the organs of that year's drowning victims were present after he'd received the bodies from the Foggy Mill morgue. The funeral director was surprised to discover that the hearts were missing from both the bodies, but Gabrielle wasn't.

I was in the middle of reading one of the Curse of Crone Lake books when the door to the motel room slammed open.

"Come on," Gabrielle motioned for me to get up, "We have to leave."

"What's going on?" I set the book down and quickly got to my feet.

"They're looking for us," she said, "It's not safe for us to stay here. We need to leave right now." After she finished speaking, she turned and walked back out to the parking lot.

"What about all of your stuff?" I asked as I stepped outside.

"It's not important," she said, climbing back into her truck. When she noticed I wasn't moving, she called out, "Are you coming or not because I'm leaving?"

"I'm coming," I said, running up to the truck and climbing inside.

The tires of the truck squealed as Gabrielle backed out of the parking space and then gunned it, racing out onto the road.

While she drove, I happened to look at Gabrielle's hands and noticed that the beds of her fingernails were stained red with dried blood. Seeing that gave me a sinking feeling in the pit of my stomach.

"How'd you find out they were looking for us?" I asked.

"What?" she replied, lifting her right arm to brush away a stray lock of hair from her forehead.

As she did that, the sleeve of her shirt rolled up far enough for me to see the watch she was wearing on her wrist. I knew that watch. I'd helped my dad pick it out for my mom's birthday several years ago.

After I saw the watch, I remembered seeing something else out of the corner of my eye as I ran to get into the truck. There was a tarp in the bed of the pickup that hadn't been there when I first got into the truck with Gabrielle that morning.

I slowly turned my head and looked through the rear window into the bed of the pickup, where part of an arm and a leg could be seen peeking out from beneath a rolled-up blue tarp.

They're not looking for us, I thought, *They already found us.*

RESPECTRE

"Aren't you going to pull over?" Abby asked.

"Why?" I replied.

"Because there's a funeral procession coming," she gestured at the pair of police motorcycles that were approaching us from the opposite direction. Behind them was a hearse and a seemingly endless line of cars with their hazard lights on.

"If I stop, we're not going to make it to the movie on time," I pointed out.

"It's not my fault," she said, "I don't make the laws."

Technically, it was her fault that we were on the verge of being late because she wasn't ready when I arrived to pick her up, despite me telling her what time I was going to be there.

I didn't want to be late, so I ignored her and kept on driving.

"Seriously," Abby scoffed, cocking her head to the side, and giving me a reproachful look, "You're going to get a ticket if you don't pull over."

"No, I'm not," I insisted, "I'm not doing anything illegal."

"Are you sure about that because that's not what I've heard?"

"I'm positive," I assured her, "I took a driving class in high school and someone asked the teacher about it and he said that as long as you don't interfere with their right of way, you can keep driving."

"Legal or not, it's still disrespectful not to stop," she chided me, "Wouldn't you want people to stop if it was a funeral for someone you knew?"

"Honestly, I wouldn't care," I said, "If the living have places they need to be, the dead shouldn't hold them up."

"That's terrible." Abby shook her head in disgust.

An uncomfortable silence settled between us we started to pass by the funeral procession. I think it was because Abby was waiting to see if I was joking about not pulling over.

I wasn't joking.

When that became clear to Abby, she made a tsking noise in her throat.

Not wanting to see the look of disdain she was giving me, I kept my attention on the road ahead.

From the corner of my eye, I could see Abby turn her head to watch as the hearse drove by. I expected her to admonish me for not stopping again, but that's not what she did. Instead she screamed and grabbed hold of me with both of her hands, digging her nails into the flesh of my forearm.

The sudden violent action startled me, causing me to hit the brakes and swerve, almost hitting a car in the funeral procession before I was able to come to a stop on the side of the road.

"What the fuck is wrong with you?!" I pulled my arm away from her, "You almost caused an accident."

Abby tried to speak but the only thing that came out of her mouth was a stuttering 'uh' sound.

"What's wrong?" I asked.

She lifted a trembling hand and pointed her finger in the direction of the back seat.

I looked up into the rearview mirror to see what she was pointing at.

"JESUS CHRIST!" I screamed, startled by what I saw. I whipped my head around so I could look into the back seat, needing to confirm that what I saw in the mirror's reflection was real.

It was.

"Get out of the car," I said to Abby as I fumbled to unlatch my seat belt.

Once I was free, I stumbled out of the car, heedless of the fact that I was fleeing into the road.

Thankfully, there weren't any cars coming at the time as all of them had chosen to pull over for the funeral procession that was still going by.

When I looked across the roof of my car, I saw Abby backing across the shoulder and into the parking lot of a small office park, trying to put as much distance between her and the vehicle as possible.

I rushed over to join her.

"Who the fuck is that?" I whispered, pointing at the pale, well-dressed, elderly gentleman in the backseat of my car, "And how the hell did he get in my car without either of us knowing he was back there?"

He was just sitting there, staring forward with an expressionless look on his gaunt face.

"I…," Abby started to say then paused for a moment, "This is going to sound crazy," she continued, "But I think it's the guy from the funeral," Abby said.

"What guy?"

"The dead one," she replied, "I think that's his ghost."

"That's impossible," I refuted the idea, "Ghosts aren't real."

"If he's not a ghost," Abby countered, "How do you explain his sudden appearance?" she gestured at the elderly man, "I saw it happen. He wasn't hiding back there. He just popped into existence." She mimed an explosion with her hands, "Why do you think I screamed and grabbed hold of you the way I did?"

I wasn't going to press the issue with her. If she wanted to believe he was a ghost, I wasn't going to refute that. How the old guy got into the car wasn't as important to me as getting him out.

"You kids alright?" A middle-aged woman had come out of one of the offices and saw Abby and I standing in the middle of the parking lot staring at my car, "Do you need me to call someone for you?" she asked.

"Can you call the Ghostbusters?" Abby muttered under her breath.

Thankfully, the woman didn't hear her.

"We're good," I turned and replied with a smile and a wave, acknowledging her offer to help.

When I turned back to look at Abby, I found her holding her phone, aiming it at my car.

"What're you doing?" I asked her.

"Watch this," she instructed.

She held her phone up in front of my face so I could see that she had her camera app open.

"What do you see?" she asked, referring to the image on the phone screen.

I saw my car, and it was empty. There was no sign of the elderly man.

"Where'd he go?"

"He didn't go anywhere," Abby lowered the phone as she replied, allowing me to see the car with my own eyes. The old guy was still sitting in the back seat.

She lifted the phone, showing me the image again, and said, "Not there," and then she lowered it and said, "There." She kept doing that until I told her to stop.

"I get it," I said.

"Told you he was a ghost," Abby smirked, "You should've pulled over like I told you to."

I wished I had listened to her. There was no way we were going to make it to the movie on time now.

"You're right," I admitted, "I should've pulled over."

Abby had a smug look on her face after hearing my confession.

"What do you know about ghosts?" I asked her, hoping she had some idea about how to get him out of the car, "How do we get rid of him?"

"You're going to have to figure that out on your own," she said, "The only thing I know about ghosts is that you don't mess around with them."

Abby turned away from me and started typing something on her phone.

"What're you doing?" I asked.

"Seeing if Beth can come pick me up," she replied, "There's no way I'm getting anywhere near your car."

Beth was Abby's sister.

"Do you think I can get a ride with her too?"

"What about your car?"

"I was going to leave it here," I said, "At least until I figure out what to do about him," I nodded toward the old guy, "Maybe he'll get bored of sitting there and just leave on his own," I hoped.

"Or you could try apologizing to him," Abby said.

I could, but I was ashamed to admit that the thought of getting anywhere near him without knowing what he was capable of scared me. I'd seen enough horror movies to know that situations involving ghosts weren't so easily resolved.

But…it was worth a try…from a distance.

I cupped my hands around my mouth and yelled, "I'm sorry I didn't stop!"

Nothing happened.

"Seriously," Abby scoffed, "That's the best you can do?"

"Is Beth coming or not?" I changed the subject.

"She's on her way," Abby replied.

***

Beth pulled into the office park 20 minutes later and stopped in the middle of the parking lot.

"Let's go," she snapped after rolling down the passenger window so Abby could hear her, "I have places to be."

Abby pulled open the passenger door and climbed into the front seat.

"Hop in the back," she said to me.

"You didn't say anything about giving him a ride too," Beth complained.

I ignored the comment and reached out to open the car door, stopping when I happened to look up and see the old man in the suit sitting in the backseat of Beth's car.

I cried out and stumbled away from the car, almost tripping over the cement parking block that was behind me.

When I looked back at the car, the man was gone.

"What the fuck's wrong with him?" I heard Beth ask Abby.

Abby glanced in the backseat of the car, "What happened?" she had a concerned look on her face as she got out of the car and came over to where I was standing.

"Seriously?" Beth complained, "If you don't get in the car in the next 30 seconds, I'm leaving the both of you here."

"What happened?" Abby repeated.

"I saw him," I said, keeping my voice low so Beth couldn't hear me, "In the backseat of Beth's car when I tried to get in."

Abby looked back and Beth's car before turning her attention to my car.

"He's gone," she declared.

"No, he's not," I shook my head, "I think he's just waiting to see which car I'm going to get inside."

"How come I didn't see him," Abby wondered.

I shrugged, "Maybe he decided you had nothing to do with me not stopping for his funeral."

"I'm leaving if you don't get in the car right now," Beth hollered at us.

"Go," I said, "I'll catch up with you later," I looked back at my car, "Once I figure out how to get rid of him."

"I'll call you later," Abby said before turning and jogging back over to Beth's car. I think she was relieved that I didn't ask her to stay with me.

I stood there and watched them leave the parking lot, returning Abby's wave as they drove by me on their way back onto the street.

Now what? I sighed.

****

Sitting there on the curb of the parking lot, wondering what I could do to get rid of the ghost that had attached itself to me, I realized I didn't know as much about ghosts as I thought I did. Most of what I knew was from the horror movies I'd seen. That prompted me to pull out my phone and start learning as much as I could about them, hoping I might find some piece of information that might help me.

"Abby was right," I muttered to myself thirty minutes later.

From what I gathered from all the contradictory information I read on the internet was that I had offended the ghost of the old man by not stopping for his funeral and that the only way I would be able to get rid of him was to make amends with him.

The question now was: How do I make amends with him?

According to the internet, there was no sure way to do that as the requirements were different for each ghost. I already knew that a simple apology wasn't enough.

Time to figure something out.

I got to my feet and looked around, wondering if there was anything nearby where I could get something to eat while I came up with a plan. That was when I saw the florist shop across the street. What caught my eye about it was the advertisement for funeral arrangements displayed in one of the shop windows.

I should go to the cemetery and pay my respects!

That's what everyone in the funeral processing was on their way to do when I disrespected the old man by not stopping.

That has to be the solution to my problem!

I rushed across the street, went into the florist shop, and used the money I had planned on spending at the movie theater on the best funeral arrangement I could afford. It wasn't anything fancy, but I thought it looked nice.

While I was waiting for the arrangement to be put together, I used my phone to look up the name of the dead guy and the name of the cemetery where he was supposed to be buried. Once I got that information, I used my map app to see how far away the cemetery was.

I sighed in relief when I saw that the cemetery was a little over a mile away from the florist.

Getting back into my car with the ghost of George Grimly, which was the old man's name, was not something I wanted to do, so I'd already resolved myself to the idea of walking to the cemetery no matter how far away it was.

***

"Finally," I panted when I rounded the corner of the street and saw the cemetery gates.

Carrying the flower arrangement took a lot more out of me than I thought it would.

When I reached the gates, I stopped to take a break while I scanned the rows of graves looking for the site where Mr. Grimly was buried. It was easy to spot. It was the only one covered in fresh dirt and flowers.

I had hoped that all the mourners would be gone by the time arrived, but that wasn't the case. One person remained. A little old lady in a black dress.

I waited a few minutes to see if she would leave, but she never did.

You can do this, I encouraged myself as I walked across the cemetery grounds and approached Mr. Grimly's grave.

The old lady turned when she saw me approaching.

Not knowing what else to say to her, I blurted out, "Sorry for your loss."

She stared at me for a moment before giving me a thin-lipped smile, "Thank you," she replied, then asked, "How did you know my husband?"

"I…I…I don't," I stammered, "I was driving by in the opposite direction when the funeral procession passed by and I didn't stop," I admitted, "I felt really bad about it afterward and decided I should come and apologize."

I didn't think telling her that her husband's ghost had appeared in my car would be a good idea.

"You didn't have to do that," Mrs. Grimly said, "I doubt George would even care."

Well, he did, I thought to myself.

To her, I said, "I'll just set these down and be on my way." I placed the vase on the ground with the other flowers. "I really am sorry I didn't stop," I said to her before I started to walk away.

I made it about a dozen steps before the ghost of Mr. Grimly materialized before me, blocking my path.

"Apology accepted, kid," he smiled at me.

"Does that mean we're square?" I asked.

"Yeah, we're square," he replied, "But, I was wondering if I could ask one small favor of you before I go?"

"What kind of favor?"

"There are some things I'd like to say to my wife," Mr. Grimly gestured at Mrs. Grimly, "Things I should've said to her a long time ago."

"I suppose I could tell her for you," I offered.

"Thanks, kid," he reached out to pat me on the back, "I appreciate that, but I really need to tell her myself."

As soon as his incorporeal hand passed through my shoulder, I blacked out.

***

When I came to, I found myself completely naked in an unfamiliar bed. Worse still, I was not alone. Lying next to me, also completely naked, was Mrs. Grimly.

She looked over at me and smiled, "That was amazing," she said.

THE VOTE

"If you're planning on voting, today's your last day," my wife Darcie said as I poured a cup of coffee.

"What do you mean?" I asked, "I thought next Tuesday was election day."

"It is," she agreed, "But we both know you're not going to wait in those long lines to vote. Today is the last day of early voting and my last chance of getting you to vote. You know how important this election is to me."

I did know how important it was to her, but I didn't share her enthusiasm for the issues that were being voted on. I couldn't even remember what half of them were about. I had more important things to worry about, like keeping a roof over our heads and food on the table.

"I went yesterday and didn't have to wait at all," she continued talking, "I just walked right in, filled out the form, and voted. It only took about five minutes. If you left a little early this morning, you could vote on your way into work."

I took a sip of my coffee instead of replying.

"Please, do this for me," Darcie begged.

"Fine," I relented, "Where do I go?" I hadn't decided if I was really going to do it or not, I just wanted her to stop talking about it.

"To the library," she smiled, "Thanks, Hun." She hugged me and planted a kiss on my cheek.

"Where's the library?" I've never been to it and had no idea where it was.

"It's over by the elementary school," she said, "If you take Sycamore Street to work you should see a big sign pointing the way."

I did take Sycamore Street to work most days and do recall seeing a large VOTE HERE sign with an arrow pointing down a side street.

"Are you sure they're open this early?" The clock on the microwave said it was 5 minutes before 8. I didn't want to get there and the place be closed.

"They open at 8. If you leave now, you can be in and out in ten minutes. I doubt there will be many people there this early."

"I guess I better head out then." I picked up my keys from the counter and walked across the kitchen to the door that led into the garage.

As I walked, Darcie reminded me of the issues I was voting on and how I should vote. I hadn't realized there were so many measures on the ballot.

"Did you get all of that?" she asked.

"Yes, on the road and school tax. No, on the corporate farm break and city council pay raises...," I rattled off the rest of the things she had mentioned, hoping I'd gotten them all straight in my head.

"Perfect," she smiled, "Make sure you get a sticker when you're done."

"Sticker?"

"Your 'I Voted' sticker. They hand them out before you leave," she explained. "I love you, but I want proof you actually voted, and that sticker is it."

"Sticker, got it," I said, "Do you think they might also give me a gold star for being such a good boy?"

"Go vote, smartass," she was still smiling as she lifted her hand and pointed for me to leave.

***

As soon as I turned onto Sycamore Street, I started looking for the voting sign that would direct me to the library. I had to drive for a few blocks before I found it.

Part of me wanted to keep driving straight to work, but another, more insistent part, told me that would be the wrong thing to do.

When I reached the street that the sign was pointing toward, I slowed down and started to turn. As I did so, I happened to glance up the road and saw another sign, a block away, similar to the first one, but it was pointing in the opposite direction.

This better be the right way.

I wasn't going to drive around and figure out which sign led to the right place. If I ended up going the wrong way, it wouldn't be my fault. It would be the fault of whoever put the signs up.

Since I'd already started my turn, I was committed to going in that direction. When I saw another VOTE HERE sign in the distance, I figured I was headed the right way.

I followed the signs for several miles before the densely packed neighborhoods gave way to sprawling farmland.

Maybe this isn't the right way.

My wife said the library was near the elementary school and I was pretty sure the school wasn't out in the countryside, far away from the town center.

I must've taken a wrong turn.

I was about to turn around when I got to the top of a small rise and saw another sign. This one was pointing towards a gated drive that led to an enormous colonial building that I assumed must have been a home at some point before being repurposed by the city.

I guess this is the place.

It could be a library. It was fancy-looking enough, although I thought the two life-sized statues of the horses that flanked the steps were a little much.

When I drove up to the building, I noticed that there was a pickup truck, a fancy sports car, a beat-up-looking hatchback, and a motorcycle parked in front of it. Since I didn't see anywhere else to park, I pulled up behind the motorcycle and got out.

On the front door of the building, hanging from the doorknob, was another sign that said WELCOME VOTER.

Shouldn't that say voters? What kind of people do they have working here that would make that kind of mistake?

"Not my problem," I muttered to myself as I reached out to open the door.

Before I could grab hold of the handle, the door swung open and away from me.

Standing in the doorway was an old man wearing a ridiculous-looking tuxedo. It reminded me of the kind I'd seen butlers wearing in the old black and white movies my mother used to watch when I was a kid.

"Welcome, voter," the man greeted me with a smile, "Please come in." He swept his hand toward the interior of the building as he stepped back, making room for me to walk through the door.

"Uh, thanks," I said, stepping into the building.

As soon as I was in the entryway, the man closed the door behind me. When he did, I happened to look back and see that the gate at the end of the drive was now closed.

That's weird, I thought, but I didn't have time to dwell on it.

"Right this way," the man said, ushering me through a set of double doors and into a room on my right.

I followed him and found myself in what can only be described as an office. A large ornate wooden desk dominated the room, behind which was a high-backed red velvet chair. In front of the desk were two smaller, but similar-looking chairs. In the center of the far wall was a fireplace. Thick curtains covered the windows, blocking out the sunlight. The room's only source of illumination came from the two oil lamps sitting on either end of the desk.

"Please have a seat," the man gestured to the two smaller chairs, "Your host will be with you momentarily." When he finished speaking, he turned and started to walk out of the room.

"Wait a minute," I called after him, "I think there's been a mistake." I was confused about why all this attention was being spent on me. "I'm just here to vote."

The old man spun around to face me, "I know," was all he said before he reached out and closed both doors.

This is ridiculous!

I stormed over to the doors, intending to leave, but found them locked.

"Excuse me!" I rattled the door, "I've changed my mind. I'd like to leave now."

"I'm afraid that won't be possible, Mr. Mills," the voice of the person speaking behind me was deep and hollow sounding. Hearing it sent a shiver up my spine. "Not until you've voted."

"But I don't want to vote any longer," I replied without turning around.

"You must," the speaker insisted, "Only then will you be allowed to leave."

When I turned around, I was shocked to see a tall figure in a thick black robe standing behind the desk. His face was obscured by the heavy cowl over his head. Leaning against the wall behind him was a scythe. The anger and defiance I was feeling at being locked in the room quickly melted away at the sight of the impressive figure.

"Please sit." A skeletal hand emerged from the robe and gestured across the desk at the two chairs, "And I'll explain everything."

I hesitantly walked over and sat down in the chair closest to the door. Once I was seated, the skeletal figure pulled out his chair and sat down.

"Are you Death?"

I'd seen enough movie and television depictions of the character to hazard a guess. The one thing those shows didn't mention, however, was the smell that clung to him. He smelled musty. Like an old piece of leather that's been left to rot in a damp cellar.

"I am," he confirmed, "Can I get you something to eat or drink before we begin?"

As imposing as he was, I was taken aback by his politeness.

"Uh…a cup of coffee would be nice if it's not too much trouble."

Sitting on the desk in front of Death was a bell. He picked it up and gave it a brief ring before setting it back down.

The doors to the office swung open and the old man appeared, "You rang, sir?"

"Our guest would like some coffee," Death said, gesturing at me with his bony hand as he spoke.

"Of course, sir." The old man bowed and then backed out of the room, closing the doors behind him.

"This isn't the county library, is it?" I stated the obvious.

"No, it isn't," Death confirmed, "This is the Apocalyptica Estate. A refuge of sorts for my brothers and me."

"How long has it been here?" I found it odd that in all the places in the world to have built an estate, they chose to build it in the small backwater town of Franklin.

"Since this morning."

When Death saw the confused look on my face, he elaborated, "The estate resides wherever we need it, whenever we need it. This morning, after we put out the call for the Electus Vet. The estate appeared here because that is where it was needed."

Before I could ask what the Electus Vet was, the old man returned to the room, carrying a large silver platter upon which sat a silver coffee pot, a bowl of sugar cubes, a small carafe of cream, and a single mug.

"Your coffee, sir," he announced, setting the tray on the desk before me.

He started to pick up the coffee pot to pour me a cup, but I stopped him with a wave of my hand.

"I can do that," I said.

"As you wish." He turned and strode out of the room.

Death sat there patiently as I poured my coffee and stirred some cream and sugar into it.

"What's an Electus Vet?" I asked before raising the mug to my lips and taking a sip.

"Not what, who," Death corrected me, "The Electus Vet is the chosen voter for mankind. The one person whose vote will determine the fate of millions. Today, that person is you, Mr. Mills." He pointed his bony index finger at me.

"Me?" I sputtered, "I think you must've made a mistake. I'm not qualified to make a decision like that."

I thought about this morning's conversation with my wife and how she had to tell me which issues I was voting on and how I should vote.

"My wife would've been a better choice."

"The fates have chosen you, so you it must be. If you refuse, you will not leave the estate." I could feel his gaze upon me, "Do you understand?"

"Yeah," I agreed quickly, "I understand." I took another sip of my coffee before asking him if anyone had ever refused to vote before.

"It happens from time to time," Death replied.

"The butler?" I asked on a whim, nodding toward the door the old man had delivered the coffee through, "Did he refuse to vote?"

"He did," Death admitted, "And if you refuse, you'll take his place."

"I have no plans on refusing." I didn't want to be stuck in that place answering doors and serving coffee to people.

Death leaned forward, "Shall we begin then?"

"Sure," I set my cup down.

"First," Death said, reaching into the desk drawer and pulling out an old leather bound book, "A little background."

He set the book on the desk and turned it to face me before opening it

"This is my brothers and me," Death declared, pointing at a page in the book depicting a painting for the four horsemen of the apocalypse. "That's me, War, Famine, and Pestilence." He pointed at each rider as he said their name.

"We were created for a single purpose," Death continued, "To remind mankind of his proper place on this planet until judgment day when we are called forth to ride together."

As he spoke, he turned the pages of the book, stopping long enough for me to see the images and for him to explain what they meant.

The first one showed Death surrounded by dead people of all ages. He said it was a reminder that there is no guarantee of how long each of us will live. The next page showed War. Around him, warriors clashed in a bloody battle. Death said that was a reminder that free will comes with a price. After that was Famine. He was surrounded by well-dressed, emaciated people, all reaching their hands out, begging for food. Death said that was a reminder that even the most entitled people may end up wanting. The last page showed Pestilence. Diseased and fly-riddled corpses lay at his feet. Death said that was a reminder that even the healthiest of people can fall.

"The point," Death said after he'd finished explaining, "Is to remind you that you are mortal and that your life comes with no guarantees. That is why, every ten years, the Electus Vet must choose which of the three catastrophes mankind will face." When he was done talking, he closed the book and put it back in the drawer.

"Three?" I asked, confused, "But there are four of you. Why are there only three catastrophes?"

"War, famine, and pestilence all result in death. It would be unfair for me to have my own catastrophe while still getting to take part in the catastrophe of the others. That is why I am the arbiter of the vote."

"I guess that makes sense."

"Do you have any questions before we begin?" Death asked.

"This isn't a dream, is it?"

"I'm afraid not."

"Then I guess we best get on with it."

Death picked up the bell and rang it again. When the old man appeared in the doorway, Death told him to send in the first candidate.

A moment later, a mountain of a man dressed in a burgundy suit ducked through the doorway.

"Greetings, brother!" his deep voice boomed, "And to you, Electus Vet," He bowed slightly.

"Mr. Mills," Death said to me, "Allow me to introduce my brother, War." He gestured at the large man, "If you vote for him, you will be voting for a catastrophe centered around armed conflict."

War stood tall and clasped his hands behind his back as Death introduced him.

"Do you have any questions for him?" Death asked me.

"Uh," my mind went blank. I hadn't expected to be put on the spot like that.

"War is pretty straightforward," I said, taking a moment to gather my thoughts, "The only thing I'm wondering about is what kind of war are we talking about and where would it be fought?"

"Fair questions," War bellowed, "Unfortunately, I cannot accurately say."

"Why not?"

"The seeds of war are like weeds planted across the globe," War explained, "I never know which ones will prosper and which ones will wither and die. I can only nurture them as they sprout and see what fruits they bear."

"So, if I understand you correctly, you're telling me that war can break out anywhere if I vote for you."

"That is correct," War confirmed.

"Even here," I was referring to the United States.

A shadow passed over War's features as he nodded his head. I got the impression he felt like that little fact made it less likely that I would vote for him.

"Would it be another world war or something smaller?"

"That depends on the parties involved," War said, "Once a conflict begins, it must be allowed to run its natural course without any interference from me and my brothers."

"I think I've heard enough, thank you."

"War is nasty business, there's no doubt about that, but there are worse ways to die," That was the last thing War said before he left the room.

A moment later, the next candidate walked into the room. He was much shorter than his brothers and extremely thin, making the black suit he was wearing look way too big on him. The skin on his face was so thin that it accentuated the bone beneath, giving him a corpse-like appearance.

This must be Famine.

"Hello, brother," Famine said to Death, "You're looking well, Electus Vet," he said to me. I assumed he was remarking on my weight since I could stand to lose a few pounds.

"Mr. Mills, as I'm sure you've already guessed, this is my brother Famine," Death said.

Famine nodded his head at me and I nodded in return.

"If I voted for you, what would your catastrophe be?" I asked.

"Businesses will fail, the stock market will crash, people will lose their jobs and their livelihoods, crops will wither and die, and people will go hungry," Famine answered.

"So…people will starve to death?" I was trying to figure out what the end result of everything he mentioned would be.

"Some will, yes," he agreed, "But not all affected by my catastrophe will die that way. Some will take their own lives while others will choose to take the lives of those who aren't suffering the way they are. A hungry man is an angry man."

As bad as War sounded, Famine sounded worse.

"Thank you," I said, "I don't have any other questions for you."

After Famine left, I drained my cup of coffee and then went to pour myself another from the carafe but was surprised to find it empty.

"My apologies," Death said, "Famine's presence has a way of making things scarce."

I set the cup and carafe back onto the tray.

"Would you like another cup?" he asked.

"I'm fine," I waved away the offer, "Let's just get on with it."

"As you wish."

A few moments later, the door to the office opened again, allowing a cloud of flies to swarm into the room. They were quickly followed by the final candidate, Pestilence. He was not dressed as nicely as War or Famine. His clothing appeared to be nothing more than a plain white hospital gown that was soiled with stains.

Seeing his pale green, pustule-covered skin made me sick to my stomach. The flies that kept flitting about him, crawling in and out of his wounds, didn't help.

"I think that's close enough, brother," Death said, holding out a hand toward Pestilence to keep him from getting any closer to me.

I was thankful for that because I could already smell the overpowering stench of his open sores from across the room.

"Mr. Mills, this is…," Death didn't get to finish what he was going to say.

"I don't need an introduction, brother," Pestilence cut him off, "The Electus Vet knows who I am and what my purview is, don't you?" he turned his milky eyes to me.

I nodded my agreement.

"Alrighty then," Pestilence said, "I guess that means we can cut to the chase and wrap things up here."

"Are you ready to vote, Mr. Mills?" Death asked me.

"I'd like some time to think about it first, but yes, I think I've got all of the information I need to make my decision."

"Very well, we will leave you to it." Death opened a different desk drawer and pulled out a rolled-up piece of paper and an inkwell, "Once you've made your decision, write it on this parchment and tossed it into the fire." When he gestured at the fireplace, it flared to life.

"I think I can manage that," I said, pulling the inkwell and parchment across the desk toward me.

I waited until Death and Pestilence had left the office before I let myself relax. I was surprised at how well I'd been able to keep myself together in the face of the absurd task that was being asked of me.

"Holy shit," I sighed.

Who would Darcie pick?

That was the only way I knew how to approach the issue. My wife had always been better than me at approaching an issue from all sides before forming an opinion.

While I sat there, I did my best to weigh the pros and cons of each catastrophe the way I've seen Darcie do. I went over everything a dozen times before I think I had the right answer.

That's who Darcie would vote for, I said to myself as I picked up the pen and wrote the name of the horseman I was voting for. When I was done, I rolled the parchment back up and tossed it into the fire.

A few moments later, the doors opened and the old man entered the office, "Are you finished, sir?" he asked.

I nodded my head, "I am."

"Allow me to show you out." He swept his hand toward the door.

I followed the old man out to the driveway and saw that the vehicles that had been parked outside were gone. All that remained was my truck.

"There's one last thing before you go," the old man said.

"What's that?"

He handed me an I VOTED sticker.

After I left the estate grounds and returned to the road, I glanced up at the rearview mirror and wasn't surprised to see that the large house was gone. All that was there now was a pasture.

I know you're wondering who I voted for, but I'm not going to be the one to tell you. If you really want to know though, all you have to do is turn on the news. Once you see the morning headlines, it should be obvious.

FLOTSAM AND JETSAM

"Find anything interesting?" I called out to my 8-year-old daughter, Tanya. She was several steps ahead of me, combing through the driftwood and dried seaweed that had collected on the beach that morning.

She'd woken me up at dawn, unable to contain her excitement at getting to visit the beach for the first time. Wanting to let her mother sleep in, I decided it was best to just get dressed and take her down to the water myself.

"I found a dead crab," she announced, lifting the lifeless crustacean by one of its claws so she could show it to me.

"Put that down." I gestured for her to drop it.

She ignored me, choosing to fling the dead crab over to a flock of seagulls that had been gathering on the beach behind us. The birds pounced on the free meal, squabbling with each other as they picked it apart.

"Now they're never going to leave us alone," I said as the birds started moving closer, squawking for more food.

Tanya liked having the attention of the seagulls and began looking for more things to feed them. That prompted the birds to take to the air and start circling her.

"Ugh," Tanya cried out a few minutes later, looking at the splatter of crap that had fallen onto a piece of driftwood near her, "That bird almost pooped on me."

"That's what they do, eat and poop," I said with a smile, "If you don't want to get pooped on, you shouldn't feed them."

Tanya leaned down and picked up a long, twisted length of driftwood and began waving it in the air, "Shoo," she yelled at the birds, trying to drive them away.

"Just ignore them and keep walking," I said to her, "They'll leave once they realize you're not going to feed them anymore."

In typical Tanya fashion, she decided to ignore me instead and take matters into her own hands by throwing her stick at the birds. When that didn't have the desired effect, she scooped up a handful of sand and threw that at them.

"Alright, that's enough," I said, walking up to her and placing my hands on her shoulders so I could turn her around and get her to start walking up the beach again.

"I hate seagulls," she huffed.

"I don't like them much myself," I replied, "They're very annoying."

Tanya and I continued walking for about ten more minutes before the sounds of the birds that had been following us started to fade. When I looked back to see why, I saw the flock hovering in the air a few hundred feet behind us.

"I guess they decided to finally give up," I said, surprised that the seagulls had stopped hounding us so abruptly. I figured we were stuck with them until we went back into the rental house.

I didn't dwell on the bird's behavior for very long because, at that point, Tanya called out and distracted me by saying something that initially alarmed me.

"I found an arm!" She sounded excited.

"A what?"

I rushed over to where she was pointing at something partially buried in the sand, expecting to see a real arm. I sighed in relief when I saw that it was the plastic arm of a doll, sun-bleached and dotted with barnacles.

Tanya pulled it free from the sand and brushed it off.

"Where's the rest of it?" she asked, scanning the shoreline.

"That thing looks like it has been floating in the ocean for years," I said, "You're not going to find the rest of it. It's long gone by now." I was certain of that, but Tanya proved me wrong.

"I found a leg!" She had a huge smile on her face as she pulled the plastic doll part out of the sand by the toes.

"Why don't you look for shells," I said to her and then muttered to myself, "Like a normal kid."

I said that because Tanya's interests tended to be a bit darker than most girls her age. She preferred dragons to unicorns and vampires to princesses. She had a growing collection of Goosebump books and Monster High dolls and had recently started requesting more black clothing, wanting to be more like Mavis in the Hotel Transylvania series.

"These are so much cooler than shells." She smiled as she held up the barnacle-covered arm and leg. "Can you hold them for me so I can look for the rest of it?" She walked over and thrust the limbs into my hands.

"Uh…sure," I replied, "But we can't stay out here looking for too long. Your mother is going to be up soon and wanting breakfast."

She'd already turned around and hurried back to the water line before I'd finished speaking, meaning she probably didn't hear a word I'd said.

Ten minutes later, Tanya came running back over to where I was standing, waving another plastic leg in the air.

"I found another piece!" She practically threw it at me before running off to continue her search.

Knowing I was going to be there for a while, I moved further up the beach where the sand was dry and sat down, depositing the doll limbs on the ground beside me.

Not long after that, Tanya came running over to where I was and kicked off her sandals.

"What're you doing?" I asked.

"I saw another piece floating in the water." As soon as she was done speaking, she was dashing back to the shoreline.

Feeling a little concerned about her going into the water by herself, I stood up and watched to make sure she didn't go out too far.

She waded out until the waves were crashing against her thighs before stopping to snatch something out of the foamy water

"I got it," she called out, waving an oddly shaped object in the air.

It took me a moment to realize that it was the doll's body, missing all its limbs and covered in barnacles. When she returned with it, she grabbed one of the legs and began trying to reattach it.

"Be careful," I warned, "Those barnacles are sharp."

I watched her struggle for a moment, trying to force the plastic tab at the end of the leg into the hole in the doll's body, before I reached out and said, "Give it here."

It took a lot of effort to force the stiff plastic of the leg back into place, but I managed to do it eventually. As soon as I had,

Tanya handed me one of the arms which was a little bit easier to reattach.

"There you go." I handed Tanya the partially assembled doll after reattaching the other leg.

"This is so cool!" She held it up with two hands so she could examine it.

"What's so great about it?"

The barnacles, along with the discoloration of the plastic, made it look like the doll was covered in cancerous growths, and that made it unsightly. The briny smell of fish that wafted from it wasn't very pleasant either.

"It looks like a sea monster baby," was her excited reply as she brushed the sand from her feet and slipped her sandals back on, "I hope I can find the rest of it."

"We can look for ten more minutes, but then we have to go back to the house." When she didn't acknowledge that she'd heard me I said, "Okay?"

"Okay," she grumbled, unhappy that I was putting a time limit on her search.

"If you don't find the missing pieces, we can come back out and search later this afternoon with Mom," I offered.

That was the only time I could promise to bring her back to the beach. We had plans to do some shopping after breakfast and would probably end up eating lunch at one of the restaurants in town. That meant we wouldn't return to the beach house until one o'clock at the earliest.

"Can you help me look?" she asked.

"Sure," I agreed, following her down to the water.

***

I let Taya search for fifteen minutes instead of the ten I originally told her I'd give her before telling her it was time to go.

"Five more minutes," she begged.

"We don't have five more minutes," I replied, "Your mother is waiting for us and you know how cranky she can get if she has to wait too long."

"Fine," she dropped her head and pouted.

"We can come back and look later," I reminded her.

"They'll probably be gone by then," she whined.

"I'll tell you what," I sighed, feeling bad that I had to cut her fun short, "We can keep searching…"

"Really?" she cut me off with a smile.

"On one condition." I held up my index finger.

"What?" The smile dropped from her face.

"You have to search that way," I moved my index finger so that it was pointing back towards the beach house.

"But…" she opened her mouth to protest.

"It's been a while since you've found anything," I said, "The other pieces might not have come this far, they may have washed up closer to the house."

I could tell she was considering my words when she lowered her head and furrowed her brow.

"Remember all of that driftwood and seaweed we saw?" I said, trying to give her a better reason to agree with me, "Where you found the dead crab?"

"Yeah."

"I bet you're more likely to find the pieces back there than in that direction," I gestured up the beach.

"Okay," she reluctantly agreed, turning, and heading back the way we'd come.

We walked for about ten minutes before Tanya stopped.

"Find something?" I asked.

"No," she replied, looking around for a moment, "I was just wondering where all of the seagulls went."

I hadn't realized they were gone until she mentioned it.

"Something must have gotten their attention." That sounded like a plausible explanation considering how quickly the birds flocked around Tanya when she fed them the dead crab. "I'm sure they're around here somewhere. Just be thankful they haven't come back to harass us."

"Hold this!" Tanya suddenly declared, thrusting the doll's body into my arms before rushing out into the water without bothering to take off her shoes.

"What are you doing?" I asked as I watched her push her way through the waves into thigh-high water.

Tanya lifted a knot of seaweed out of the surf and held it up so I could see it, "I found them!" She had a huge smile on her face. Tangled up in the fronds of kelp were the head and missing arm of the doll.

She quickly freed the pieces and returned to the beach, panting from the exertion of fighting against the waves.

"Here." She handed me the arm, wanting me to put it on first while she examined the doll's head, "This is so cool," I heard her mutter to herself as I forced the limb into place.

"Done," I said, showing her the doll, "Hand me the head." I held my hand out to her, wanting to finish putting the thing together as quickly as possible so we could return to the beach house.

Ugh, that's hideous, I thought as I looked down at the plastic doll's head that Tanya had placed in my palm.

It was missing most of its hair, exposing the holes where the strands had originally been stitched into place. Like the other pieces of the doll, the head was discolored and covered in barnacles, one of which was centered directly over the left eye, adding to its monstrous appearance.

"This thing really stinks," I grimaced. The fishy odor coming from the head was worse than all the other pieces combined. "You should probably soak it in the tub with a lot of soap when we get back," I suggested as I lined up the tab of the plastic neck with the hole in the body.

As soon as I popped the head into place, a strange sensation came over me. I felt like I was floating. My body felt light and airy. That feeling only lasted for a moment before it was replaced with a dizzying sense of disorientation. The world around me became foggy and indistinct.

"Dad?" Tanya's concerned voice sounded far away, like she was standing at the end of a very long tunnel, "Are you okay?"

No, I'm not okay, I tried to say, but found myself unable to talk. That was the last thought I had before the ground came rushing up at me and the world went dark.

***

When I came to, I was lying on a small bed, in a bedroom that looked like it belonged to a young boy. An assumption I made based on all the sports memorabilia and toys that filled the room.

"How are you feeling?" someone asked.

I turned and saw a middle-aged blond woman standing in the doorway. She was dressed in a loose-fitting blue sun dress. The kind that was popular along the coast during the summer.

"Where am I?" I swung my legs out of bed and sat up.

"You're in my home," the woman smiled, closing the door behind her before walking across the room to join me.

"How did I get here?"

"I brought you here," she explained, "After I found you on the beach." She gave me a concerned look, "Don't you remember?"

I had no memory of ever meeting the woman.

Why can't I remember her?

As I sat there, trying to make sense of what was going on, I realized I couldn't remember anything that had happened to me before I woke up in the bed, not even my name or where I came from.

"Are you okay?" the woman asked after seeing the look of worry on my face.

The question echoed in my mind, bringing with it the fleeting image of a young girl and a doll, but the image faded before I could make sense of it.

"I can't remember anything from before I woke up," I said, "My mind is a complete blank."

"Nothing?" she inquired.

"Nothing," I confirmed, "I can't even remember my name…I don't suppose you know it?" I asked, desperate for any shred of information about myself.

"Sorry," she shook her head, "You were barely conscious when I found you. We didn't have time for introductions before you passed out."

"You said you found me on the beach…what beach?" If I knew where I was, I might be able to remember something about why I was there.

"Calliope's Cove," she said, "It's…"

"In South Carolina," I interrupted. The location popped into my head when I heard the name of the beach.

"That's right," she sounded surprised, "Do you remember anything else?"

I tried thinking about Calliope Cove and South Carolina, hoping some other tidbit would be revealed to me but nothing came to mind. "No," I shook my head and sighed, "I just know that Calliope Cove is somewhere along the South Carolina coast."

"That's not much, but it's a start," she smiled, "Perhaps a little breakfast would help jog some other memories loose." She turned and started to leave,

"You don't have to do that," I said, but she either didn't hear me or chose to ignore me.

"I'll be right back," she declared, stepping out into the hall and shutting the door behind her.

I got up, intending to stop her, but I didn't get very far. When I tried to leave the room, the doorknob jiggled in my hand but would not turn. I twisted the knob as hard as I could while tugging on the door, but I couldn't get it to budge.

I'm locked in!

I pounded on the door, "Hello…Miss…" I called out to the woman, realizing that she'd never told me her name. "I appreciate you helping me, but I think I should probably go to the hospital."

When she didn't respond, I rattled the door in frustration before walking over to the window to see if I could get out that way.

I couldn't.

The window was sealed shut and the storm shutters were closed, blocking my view so that I couldn't tell what floor of the house I was on.

As I stood there, weighing my options, I heard the muffled sound of a girl screaming. The sound was so faint that I couldn't tell if it was coming from inside the house or outside.

I walked to the center of the room and waited to see if I would hear it again, wondering if someone else was trapped in the house like I was.

"Daddy," a girl sobbed, "Please stop," Her voice was faint but clear enough for me to tell that she was outside somewhere.

Hearing her plea wasn't the only thing that troubled me. There was something familiar about her voice. I felt like I should know who she was, but no matter how hard I tried, I couldn't recall a name or a face.

I returned to the window and tried to look out, seeing if I could catch a glimpse of the girl, but nothing was visible through the narrow gaps of the storm shutters that blocked my view.

Why are the storm shutters closed? It seemed like a nice sunny day outside.

"Hello," I yelled while pounding on the window, hoping to get the attention of the girl or anyone else who might be outside with her.

"She can't hear you."

I whirled around to find the woman standing in the center of the room with a tray full of plates loaded with pancakes, eggs, and bacon.

"I need to leave." I tried to dodge past her to get out of the room before she had time to react, but the door slammed shut in my face before I could make it out into the hall.

"I'm afraid you're not going anywhere," she said, setting the tray down on the bed before turning to face me, "Not yet at least."

"HELP!" It was the girl again, screaming at the top of her lungs.

Tanya, the name flashed across my mind. With it came the knowledge that I knew the girl. She was someone close to me, but I wasn't able to discern the connection yet.

I ran back over to the window and yelled the name, "Tanya! Can you hear me?" I pounded on the window again.

"I see your memory is returning," the woman remarked.

"Who is she?" I stomped across the room to confront her, towering over her, "And why won't you let me leave?"

She held my gaze for a moment, seemingly daring me to do something rash. The way she smiled up at me warned me that she wasn't intimidated.

"You're stronger than the others," she sounded amused, "Therefore, I'm going to give you a choice."

"A choice?" I repeated.

She nodded, "You can go over there and enjoy your breakfast and forget about what's happening outside and live the rest of your life in blissful ignorance." She gestured from the tray of food on the bed to the window as she spoke, "Or I can restore your memory..."

"Restore my memory," I cut her off before she could finish. As far as I was concerned, that was the only choice that made sense.

"You might want to let me finish before you decide," she warned, "Your fate will remain unchanged regardless of what you choose. The question you must ask yourself is if you want to know what that fate is."

As ominous as that sounded, not knowing anything about who I was or why I was there felt worse to me. Plus, I felt like I had an obligation to help Tanya, whoever she was.

"I need to know what's going on," I said.

"Even though you'll likely regret knowing?" was her reply.

"That's the chance I'm going to have to take," I kept my eyes locked on hers, trying to sound more confident than I felt.

"I can see where your daughter gets her resolve from," the woman remarked.

Daughter? Was she referring to Tanya?

I opened my mouth, wanting to confirm my thoughts, but the woman stopped me with a wave of her hand.

"Save your question," she said, "In a few moments you might find that you already know the answer."

She walked closer to the bed, "Sit," she gestured at the mattress.

I did as she requested.

"This is going to be unpleasant," she said as she reached out toward me, stopping when her hands were inches away from my cheeks. "Last chance to change your mind."

I took and deep breath and let it out with a sigh, "Do it."

She grabbed hold of my face. As soon as she did, my eyes rolled into the back of my head, and I began to convulse as my memories returned. When it was over, I slid off the bed and onto my knees.

"Calliope," I spat the name out as I pulled myself to my feet to confront her, "It was your doll we found on the beach."

The woman no longer looked like the pleasant motherly figure she was when she first came into the room. She now looked like a waterlogged corpse covered in seaweed and barnacles.

"And you have my gratitude for putting her back together again," Calliope smiled, "If you hadn't, we wouldn't have had this opportunity to get acquainted."

I became aware of Calliope's identity when I inadvertently freed her spirit from the doll, allowing her to take possession of my body. I'd only gotten a glimpse of who she was before she managed to imprison me within one of my childhood memories, making me forget myself.

"Why are you doing this to me?" I asked.

"It's nothing personal," she replied, "You just happened to be in the right place at the right time," she smirked and then added, "Or if you prefer, the wrong place at the wrong time."

"What do you want from me?"

"Isn't it obvious?" Calliope spread her hands to indicate that I should already know the answer to that question.

Tanya!

I could still hear the distant cries of my daughter calling for help. That's when I realized I hadn't heard anyone else, just Tanya.

"Where's Michele?" I took a step towards Calliope. Michele was my wife.

Her smile widened, showing her blackened teeth, "She's around," Calliope said, "Would you like to see her?"

I closed the distance between us until I was looming over her again, "You better not have hurt her." I growled.

Calliope laughed at my bravado. When she was done, she leaned in close to my ear and whispered, "I ripped her heart from her chest with your hands and I enjoyed every second of it."

Before I could respond, she lashed out and grabbed hold of my head.

"See for yourself," she hissed.

I was suddenly back in control of my body again, finding myself standing in the doorway of the master bedroom of the beach house. The first thing that hit me was the overwhelming stench of blood. It was everywhere. But that's not what my eyes focused on. They were glued to the eviscerated body of my wife, lying spread eagle on the bed. Her lifeless eyes staring at the ceiling.

"I'm sorry," I whispered.

"HELP!" Tanya yelled from the adjoining bathroom.

"Tanya!" I said, rushing over to the door.

"STAY AWAY FROM ME!" she yelled.

"It wasn't me," I insisted, "I would never hurt you or your mother. You know that."

My vision went black, and I found myself standing in the room with Calliope again.

"I told you that you'd regret knowing," Calliope said.

I lunged for her, but my hands passed through empty air as she disappeared and reappeared behind me.

"I also told you there was nothing you could do to change your fate," she said.

I lunged again, but she disappeared well before I was within striking distance. When she reappeared, she was standing in the doorway.

"This has been entertaining," she smiled, "But I really must get back to work." She turned and walked down the hall. The door slammed shut behind her, leaving me trapped in the room.

Even though I couldn't see what was going on outside of my body, I could still hear it.

I could hear Calliope using my voice, trying to convince Tanya that it was safe to come out of the bathroom.

A short time later, there was a loud clatter followed by the sounds of a struggle. That went on for several minutes until I heard Calliope cry out.

"Put that down," she yelled, but it was my voice I heard.

"Fuck you!" Tanya screamed.

Something strange happened then. I blacked out again, but only for a moment. When I came to my senses, I found myself back in control of my body, standing in the middle of the kitchen.

"Dad?" Tanya asked, "Is that you?" She was standing across the room from me.

In her right hand was the body of the doll, and in her left was the doll's head.

"It's me," I confirmed. I no longer felt the presence of Calliope in the back of my mind. "How did you know that would work?" I nodded at the doll in her hands, assuming that Calliope's hold on me had been broken when Tanya had removed the head.

"Lucky guess," she replied, "When you said it wasn't you, I thought that maybe the doll had done something to you. I read a story like that once."

"Remind me to send the author of that story a thank you note," I smiled at her.

"FREEZE," someone yelled.

I turned around and saw a police officer standing in the doorway with his gun pointed at me.

"DROP THE WEAPON," he commanded.

I looked down and saw that I was clutching a knife in my hand. I hadn't realized I was holding it.

"This isn't what it looks like." I started to raise my hands.

The sudden movement must've spooked the officer because he fired his pistol.

The bullet struck me in the chest, knocking me backward onto the floor.

As I lay there, bleeding out, I could see Calliope standing above me, with a smile on her face. Nobody else seemed to notice her.

The last thing I remember before the darkness claimed me was Calliope's voice saying, "Two out of three ain't bad."

KEEP ON ROCKING IN THE FREE WORLD

"Shit," I cursed as the car's engine suddenly died.

I tried to restart it, but nothing happened when I turned the key. Everything just turned off and never came back on.

Not wanting to leave the car in the middle of the road, I turned the wheel and let the car coast to a stop on the side of the country road.

"What's going on?" Elena asked, "Why'd you stop?" She had her eyes closed and was starting to doze off when I pulled the car over to the shoulder.

"Car's dead," I pointed at the dashboard.

Elena sat up and looked around, trying to get an idea of where we were. When she didn't see any street signs or buildings, she pulled out her phone and tried to open her map app.

"No service." She turned the screen so I could see it before putting the phone away, "Do you have any idea where we are?"

"No clue," I admitted, "I was following that shortcut the guy at the gas station told us about. All I know is that this road is supposed to reconnect with the interstate at some point." I gestured off into the distance.

I had asked the gas station attendant about an alternate route around the city when I saw that an accident had closed all lanes of the interstate, potentially adding hours to our drive.

"What's the last town we drove through?"

"Some place called Wrong Way about twenty miles back," I replied.

"Wrong Way?" Elena scoffed, "Seriously?"

"That's what the sign said."

"Does your phone have service?" she pointed between my legs where my phone was sitting on the car seat.

My phone was a newer model than hers and I had a much better cellphone plan, so she was hoping it had better reception.

"Nope," I said after lifting the phone to check it, "I haven't had service since we left Wrong Way."

Elena turned in her seat and looked back the way we had come, scanning the road behind us.

"Have you seen any other cars?" She was hoping we'd be able to flag down another driver that could help us.

"Not since…" I started to answer, but Elena cut me off.

"…Wrong Way," she finished. She took a deep breath and exhaled it with a sigh, "I guess that means we're walking."

***

Five minutes later Elena and I were standing next to the car, adjusting our backpacks. We'd packed light because we were only supposed to be gone for a couple of days.

"Looks like we're not going to make it to the music festival in time to see the opening acts," I sighed as we started walking away from the car.

"That's fine with me," Elena replied, "All of the bands I'm most excited about seeing aren't playing until tomorrow anyway."

We continued talking about the music festival until I realized we'd walked a couple of miles and hadn't seen a single car or house or any other sign of people in the area.

"Maybe we should turn around," I suggested, wondering if it would've been smarter to walk back to Wrong Way, instead of going forward.

"This road leads to the interstate, right?" Elena asked, "If it does, we're bound to run into someone eventually, don't you think?"

"I guess," I reluctantly agreed.

"We can go back if you want," Elena offered, even though she didn't want to do that. She figured the next town had to be a lot closer than returning to the previous town.

"No," I said, "We can keep walking this way."

"I'm sure we'll come across a house or a gas station soon," she hoped, "Certainly within the next mile or two," she sounded confident.

We walked the next mile in silence before I spotted something in the distance.

"What's that?" I pointed across an expanse of tall grass where the top of a white dome was peeking above the tree line.

Elena, who was walking a couple of steps in front of me, stopped and turned so she could see what I was pointing at.

"It looks like the top of a water tower," she smiled, "I told you the next town had to be nearby." She left the road and started to cross the field, "Come on," she motioned for me to follow her.

"Where are you going?"

"I'm taking a shortcut," Elena called back.

"Shouldn't we just follow the road?" I gestured in the direction we'd been walking.

"We could," she stopped and turned around, "But this way will be faster."

"How do you know that?"

"Because of the water tower," she hooked her thumb over her shoulder, "The closer we get to it, the closer to town we should be." When I didn't make a move to join her, she said, "We can keep walking along the road if you want, but it'll probably take us twice as long to get there, assuming the road doesn't bypass the town altogether."

I hadn't thought of that. I didn't like the idea of walking any further than I had to, and I certainly didn't want to risk walking past the town.

I pulled out my phone and checked it, something I'd done frequently as we walked. When I saw that it still had no service, I slid it back into my pocket and walked out into the field to join Elena.

***

"Almost there," Elena huffed, stopping to finish the last drop of water from the plastic bottle she was carrying. When she was done, she put the empty bottle into her backpack.

The walk to get to the water tower was a bit more arduous than it looked. Once we passed through the field and made it into the trees, the ground began to rise and fall in a series of rolling hills. What I thought was going to be a quick walk ended up being an hour-long hike.

"Do you want to take a break?" Elena asked after seeing me pull out my water bottle to take a drink.

The tower was about 500 feet away from us at the top of the next hill.

"Nah, I'm good," I replied, recapping my water bottle and sliding it into the little pouch on the side of my backpack, "We can take a break when we get to the top." I nodded up the hill.

We were halfway up the hill when Elena suddenly stopped and tilted her head, listening to something.

"Do you hear that?" she asked.

I stopped so I could listen too. When she'd asked, all I could hear was the sound of my footsteps crunching through the tall grass covering the hill.

"It sounds like music," I said after hearing the faint pounding of drums. As I continued to listen, I could make out the whine of an electric guitar and the screaming vocals of a heavy metal singer. "That's definitely music," I confirmed.

Elena smiled, "I know this song," she said as she started walking again.

"I don't recognize it," I admitted as I followed behind her. It didn't sound like anything I or Elena normally listened to.

"It's *Rainbow in the Dark* by Dio," Elena said, "It was one of my dad's favorite songs," she revealed before singing along to the song's chorus.

"I think it's coming from down there." I pointed.

We'd reached the top of the hill where a cracked and rutted road led to the left and right of our position. I was pointing to the left.

As we stood there, *Rainbow in the Dark* ended and a new song began.

"Whoever's playing this stuff really loves their 80s metal," Elena smiled, once again recognizing the song that was playing.

"I didn't know you were a fan," I replied.

In the 8 months I'd known Elena, I'd always assumed our taste in music was the same. It was the topic we'd bonded over, especially our love for The Lumineers and other modern folk bands. We were actually on our way to a folk music festival when the car broke down.

I didn't think liking heavy metal was a bad thing, I was just surprised to hear that Elena liked it.

"I grew up on this stuff," she said, "My mom and dad were huge metal heads in the '80s." She laughed as she recalled some of the pictures she'd seen of her parents, "You should've seen their hair." She held her hands up to both sides of her head, "So much hairspray."

As Elena talked, I pulled out my phone, checking to see if service had returned.

"Anything?" Elena sounded hopeful after checking her phone and seeing that it didn't have any service.

I shook my head, "Nope."

"I guess that means we should find whoever's blasting that music and see if they have a phone we can use," she replied.

In my mind, I pictured a bar full of burly bikers, sitting around drinking beer and listening to loud music. That made me uncomfortable with the idea of seeking out the source of the music, but we didn't really have any other options at the moment.

As I followed Elena up the road, I silently hoped that we'd find someone else to help us before we found out where the music was coming from.

Elena, who had started singing along to Judas Priest's *You've Got Another Thing Comin'*, the song that was currently playing, didn't seem to share my concerns.

****

"I think I see a house," Elena declared.

We'd been walking for about ten minutes, following the music, when she saw the roof of a structure behind a line of trees a few hundred meters from the road.

"Never mind," she sighed as she came to the other side of the tree line and saw the broken windows and missing door of the house.

"This one is abandoned too," I pointed at a house on the opposite side of the road.

Elena had been so focused on the house she'd seen that she hadn't noticed the one across the street from it that was in a similar state of disrepair.

"Sounds like the music is coming from both houses." Elena stopped and looked from one house to the other while tilting her head to listen.

I stopped and listened too. The music did sound like it was coming from both houses, but it also sounded like it was still coming from further up the street.

"Want to check it out?" I asked, hooking my thumb toward the nearest house.

"Sure," Elena replied.

The music coming from the abandoned houses had piqued her curiosity. She followed me through the weed-infested yard and up onto the porch. The closer we got to the house, the louder the music got.

"It sounds like it's coming from the back," I said as I peered through the doorway.

A moment later, I stepped off the porch and began circling the house, peering through the broken windows.

"What are you doing?" Elena asked as she followed behind me.

"Making sure there's nobody inside," I replied.

Someone had to have set up the speakers that were playing the music and I wanted to make sure they weren't still around. Plus, I'd started to an uneasy feeling. The kind you get when you think someone is watching you.

"See anything?" Elena asked as we moved to the back of the house.

"No," I shook my head, "I couldn't tell where the music was coming from either," I added.

"Well, let's find out," Elena stepped onto the back patio, through the remains of the sliding glass door, and into the house.

I turned in a circle, scanning the surrounding area behind the house, trying to figure out why I couldn't shake the feeling that someone was watching me. When I didn't see anyone, I joined Elena.

"It sounds like it's coming from up there." Elena had to raise her voice to be heard over the music as she pointed at the ceiling, "In the attic."

"This doesn't feel right," I verbalized the anxiety I was feeling, "I think we should leave."

Elena looked over at me and then back up at the ceiling, "It is pretty weird," she agreed.

The two of us left the house. When we returned to the road, I started walking back the way we had come while Elena went in the opposite direction.

"Where're you going?" Elena asked. She was the first to realize that we weren't walking in the same direction.

I looked over my shoulder at her, "Back to the car," I said.

"Seriously?" Elena scoffed, "We're already here. Let's just keep going until we find someone who can help us." She gestured in the direction she wanted to go.

"Okay," I relented, "But if we don't find anyone in the next half hour, we're going back to the car."

"Fair enough," Elena agreed.

We continued walking up the road without talking to each other. Even if we had anything to say, the increasing volume of the music would've made it hard for us to hear each other clearly.

As we walked, I kept my phone in my hand so I could periodically check for service and to see how much time had passed. If we didn't find anyone soon, I was planning on walking back to the car with or without Elena.

"Look!" Elena said, raising her voice to be heard over the music.

I looked up from my phone to see her standing in the middle of an intersection, pointing at a building down a side street.

"I bet whoever is playing the music is in there," she said.

The building Elena was pointing at was a small brick structure with remnants of a large antenna tower on the roof. Mounted on the side of the building facing us were four large, heavily weathered letters identifying the structure as a radio station.

"K, L, L, D," I announced the station's call letters, "Never heard of it." I had to practically yell to be heard over the music, which seemed to me coming from all the buildings that lined the street.

"I don't think many people have," Elena replied, "I doubt they can broadcast very far with a broken antenna." She gestured at the roof of the building.

"Do you really think there's someone inside?" I asked while looking at the empty parking lot in front of the station, "I don't see any cars."

The fact that we'd seen so many abandoned houses but not a single person was making me feel anxious. I didn't want to go any further. I wanted to turn around and leave.

"There has to be someone," she insisted, "The music isn't playing itself."

"Maybe it's automated…programmed to play random songs," I countered.

"Even if it is, there should still be someone around to make sure it's running properly," Elena said.

"Not if they've left town like everyone else seems to have," I swept my arm behind me to gesture at the row of empty houses we'd just walked past.

"Well, I guess there's only one way to find out," Elena declared as she started walking up the street.

***

When we made it to the entrance of the radio station, Elena reached out and tested the glass door to see if it would open.

"It's unlocked," she rasped. Her throat was dry from talking with her voice raised and not having anything to drink.

I pressed my face to the dirty glass so I could see inside.

"See anyone?" Elena asked.

I shook my head, "No." All I saw was a reception desk with two large speakers sitting on opposite ends of it. Currently blaring from them was the Quiet Riot song *Cum on Feel the Noize,* but I didn't know that at the time.

Elena pulled the door open and walked inside, holding it open for me to follow. As I walked by her, she threw up her hand, making the sign of the devil, and began singing the chorus to the song while banging her head to the beat.

"I love Quiet Riot," she said when she was done.

"I couldn't tell," I replied with a lopsided grin on my face.

The two of us stood in the entryway, examining our surroundings.

"Which way?" Elena eventually asked.

Two doors led further into the building, one on either side of the reception area.

"Why don't you check that door?" I pointed to the door closest to Elena, "And I'll check this one." Using the same hand, I hooked my thumb over my shoulder at the door behind me.

"Sounds like a plan," Elena said, turning and approaching the door I'd indicated.

I waited until she opened the door and peeked inside before I opened the door in front of me.

On the other side of the door, I saw the booth where the DJs sat and played music. When I saw that someone was sitting inside the booth with a pair of headphones on, I quickly shut the door and spun around to look at Elena.

"What'd you find?" Elena asked when she saw me looking at her.

I considered lying and telling her that there wasn't anything there, but I couldn't bring myself to do it.

"There's a guy in there," I gestured at the door.

"Great! Let's go talk to him," Elena said, brushing past me as she rushed across the entryway and through the door.

I stood in the doorway and watched as Elena approached the window of the booth and knocked on it, trying to get the man's attention. It took her several tries, knocking louder and louder each time, before the man, who was sitting with his back to us, swiveled in his chair and saw her.

Elena waved at him.

The man, who appeared to be in his late fifties or early sixties, was clearly shocked to see us. He stared at us for what seemed like an eternity before removing his headphones and slowly rising from his chair before walking out of the booth.

"What are you doing here?" he asked, raising his voice to be heard over the music.

Elena looked back at me before answering, "Our car broke down on the way to the interstate," she said, "We saw the water tower from the road and figured there was a town nearby so we cut across the woods and headed this way. From there we just followed the music until we found you." She paused for a moment. When the man didn't say anything, she added, "We're just looking for a phone so we can call someone to come help us."

I walked over to join them as Elena spoke.

The man opened his mouth to say something, but stopped and looked back at the booth instead because the Quiet Riot song had just ended.

"One second," he raised his index finger and rushed back into the booth, removed the Quiet Riot record from the player, grabbed a new record without looking at it, and started to play it. A moment later, the guitar intro for Metallica's *For Whom the Bell Tolls* roared from the speakers.

When the man returned, he shuffled over to a desk in the corner of the room, grabbed something, and returned to where Elena and I were standing.

"You said you came into town over by the water tower, right?" the man asked as he unfolded the thing he'd grabbed from the desk and held it up, showing us that it was a map.

Elena and I both nodded.

"Can you show me the route you took to get here?" he asked.

"Sure," I said, wondering why that was so important to the guy.

"This is where we are," the man pointed to a spot near the center of town, "And this is where the water tower is," he slid his finger to a spot outside of town.

"This is the way we came," I said, stepping forward and placing my finger on the spot where the water tower was and moving it diagonally to the edge of the map. The map didn't show enough of the surrounding areas to have the road we'd broken down on it.

"Did you follow this road to get into town?" The man pointed at the road that ran in front of the water tower, "Or did you cut through here?" he moved his finger in a straight line from the tower to the radio station, cutting across a couple of fields and side streets.

"We followed the road," I replied, "Why does that matter?" I snapped, getting irritated at being questioned. I just wanted to use the phone and get the heck out of there.

The man ignored my question and asked one of his own, "Do you know how to use a record player?" He looked from me to Elena.

"No," I admitted. I was sure I could figure it out, but I wasn't going to offer.

"Of course," Elena declared at the same time.

The man motioned for Elena to follow him into the booth. Once inside, he pointed at the record player. "When that song ends, start another one." He moved his finger from the player to the crates of records that were stacked up against the wall.

Elena walked over to one of the crates and lifted a record out, "You only have singles?" she asked, holding up the small record that was only large enough to contain a single song per side.

"What you see is what I got," the man swept his arms across the room,

Elena put the record back and started flipping through the crate until she found a record that caught her eye. It was Queensryche's *Operation Mindcrime*. She pulled it out and turned around to show me.

"I'd completely forgotten this band existed," she smiled, "I'm playing this next."

"Play whatever you like," the man said, "Just keep it playing." He jabbed his finger at the record player.

"Why?" I asked.

Once again, he ignored my question.

"I need to run over to my trailer to get my phone so you can make your call," the man said, "I'll explain everything when I get back." He shuffled out of the booth and toward the exit of the radio station.

"What's wrong with that phone?" I followed the man and was pointing at an old phone that was sitting on one of the desks.

"It doesn't work," the man replied, "None of the phones in town do. If you want to make a call here, you need a satellite phone…which I have in my trailer."

I was about to suggest that maybe I should go with the man, but Elena interrupted me.

"Leave him alone," she snapped, "He's just trying to help." To the man, she said, "Do you have anything to drink around here? My throat is killing me." She placed her hand on her neck.

"There's a fridge in the breakroom," the man pointed to the other side of the building, "Help yourself to whatever you want."

"Cool," Elena replied. Right after she finished speaking, the Metallica song ended. "That's my cue," she smiled, returning to the booth to put the Queensryche record on.

The man waited until the song began to play before he left.

"Wait a minute," I stopped him as he was about to step out into the parking lot, "Where's your trailer?"

"See that stop sign?" the man gestured up the street.

"Yeah," I answered.

"Take that left and it's two blocks up on the right-hand side. You can't miss it." When he was done talking, he pushed the door open and walked outside.

I considered following behind him to see if he really was going to his trailer, but I decided against doing that. I didn't want to leave Elena alone.

"Do you want something to drink?" Elena asked loudly from behind me, startling me. "Sorry," she quickly apologized, "I didn't mean to scare you." When I didn't acknowledge her comment, she said, "Are you okay?"

"Not really," I admitted, "This place gives me the creeps. Where is everyone? And what's up with all of this?" I gestured at the speakers on the desk. "None of it makes any sense."

"You're right, it doesn't," Elena agreed, "But we're here so let's try not to make a big deal out of it. When he comes back, we'll call a tow truck and get the heck out of here, okay?"

"Okay," I sighed.

If he comes back, I thought.

"In the meantime, let's see what he has to drink," Elena tugged on my arm, pulling me toward the door that led to the breakroom.

****

"What do you want?" Elena stood before the open door of the refrigerator and gestured at the various brands of beer and soda that filled its shelves.

"I haven't had one of those in a while," I pointed at a bottle of IBC Root Beer.

"Sounds good to me," she grabbed two bottles and held one out to me.

After I took the offered bottle, Elena reached into the fridge and grabbed two more bottles before shutting it.

"Let's get back before the song ends," she nodded in the direction of the booth, "I need to figure out what I'm going to play next." She seemed to be enjoying the idea of being a disc jockey.

As we passed back through the entryway, I stopped by the doors and chugged my root beer as I looked outside at the deserted street.

"I don't think he's coming back," I blurted out after I'd finished my drink.

"Why do you think that?" Elena asked.

"Just a feeling," I replied, keeping my attention focused on the street.

"You can go look for him if it'll make you feel better," Elena offered.

"And leave you here?" I turned to look at her.

"I'll be fine," she insisted.

"Are you sure?"

"Positive. Now, go," she gestured outside, "The sooner you make that phone call the sooner we can get the hell out of here."

I pulled my phone out and checked it for the millionth time, hoping it would have service and I wouldn't have to go looking for the man, but that wasn't the case.

"Okay, I'm going," I sighed, pushing my way through the door, and walking out into the parking lot.

Elena returned to the booth to start looking for the next song she was going to play.

****

"Two blocks up on the right-hand side," I muttered to myself after I'd reached the stop sign.

I stood there for a moment, looking in the direction the man had indicated, but I couldn't see a trailer, just a row of shops. Wanting to give the man the benefit of the doubt, I decided to walk up the road to see if I could find the trailer.

I did find it, on the other side of an auto body shop, set back a couple hundred feet from the road on a heavily wooded lot. And I didn't like what I found. The door to the trailer was wide open and there was no sign of the man.

"I knew it," I hissed after I'd poked my head through the doorway of the trailer, confirming that it was empty.

As I looked around the interior of the trailer, I noticed feminine items scattered around. Items that most men wouldn't have a use for. And they all looked like they'd been recently used.

There's someone else here, I thought.

I whirled around and scanned the road, looking for any sign of the man or the woman who was likely with him, but the road curved out of sight, limiting my field of vision.

They couldn't have gotten far.

I was about to jog up the road and try to catch up to them, but I stopped when I saw a piece of paper, weighted down with a brick, sitting on top of a trashcan next to the trailer door.

I pulled the paper free and held it up. Written on it was a single sentence:

THE MUSIC KEEPS THEM AWAY

"What's that supposed to mean?" I asked out loud.

As soon as I asked the question, the song that was playing ended. I assumed Elena would start a new song at any moment, but she never did.

The sudden silence, coupled with the idea that something might've happened to Elena, sent chills up my spine.

"ELENA!" I yelled as I ran back towards the radio station.

I'd only managed to make it a block before strange figures began appearing in the doorways of all the nearby shops.

"Hello," I stopped and raised my hand in greeting, thinking the closest figure was a person. I quickly realized my mistake when the figure stepped out of the shadows and onto the sidewalk.

There was nothing human about it except its basic shape. Its face was featureless and its body was a pixelated mixture of gray, black, and white, the colors in constant motion like the static on a television screen. As it got closer, I thought I could hear the hiss of white noise coming from it.

The figures converged on me with slow, measured steps.

I turned and ran back towards the trailer, but again I didn't make it very far. While I was watching the figures in front of me, several more had come out of the buildings behind me. There were close to twenty of them, all making their way toward me.

I was surrounded.

I spun in a circle, looking for a way to escape, but none presented itself.

There were now more than fifty of the figures spread out around me in every direction. All walking toward me. The closest ones were less than twenty feet away.

If you're going to do something, you better do it now, the voice of reason shouted in my mind.

I tensed my muscles, preparing to run, but before I did, the drum intro to Iron Maiden's *Run to the Hills* began pounding from the speakers.

The bodies of the figures flickered, like a television screen having trouble focusing, before they dispersed with flashes of light so bright that I had to shield my eyes. When I was able to uncover them, I saw that I was alone in the street.

Not wanting to be stuck outside when the current song ended, I ran as fast as I could back to the radio station.

"ELENA!" I yelled, throwing open the doors of the station.

I kept calling her name until I saw her standing in the doorway of the booth staring at me with a concerned look on her face.

"What's wrong?" she asked.

"He's gone," I panted, "And there are these things….," Speaking quickly, I stumbled over my words, making them sound incoherent.

"Catch your breath and then start over," Elena said.

"He's… gone," I repeated, taking a deep breath between each word. Before I could continue, Elena interrupted me.

"What do you mean he's gone?" she asked.

"Gone as in gone," I said, crossing the room so I didn't have to shout to be heard over the music. "He just up and left."

"Why would he do that?"

"It probably has something to do with the weird…," I paused, trying to think of the right word to describe the figures I'd seen, "People out there." I hooked my thumb over my shoulder toward the entrance of the radio station.

"There are other people here?" Elena sounded hopeful.

I sighed in frustration, "Not people. People is the wrong word for them…they're…things…ghosts…aliens…fuck, I don't know what they are. I just know they aren't human. They appeared when you stopped playing the music…why did you stop playing the music anyway?"

"I had to pee really bad, I didn't think I was going to be gone that long," she said and then it suddenly hit her what I had said, "Did you say aliens?" she asked, raising her eyebrows, and looking at me like I was crazy.

Instead of replying, I held out the note I'd found which was still clutched in my fist, "I found this," I said.

Elena took the note and smoothed it out so she could read it, "The music keeps them away," she read it out loud, "What's that supposed to mean?"

"It's better if you see for yourself," I said. "Go and stand in the entrance and keep your eye on the street," I instructed.

"What am I supposed to be looking for?" Elena asked, "Little green men?" She laughed as she walked toward the entrance.

I wasn't amused by her attempt at humor, "You won't be laughing when you see them," I said.

Once Elena was in position, I walked into the booth and removed the needle from the record that was playing. A couple of minutes later, Elena came running back into the booth.

"What the hell are those things?"

I shrugged, "I have no idea. All I know is that the music keeps them away." I pointed at the note, "As it says there."

"Then hurry up and turn the music back on before they get in here," Elena sounded frantic.

I obliged, placing the needle back on the record, and restarting the song.

Elena peeked back through the doorway at the entrance to verify that the things outside were gone. She sighed in relief when she saw that they were.

"We can't stay here," she said.

"I agree," I said, "But we can't just walk out of here either. We won't make it out of town before the music ends."

Thinking about leaving made me recall the conversation we'd had with the man and how he was asking so many questions about the route we'd taken to get into town. He was asking those questions because he knew he'd be able to escape if he left the same way we had arrived.

"How long did it take us to get into town from the water tower?" Elena asked.

"About 25-30 minutes," I replied, "Why?"

Elena picked up the map the man had left on the desk and examined it.

"If we cut across here." She drew a straight line with her finger from the radio station to the water tower, "running the entire way, we could probably make it back in about ten minutes."

"That means we'll need a song that's at least 10 minutes long to cover our escape," I pointed out.

"Not a song," Elena replied, "We need an entire album."

"I doubt you're going to find one here," I said, "If there was one, that guy would've been playing it instead of sitting here playing song after song. Don't you think?"

"He wouldn't have been able to do that all day though, he'd have to sleep sometime," she replied, hoping we'd be able to find some easy way out of our predicament.

"He had help," I revealed, "There was someone else living in the trailer with him. They probably took shifts playing songs while the other person slept."

"That's what we can do," Elena blurted out, "You can stay and play the music while I go and get help."

"Why don't you stay and I go get help?" I countered. I didn't want to be left alone.

"Because I'm faster than you," Elena sneered, "I can make it back to the car a lot quicker than you can."

"You don't know that." I said, feeling slightly offended by her comment, "I can run pretty fast when I want to."

Elena eyed my body, the look on her face implying that I was not in the best of shape.

"I'm going," she suddenly decided, walking quickly toward the exit.

"You won't get very far," I threatened, before walking into the booth and removing the needle from the record.

"Seriously," Elena scoffed, turning around, and returning, "Don't you want to get out of here?"

"Of course I do," I snapped, "But I want us to do it together."

Elena stood with her hand on her hips and a scowl on her face.

"Let's wait an hour," I suggested, "If we can't figure out a way for both of us to leave by then, you can go and get help while I stay here."

"Fine," Elena snapped, "One hour."

Satisfied that we had settled our differences, I placed the needle back on the record.

"I guess we should see what songs we have to work with," Elena said.

After walking into the booth to join me, she started flipping through the available records.

"I don't recognize any of these bands," I admitted after looking through a few of the records.

"Look for anything by Megadeth, Metallica, or Slayer. Some of their songs are pretty long," Elena advised.

"Okay," I said, "But first I need to pee." That root beer I drank had gone straight to my bladder.

I started to walk away, but stopped when I realized I had no idea where the restroom was.

Guessing what I was about to ask her, Elena pointed the way, "It's on the other side past the breakroom," she said.

"Thanks," I replied, "I'll be right back."

After I had finished using the facilities and was washing my hands, I heard the music stop. A few seconds later, a new song started playing, surprisingly it was one that I recognized.

"I know this song," I declared as I walked back over to the booth.

But there was no reply. The booth was empty and Elena was nowhere to be found. She'd left without me, knowing I'd do the right thing and keep the music playing for her.

Through the speakers, the lead singer for the band Europe belted out the chorus of their most popular hit, *The Final Countdown.*

REUNION

"Shit," I muttered after opening the fridge.

Blaire, a friend of mine, was having a get-together at her apartment and I was supposed to bring some liquor with me, but all I had was a near-empty bottle of vodka.

I looked at the clock on the microwave and saw that it was 9:45 pm, "I still have time to pick something up," I muttered to myself. The liquor store closed at ten and wasn't that far away.

I grabbed my car keys and ran out the door.

Ten minutes later, I was walking into the liquor store.

"We close in 5 minutes," the guy behind the counter said.

"I only need 2," I replied, holding up two fingers as I rushed to the back of the store where the vodka was kept.

I quickly grabbed my usual brand and then returned to the counter to pay for it well within those two minutes.

"Need a bag?" the cashier asked. The way he said it made it sound like it would be a major inconvenience to him if I said yes.

"Nope, I'm good." I grabbed the bottle by the neck and left the store.

I was halfway across the parking lot when I noticed something odd about my car.

"Who the fuck is that!?" I snapped.

It looked like there was somebody sitting on the passenger side.

I stopped and stared at the person, trying to see what they were doing. As I did, I realized it wasn't a person at all. It was a mannequin dressed in a polo shirt. He looked like a giant Ken doll.

"That is so not funny." I placed my hand on my chest, trying to slow my heartbeat. I was ready to run back into the liquor store and call the police.

"Carly!" I called out, figuring she was hiding somewhere in the parking lot laughing her ass off, "I know it was you."

Carly was a friend of mine who managed a clothing store. If anyone was going to pull a prank like this, it was her. She had the resources and the inclination.

She once convinced me to come over to her apartment to meet a friend of hers. She insisted that I'd get along great with the guy. When I got to her place, I found her sitting on the couch with one of the mannequins from her shop.

That's why I was positive that Carly was the one who'd put the mannequin in my car.

"I'm leaving," I announced as I approached my car, "If you don't come and get it, I'm going to keep it."

I waited a moment to see if Carly would appear. When she didn't, I got into my car and shut the door.

"Hold this for me," I said to the mannequin, placing the bottle of vodka I'd just bought between his khaki covered legs. As I did so, I noticed a folded-up piece of paper wedged between two of the fingers on its left hand.

"Is this for me?" I asked, taking the piece of paper and unfolding it.

Written on it was an address and a time.

What are you up to, Carly? I wondered.

According to the note, I had fifteen minutes to get to the address listed on the paper.

"Okay." I started the car, "I'll play along."

Blaire's party wasn't supposed to start until 11, so I had a little time to kill.

I entered the address into the map app on my phone. When I saw what the destination was, it only confirmed my suspicions that Carly was to blame for the unexpected passenger in my car.

"Let's get you home," I said to the mannequin as I drove out of the parking lot.

15 minutes later, I pulled into The Sunset Plaza, a collection of shops and restaurants arranged in a U-shaped strip mall.

Since most of the stores had already closed for the evening, I was able to find a parking spot right in front of my destination, The *Berry Berry Boutique*. A high-end fashion store that my friend Carly happened to manage.

"Home sweet home," I announced.

I considered carrying the mannequin up to the shop with me, but decided against it. If Carly wanted it back, she was going to have to come outside and get it herself.

I knew the shop was already closed for the night, so I knocked on the glass doors trying to get someone's attention. The lights were on and that meant they were still finishing up their nightly closing procedures. Plus, Carly's car was parked in its usual spot, so I knew she was inside.

I had to stand there knocking for 5 minutes before one of Carly's employees finally came to the door.

"We're closed," the annoyed-looking girl snapped, "You'll have to come back tomorrow." She turned to leave.

"I'm here to see Carly," I said, "Tell her it's Samantha."

The employee glanced back at me and rolled her eyes before walking off.

A minute later, Carly came to the door and unlocked it.

"Hey, Sam," she said, opening the door and letting me into the shop, "What are you doing here?" She locked the door behind me.

"What do you mean?" I was confused by her reaction, "I came because of your note." I showed her the note the mannequin was holding.

Carly took the piece of paper and examined it.

"I didn't write this," she handed it back to me, "Where'd you get it?"

"From your mannequin," I replied, jerking my thumb over my shoulder in the direction of my car.

"My what?" She looked at me like I was crazy.

Getting the sense that she had no idea what I was talking about, I told her about my trip to the liquor store and how I returned to my car to find a mannequin sitting in the front seat.

"That's creepy," Carly said, "I wouldn't do anything like that. Plus, I wouldn't have had the time. I've been stuck here all evening."

"Do you…," I was about to ask her if she recognized the mannequin and could tell me where it might've come from but I was unable to finish the question when I turned and saw that someone had put another mannequin in my car.

"What's wrong?" Carly asked.

"There's another one," I pointed at my car, "In the backseat."

The new mannequin was a woman wearing a floral dress.

"Told you it wasn't me," Carly said as she looked at my car through the doors of the shop.

"Who the hell is doing this?" I looked to Carly for an answer, but she just shrugged her shoulders.

"They look like old department store mannequins," she said a moment later, "Like the ones they used to have at Sears and JC Penney. Do you know anyone who works at the mall?"

"No," I shook my head.

"I don't know what else to tell you," Carly said, "I will say that if that happened to me," she nodded toward my car, "I'd have left them on the side of the road."

Before I could reply, one of Carly's employees approached, needing her help with closing down one of the registers.

"I've got to get back to work," Carly said.

"Of course," I replied, "Sorry to have bothered you with all this."

"No worries," Carly said, unlocking the door to let me out, as I left, she added, "You should toss them in the nearest dumpster."

***

I stood outside my car in the shopping center parking lot, staring at the two mannequins, wondering what I should do. That's when I noticed there was another note wedged between the male mannequin's fingers.

"Now what?" I muttered, opening the car door to retrieve the note.

Written on it was another address and time.

Curious as to where the person who was putting the mannequins in my car wanted me to go this time, I used my map app to look up the address. Unsurprisingly, it was for another clothing store. One for children that was called *Bean Sprouts*.

According to the map app, it was just a few blocks away.

I didn't know anyone who worked there, but I did know someone who worked in the discount retail shop that was right next door to it. His name was Glenn, and he was one of my exes. That made me think he was the one responsible for the mannequins in my car.

Why would he put the mannequins in my car? I wondered.

I tried to come up with a reason why he'd want to mess with me like that, but I couldn't.

Our relationship only lasted a couple of months before it became clear to both of us that we weren't very compatible. As far as I was aware, we'd ended things amicably and haven't spoken to each other since.

Maybe whoever is doing it wants me to think it's Glenn.

They'd already sent me to the *Berry Berry Boutique* where I'd accused Carly of being the culprit.

Whoever it was knew me well enough to know my circle of friends and my dating history.

I got back into my car and started the engine.

Where to go?

I felt like I was at a crossroad. I could dump the mannequins, go to Blair's party, and forget about the stupid prank, or I could go to the address on the note and try to figure out who was messing with me.

I looked at the time. It was 10:39 p.m.

There's still time to do both, I reasoned.

"Fuck it," I said, putting the car into gear and driving to the destination on the note.

****

Since *Bean Sprouts* was closed when I arrived, I was able to park right in front of it.

Before I got out of the car, I eyed all the vehicles that were around me, checking to see if I recognized any of them.

I didn't.

After that, I got out and walked around the cars, peering through their windows, looking to see if there were any mannequins inside any of them.

Whoever was putting them in my car had to transport them somehow and they had to be close by to transfer them quickly without me noticing. That's why I really thought I'd find a mannequin inside one of them.

But I didn't.

Eventually, I decided to act like I wasn't paying attention to my car by walking up to the front doors of Bean Sprouts and looking into the darkened sales floor beyond.

I was only able to do that for a few minutes before my uterus let me know that it had other plans for me.

"Oh my God. Not Now," I hissed. I thought I had a couple of days before I started my period.

The mannequins were going to have to wait. As someone prone to heavy flows, I didn't want to bleed all over myself.

I grabbed my purse and rushed across the parking lot into the discount store, where I ran into the restroom and locked myself in the nearest stall.

"That was close," I sighed. A few drops of blood spotted my underwear, but not enough to need to change.

I cleaned myself up, took care of business, washed my hands, and then left as quickly as I could. But I wasn't fast enough. By the time I made it back outside to my car, I found that I was already too late to catch whoever was massing with me.

They'd already come and gone.

"God dammit!" I cursed.

My car was empty. Both the mannequins were gone.

Now, I'll never know who was fucking with me.

I whirled around hoping to get a glimpse of anything that might offer a clue as to who put the mannequins in my car but I didn't see anything near me except an elderly man putting groceries in the back of his SUV a couple of rows over from me.

"Excuse me, sir," I called out, jogging over to where he was, "You didn't happen to see anyone messing with my car, did you?" I gestured at my vehicle.

He sized me up, clearly wondering if I posed some kind of threat before answering.

"Can't say that I did," he shook his head and then offered me some advice, "If you're worried about people messing with your car you probably shouldn't park that far away from the store," he nodded towards my car, "It's not safe."

"Thanks," I gave him a weak smile, "I'll try and remember that."

I returned to my car.

When I got into the driver's seat, I looked over and saw the bottle of vodka I'd purchased, sitting on the passenger seat, with a folded-up piece of paper sticking out from beneath it.

I grabbed the paper and unfolded it. As I did, a one-hundred-dollar bill fell out of it.

"What the hell?"

I picked up the money and examined it, checking to see if it was real.

It was.

I set the bill aside and finished unfolding the note and read it. The only thing written on it was a single word: Thanks.

"Seriously?" I looked up and scanned the parking lot to see if anyone was watching me.

I had no idea why I was targeted, but I got the feeling I was the subject of some stupid prank being filmed for YouTube or TikTok. They were probably still filming me to get my final reaction.

I raised my middle finger and held it up to the window before starting the car and driving over to Blair's party, where I intended to get shitfaced and forget about the ridiculous night I'd had.

***

Late the next morning, after dealing with the hangover from the previous night's festivities, I went into the bathroom to change my tampon and saw that there were only a couple left in the box.

"Ugh," I groaned as I got dressed and headed back to the discount store, berating myself the entire time for not thinking about picking some up when I was there last night.

Well, you were a little preoccupied, the voice of reason reminded me. Which was true.

When I pulled into the parking lot, I had to pass by the children's clothing store to get to the discount store. As I drove by, I turned my head and looked at it. What I saw caused me to slam on the brakes.

In the big display window were the two mannequins that were in my car. They were posed differently and wearing different clothing, but it was them. I recognized their faces. Standing between them was the mannequin of a child.

Someone behind me honked.

I gave whoever it was a dirty look in the rearview mirror before pulling into the nearest parking space.

Someone had to take those mannequins out of my car and place them in that store window. I intended to find out who.

I got out of the car, walked into the store, and approached the nearest employee.

"Excuse me," I said.

The middle-aged woman, who was folding clothing on a rolling cart, looked up at me and smiled.

"How can I help you?" she asked.

"I have a question about those mannequins in the window," I gestured over my shoulder at them.

The smile dropped from her face, "What about them?"

"This is going to sound crazy," I said, "But, last night, somebody put them in my car and had me bring them here. I was wondering if you could tell me who it was?"

"That doesn't sound crazy," she said, "Not to me. But you're going to think I'm crazy when I tell you that nobody put them in your car." She was being completely serious.

"Somebody had to have put them in my car," I insisted.

"That would be the logical thing to think," she replied, "But that's not what happened."

"What do you mean?" she was starting to confuse me.

"When this store was being renovated," she explained, "The previous business left those behind." She nodded toward the window display. "I didn't have a use for the adult mannequins, so I gave them away. Three days later, I came in to open the shop and found them back in the storeroom. All three of them, standing together like one happy family."

"How did they get back there?"

She shrugged, "I have no idea. The doors were locked, and the alarm was set."

"Maybe one of your employees was messing with you?"

"Not possible," she said, "At the time, I was the only one who knew the alarm code and the only one who had keys to the door."

"That's crazy."

"You're right. It is," she agreed, "I didn't know how they found their way back here until a young man came into the store and told me about how he'd returned to his car to find one of the mannequins sitting in the passenger seat with a note instructing him to bring them here...Sound familiar?"

"That's what happened to me," I admitted.

"It's happened to someone every time I've tried to get rid of them," she said. "That's why, when I saw them in the storeroom this morning, I decided to just go ahead and let them stay." She gestured at the happy mannequin family.

WELFARE CHECK

"Unit 22, come in," the dispatcher's voice called out from the car's radio.

I picked up the handset and responded, "Go for unit 22," I said.

"We just got a call about a possible 270 in your area," the dispatcher replied.

270 was code for child neglect.

I acknowledged the code, got the address from the dispatcher, and then let them know I was headed to the location.

When I arrived, a woman rushed out of a nearby convenience store and flagged me down.

"Are you the one that called?" I asked as the woman approached.

She nodded her head, "Yes, I called, but she's not here anymore."

"Where is the child now?"

"She's over there," she pointed to a little girl who was walking along the sidewalk a block and a half away from where we were, "I tried to get her to stay but she wouldn't listen to me."

I thanked the woman and then drove up the street, pulling over about 25 feet in front of the girl. I waited until she got closer to my cruiser before stepping out.

"Can I talk to you for a second?" I said to the little girl, blocking her path.

As I waited for her to reply, I looked her over.

The first thing I noticed was that the dress she was wearing was dirty and looked like she'd been wearing it for several days. The next thing I noticed was that she was barefoot and her feet were even dirtier than her dress. In her equally dirty hand was a half-eaten hot dog that she'd bought from the convenience store.

"Okay," the girl replied.

"What's your name?" I asked.

"Molly," she said.

"Where are your parents, Molly?"

The girl took a bite of her hot dog and shrugged.

"Where do you live?"

She shrugged again.

By this time a small crowd of people had gathered on the street corner to see what was going on. I turned and addressed the closest people.

"Do any of you know this young lady?" I gestured at the girl.

Several people shook their heads, and a few others murmured, "No."

"I saw her come out of a house over on Wright Street," an older gentleman called out.

"Which house?" I asked him.

He didn't know the address, but he described it to me.

***

"Do you recognize this house?" I pointed.

I'd coaxed Molly into the cruiser and then driven down the street until I found the house the man had described.

She nodded.

"Is this where you live?"

She shook her head.

Molly's conflicting answers confused me, prompting me to get out of the cruiser and approach the residence, hoping whoever was inside could shed some light on what was going on.

"Stay put," I said to her before closing the car door, "I'll be right back."

When I made it to the porch, I noticed that the door was slightly ajar. My first thought was that the girl must not have shut it all the way when she left.

I knocked on the door and identified myself.

"Police!" I called out, "Anybody home?"

When nobody answered, I knocked again, loudly repeating myself.

There was still no reply.

At that point, given the condition of the child in my cruiser, I assumed I had probable cause to enter the premises.

I pushed the door open and entered the house, periodically calling out, letting anyone who may be inside know I was there.

Nobody ever responded as I went from room to room searching the house.

While I was looking around the kitchen, I heard a faint shuffling sound behind me. Thinking that someone was trying to sneak up on me, I quickly drew my pistol and whirled around.

"Freeze!" I yelled.

When I saw Molly standing there with a vacant expression on her face, I took a deep breath and exhaled as I re-holstered the gun.

"Jesus Christ, kid," I cursed, "You scared the shit out of me! I thought I told you to stay in the car!"

She just stared at me.

"Is this your house or not?" I asked her.

She shook her head.

I sighed in frustration.

"Do you know whose house this is?"

She shook her head again.

Feeling at a loss about how to proceed, I decided it would be best to hand the child over to protective services and let them figure out where she came from. But, before I did that, I had one final question for Molly.

"Have you ever been inside this house before?"

To my surprise, Molly nodded her head.

"You have?"

She nodded again.

I took a moment to process everything I'd learned from Molly. Which wasn't a lot. But it was enough to lead me to a possible conclusion.

"Was someone holding you here against your will?"

The fact that she'd been in the house, but it wasn't hers, coupled with her dirty appearance made me think it was possible she'd been abducted by whoever lived in the house.

Molly nodded her head.

That's probably why nobody was here when I arrived.

They either fled once they realized the girl was gone or when they saw me pull up to the curb.

"Where were they keeping you?" I asked, wanting to make sure there weren't any other children in the house.

"Down there," she pointed at one of the doors in the kitchen behind me.

"In the basement?"

Molly nodded.

I was surprised by her answer. As far as I knew, none of the houses in the city were supposed to have basements. The reason why had something to do with the water table being too high, making them prone to flooding. If the house had a basement, it was constructed by the homeowners without the city's knowledge.

"I need you to go outside and wait for me by the car," I motioned for her to leave.

Since the rest of the house was empty, I had to assume that whoever was holding Molly captive might not have fled as I'd originally thought. They could be hiding in the basement and if that were the case, it meant it wasn't safe for her to be inside the house with me.

I waited until she stepped out onto the porch before drawing my gun again and returning to the kitchen.

"This is the police," I called out while standing to the side of the door Molly had said was the entrance to the basement, "Come out with your hands up."

I waited and listened for footsteps. When I didn't hear any, I reached out and quickly swung the door open.

"Come out where I can see you," I aimed my pistol down the stairs and into the darkness of the basement.

With my free hand, I tried the light switch that was on the wall at the top of the stairwell, but it didn't seem to work. That's when I slipped the flashlight out of my belt and shined it into the basement. What it revealed sent me running down the steps.

"Unit 22 to dispatch," I spoke into my radio as I rushed down the steps.

"Go for dispatch," the dispatcher replied seconds later.

"I need an ambulance at 1804 Wright Street."

When I shined my flashlight into the basement, the beam illuminated two people lying on the floor. From my original vantage point, I could only see their feet and had no idea if they were alive or not, which is why I rushed down the steps.

Before I checked the bodies, I swept my light across the basement making sure nobody else was down there with me. Satisfied that I was alone, I approached the closest of the two bodies.

I didn't need to check the young woman's pulse to know that she wasn't alive. I could tell by the angle of her neck that she was dead. The young man lying nearby was also dead. His neck had also been broken.

Judging by the color of their skin, I could tell that they'd died recently.

"What were you doing down here?" I whispered the question, no longer looking at the bodies of the two deceased people. I was now looking at the hole that had been dug on the floor between them.

It looked like someone was in the process of digging a grave.

I stepped back and surveyed the scene as I called dispatch on the radio again.

"Cancel the ambulance," I said, "Send the coroner and a couple of homicide detectives instead."

What the hell happened here? I wondered as I stared at the hole and the two bodies lying next to it.

Was the hole meant for them? If it was, it looked too small.

The stairs creaked.

I whirled around to find Molly descending into the basement.

"Don't come down here." I jabbed my finger at her, "Go back upstairs and wait for me."

She ignored me and continued walking down the steps.

"What the hell is wrong with you, kid?" I snapped while moving to block her view of the bodies. I was getting tired of her disobeying me.

My comment must have struck a nerve because she narrowed her eyes and glared at me.

"Go upstairs!"

She refused to move.

"Fine," I sighed, "If you won't leave, you can at least be helpful." I stepped aside so she could see the bodies. "You said you were being held down here. Do you know these people?"

She shook her head.

"Do you know who did this to them?"

Molly's face lit up and she smiled, "I did," she said.

"Oh, really?" I scoffed, "You managed to break both of their necks all by yourself?"

She nodded.

"Were they the ones who were keeping you down here?" I asked, figuring she knew who they were and what had happened to them.

Molly shook her head, "They weren't the ones who put me down here. My parents did."

"I thought you said this wasn't your house?" I confronted her.

"It's not," she replied, "Not anymore."

I felt like Molly was talking in circles, giving me the runaround.

"Where are your parents now?"

She shrugged, "I don't know."

"Did they do this?" I gestured at the bodies.

"No. I did that," was her reply.

She had to be lying. There's no way that scrawny little girl could have killed anyone, which meant she was covering for someone, most likely her parents.

"When was the last time you saw your folks?"

She shrugged again.

"Think," I demanded.

"When they put me in there," Molly pointed at the hole in the ground, "And left me. They said I was bad and needed to be punished."

When I first saw the hole in the basement floor, I assumed whoever was digging it didn't get to finish and that was why it looked so small. As I stood there looking at Molly, I realized the hole was the perfect size for her little body.

"Your parents were going to bury you?" I looked from her to the hole. Her story was getting crazier by the second.

"My parents did bury me," she replied, "And then those two people dug me up." She pointed at the bodies lying next to the hole.

"Let me get this straight," I tried to organize everything she'd told me into a cohesive narrative I could tell the detectives when they arrived, "You used to live in this house, and for some reason, your parents brought you back here to bury you in the basement but those people found you and were killed because of it. Does that sound about right?"

Molly shook her head.

I sighed and rolled my eyes in frustration, "Then explain it to me so that I can make sense of what happened."

"What year is it?" she asked, changing the subject.

"You don't know what year it is?" I replied.

She shook her head again.

"Seriously?"

"I really don't," she insisted.

Great, I sighed. If she didn't know what year it was it would call into question everything that she'd told me, including her name.

"It's 2023," I said.

She stared at me for a moment, clearly thinking about something.

"I was buried for 20 years," when she spoke it sounded like she was talking more to herself than to me.

"That's not possible." It was clear there was something seriously wrong with the girl. "Why don't we go upstairs and wait for CPS to arrive?" I nodded toward the stairs.

All I wanted to do at that point was hand Molly over to them and be done with her.

"I thought you wanted to know what happened here?" She tilted her head in an odd manner.

"I do. But I don't think you're capable of telling me the truth."

"I will tell you the truth," she said, "I promise."

I threw out my hands, "Okay, lay it on me." Whatever she said was likely going to be a lie, but I might be able to glean some shred of truth from her and decided to hear her out.

"I'm not like other kids," Molly began.

You got that right!

"I was born bad," she said, "That's what my mom used to say to me."

"Why would she say that?" That seemed like a horrible thing to say to a child.

"Because I could do things other people couldn't," she said.

"Like what?" Molly was sounding crazier by the second.

"Move things with my mind, hear people's thoughts, those sorts of things," she replied.

I couldn't help but laugh at that.

"I don't like being laughed at," she growled.

I was going to apologize, but I couldn't open my mouth. When I tried to reach up and touch my face, I found that I couldn't move my arms.

"My parents were afraid of me," she said, "They thought I was evil. That's why they buried me down here. They thought they could just erase me and pretend I never existed."

I could feel my body being lifted off the ground, but there wasn't anything I could do to stop it.

"I didn't know how long I'd been buried down here before they dug me up," Molly gestured at the bodies again. "I was as confused as they were when they pulled me out of the ground. If I had known who they were, I wouldn't have killed them. The only reason I did is because I thought they were my parents coming back to free after realizing they'd made a mistake."

When she was done talking, she walked up to me and removed the handcuffs from my belt. Then she forced my hands behind my back and put the cuffs around my wrists.

"I could kill you just as easily," she warned, "But I won't. Not if you leave me alone."

The faint blare of sirens could be heard in the distance.

"If you don't want anyone else to get hurt," Molly said, "All you have to do is leave me alone." She fixed her eyes on mine, wanting to make sure I understood what she was saying. "If anyone comes looking for me, I'm going to have to punish you for telling them about me."

When she was done speaking, she turned and walked up the basement steps.

A few minutes after Molly left, I could move again.

I quickly unlocked the cuffs and went upstairs to wait for the detectives to arrive. While I waited, Molly's final words echoed in my mind.

MICROWAVEABLE

"That thing is a beast," Harvey said when he saw the microwave sitting on the kitchen counter next to the stove.

I'd bought the microwave for $25 from an estate sale that I passed while driving home that afternoon. The person in charge of the sale assured me it worked, but encouraged me to give it a try once I got it home. If it didn't work, she said I could bring it back before the sale ended on Sunday. If she hadn't offered me that guarantee, I wouldn't have taken a chance on the old device.

"It goes with everything else in here," Harvey added while looking around, making fun of how big, bulky, and old the other kitchen appliances looked.

A few months back I got a promotion, which allowed me to move out of the apartment I shared with Harvey and mortgage a modest home in an old subdivision that was built in the early 70s. The house I bought, which came with all the appliances I needed except a microwave, wasn't much bigger than the apartment we were living in, but it was all mine.

I didn't mind how outdated everything was. I planned to upgrade things piece by piece as I could afford it.

"Do you know what brand it is?" Harvey examined the visible surfaces of the microwave, looking for a company logo but couldn't find one.

"I have no idea," I admitted, "Why do you care?"

"Just curious."

Harvey stepped away from the microwave and began walking around the kitchen opening cabinets.

"What're doing?" I snapped. I was already annoyed that he'd shown up at my house uninvited, having him going through my things like we were still roommates was starting to piss me off.

"Looking to see if you have any popcorn," he replied, "So we can test out the microwave."

"I don't have any popcorn."

Harvey stopped searching, "Well, what do you have that I can microwave?"

"Nothing for you," I said, "If you're hungry, you need to go and buy your own food."

I was certain the only reason he stopped by was to help himself to my kitchen. When we lived together, he would frequently steal my food and never offered to replace any of it.

"Oh, come on, man, don't be like that," he whined.

I didn't want to give him anything, but I suddenly remembered that I did have something I could give him. Something I had no intention of eating.

I walked over to the pantry, opened the door, and pulled out a box of generic toaster pastries that I had bought when I first moved in. I'd eaten one pack and decided I didn't like them. I couldn't convince myself to throw them away, so they've been sitting on the shelf ever since.

"You can have these," I handed the box to him.

He took the pastries and walked back over to the microwave.

"You got this at that estate sale, right?" Harvey gestured at the microwave as he pulled a package of pastries out of the box, "Do you know what happened to the previous owners?"

"What do you mean?"

"They don't normally do sales like that unless somebody's died without a will," Harvey explained, "Since you live in the neighborhood, I was wondering if you knew what happened to them."

I hadn't really thought about it. I assumed the estate sale was just a fancy name they were using for their garage sale.

Harvey put the toaster pastries on the counter so he could pull out his phone and search the internet for information about the occupants of the house that was having the estate sale.

"Holy shit! Somebody killed them!" he said a few minutes later, turning his phone so I could see the headline of a news article that read: Harvest Woods Family Massacred at Home.

I took Harvey's phone and scanned the article. According to what I read, a week or so before I moved into the neighborhood somebody entered the Porter family home and savagely butchered them. The article went on to explain how the police have been unable to find a single piece of evidence linking anyone to the scene of the crime.

"Do you still want it?" Harvey gestured at the microwave, "Now that you know where it came from?"

"Why wouldn't I?" I said, handing the phone back to him. "It's just a microwave. It's not like it was used to kill the family."

"But it's a microwave from a murder house," he clarified, "Aren't you afraid that it might be haunted or something?"

"Haunted?" I scoffed at the idea, "Have you ever heard of a haunted microwave?"

"No," Harvey admitted, "But I did see a show on the SyFy channel about other types of haunted objects. There was a hairbrush, a jewelry box, a pair of sunglasses, and a car."

"Even if I did believe in stuff like that, I'd never believe a microwave would be haunted," I said, "Nobody has that much personal attachment to one. Not the way they become attached to the things you mentioned."

"You're probably right," he replied, tearing open the outer wrapping of a package of toaster pastries, "I guess that means it's safe to use." He opened the microwave door and started putting the pastries inside.

"I have a toaster, you know?" I snapped at him while gesturing at the toaster sitting on the other side of the stove.

"I know," Harvey said, "I was just going to test the microwave for you."

"You might want to put those on a plate or a paper towel," I said, "I haven't cleaned it yet."

"I'm not worried about that," he said, "It looks clean enough to me. Besides, if there were any germs inside, the microwaves will kill them."

"Have at it then," I declared, letting him proceed. If he wanted to use it before I cleaned it, that was on him.

"Any idea how this thing works?" Harvey had put the pastries in the microwave and shut the door before examining the display panel, "It doesn't look anything like the one back in the apartment."

"I think you just push the number of minutes you want it to cook," I pointed.

The display panel just had a series of numbers from 1 to 10. Having worked in a fast-food restaurant with an industrial micro-

wave that had a similar panel, I assumed each number correspond-
ed to a cooking time in minutes.

"A minute should be good enough," Harvey said, reaching out
and pressing the 1 button.

The microwave began to hum before a bright light suddenly
started pulsing within it.

"Is it supposed to do that?" Harvey asked, taking a step away
from the device.

"I don't think so." I also stepped back.

The microwave continued to hum as the pulses of light got
brighter and brighter. The light got so bright that Harvey and I had
to shield our eyes.

I was certain that there was something seriously wrong with
the microwave and had decided that I was going to return it to the
estate sale as soon as it finished doing whatever it was doing to
Harvey's pastry.

"It's been longer than a minute," Harvey pointed out,
"Shouldn't it be cutting off by now?"

"Maybe you should unplug it," I said.

"I'm not going anywhere near that thing," was his reply, "You
unplug it."

Knowing that I wasn't going to be able to convince Harvey to
do it and because it was my house that was in potential danger, I
approached the microwave.

"What a minute," Harvey stopped me as I reached out blindly,
searching for the microwave's cord.

"Why?" I withdrew my hand

"Do you have any rubber gloves?"

"Why do I need gloves?"

"To insulate your hands so you don't electrocute yourself."

His comment worried me enough to the point that I didn't
want to risk touching the microwave at all.

But I still needed to find a way to turn it off.

The obvious answer hit me a moment later.

The fuse box!

I could cut power to the entire kitchen without having to touch
the microwave.

With my eyes squeezed shut, I felt my way across the kitchen,
heading toward the garage where the fuse box was. I made it about
halfway there before the microwave quit humming and the pulses
of light ceased.

"Is it over?" Harvey asked.

I waited a moment to see if anything else would happen. Thankfully, nothing did.

"I think so," I said.

Hesitantly, I opened my eyes and looked around. What I saw when I opened them shocked and confused me.

"What the fuck's wrong with your house, man?!" Harvey was just as shocked as I was.

Everything around us had become translucent, like a barely visible holographic image. When I tried to touch the nearest countertop, my fingers passed right through it.

"I have no idea," I said, withdrawing my hand and examining it, looking to see if it had changed too. I was glad to see it was still solid.

"I bet it has something to do with that microwave?" Harvey declared.

"What makes you think that?"

"Look at it," he pointed.

Like everything else that was around us, the microwave was also affected by whatever was going on. Because of that, I had to get closer to where it was to see what Harvey was pointing at.

"I think you're right," I agreed.

On the glass door of the microwave, a digital countdown had started. Fifty-five minutes remained.

"I don't think that thing is a microwave," I said, "It may have been at one time but now it's something else."

"What do you think happened?" Harvey asked.

"I haven't the slightest clue," I said, "But there might be a way to find out."

I walked across the kitchen and into the dining room, avoiding touching any of the walls or furniture. Even though it was all intangible, I didn't want to be walking through something if it suddenly became solid again.

"Where are you going?" Not wanting to be left behind Harvey followed me.

"I was going to have a look outside," I pointed at the image of the blinds that were covering the sliding glass door.

"Why?" he replied.

"To see what's out there."

"We can see through the fucking walls." Harvey made a sweeping gesture with his hand, "If there were something out there, we'd be able to see it."

He was right. If there were something out there, we'd be able to see it. The only thing we could see was a vast gray emptiness. The house that once surrounded mine were gone.

"I still want to check," I said.

I took a deep breath and stuck my foot through the blinds and sliding glass door, testing to make sure the ground was there. I sighed in relief when I felt a hard, flat surface beneath my foot.

"It's safe," I said, before stepping fully out of the house.

Harvey joined me a moment later.

"What the fuck is this place?" He gazed at the nothingness around us.

"I've been thinking about that," I said, "I think that the microwave may have sent us into another dimension."

"Another dimension?" Harvey repeated.

"Or maybe a liminal space."

"What the hell is a liminal space?" He turned to me for an answer.

"It's…," I had to stop and think of how best to describe it in a way that would be easy for Harvey to understand. I settled on saying, "It's a place between places."

"Like a pocket dimension?" he asked, "I read about one of those in a comic book once."

"Yeah, sort of like that," I agreed. It was a good enough definition for me.

"HELLO!" Harvey suddenly called out, "ANYBODY THERE!"

I didn't expect any kind of a reply, which is why I was shocked when his words were repeated back at us several times, but not as an echo. The repeated words didn't sound anything like Harvey. They were distorted and varied in pitch from very high to very low.

"That's creepy," I said, "We should probably go back inside." I made a move to return to the house.

"Hold up," Harvey held his hand out for me to wait, tilting his head to the side, listening to something, "Do you hear that?"

I stopped and listened. At first, I didn't hear anything, then I started to hear a rapid clicking sound. It was very faint, but growing louder.

"What is that?" I whispered.

"Did your family ever have a dog?" Harvey asked.

"No, what does that have to do with anything?"

"Whenever my dog needed his nails clipped, he would make a sound like that when he ran across the tiled floor," he explained.

The sudden image of a vicious dog running towards us filled my mind. That was quickly replaced by the image of bodies mauled beyond recognition as I recalled the article Harvey had shown me.

"What's wrong?" Harvey asked when he saw the look of dread descend upon my face.

"Remember that article you showed me?" I said. "The one about the family that was massacred. The one who used to own the microwave."

"Yeah."

"I think we're about to find out what happened to them."

HIGHWAY TO HELL

"What're you doing in here, Josh?" my father asked after finding me in the garage behind the house.

"I was just looking at the car." I pointed at his 1973 red pepper Ford Falcon. The car my mother claimed he loved more than her.

The Falcon was in pristine condition and looked like it had just rolled off the assembly line. Its red paint and chrome fixtures always looked freshly polished. The car was originally owned by my grandfather, but he gave the car to my father for his 18th birthday. My 18th birthday was the next day, and I was hoping my father would continue the tradition and hand the car off to me.

I never mentioned that to him though. I was afraid he'd laugh at the idea, crushing my dreams of one day sliding behind the wheel and hearing her engine roar as I pressed down on the gas pedal. I'd rather hold onto the fantasy that it would one day be mine for as long as I could.

"She's a beauty, isn't she," my father said, lightly running his hand along the edge of the roof.

"She really is," I agreed.

The two of us admired the car in silence for a moment before I remembered what day it was.

"Are you taking her out?" I asked.

I would be surprised if he didn't. He took the car out like clockwork every three months and never missed a trip. I once asked my mother where he went when he left because he was usually gone all weekend, but she just shrugged her shoulders.

My father walked around the car to come stand beside me. He placed his arm around my shoulder and held out the keys to the car with his free hand, "We're taking her out," he said.

"Are you serious?" I asked, reaching out to take the keys from him. I felt like I was in a dream and would wake up disappointed at any moment.

"Absolutely," he replied, releasing his hold on me and walking over to the passenger side of the car.

"Right now?"

"Do you have something more important to do?" He opened the car door and got in.

"No," I shook my head, opening the door and easing myself down into the driver's seat. "Should I text Mom and tell her I'm going with you?" I slid my phone out of the back pocket of my jeans.

"I already told her we were going for a ride," he said, "Plus, that won't work in here." He pointed at my phone.

I looked down at the phone and used my thumb to press the button on the side of it, trying to wake it up, but nothing happened.

That's weird, I thought. The battery shouldn't be dead, it was over 90% full when I walked into the garage.

"Put it away," my father said, a slight smile tugging at the corner of his lips. "You won't be needing it."

I turned to face him, expecting him to give me an explanation for why the phone wasn't working, but he ignored me and instead said, "Start her up," nodding towards the steering column as he talked.

I put the phone back into my pocket and then slide the key into the ignition. The engine roared to life when I turned the key.

My father reached up and tapped the button on the garage door opener that was clipped to the visor above my head.

"Where are we going?" I asked, wrapping my fingers around the leather steering where cover.

"That's a good question," my father replied.

He leaned forward, opened the glove compartment, and pulled out what appeared to be a brand-new map.

"Looks like we're going to Tennessee." He turned the map towards me so I could see it for myself.

"Tennessee?" I was surprised by his response. The Tennessee state line was at least a four-hour drive. I thought we'd be staying in town. "Why Tennessee?" I asked.

"Because that's what the map says," was his response.

"Where in Tennessee?" I wasn't going to argue with him. If he said we were going to Tennessee, then that's where we were going. I didn't want him to change his mind about letting me drive.

My father unfolded the map and studied it for a moment, "Duncan Hollow." He placed his finger on a part of the map that looked like it'd been circled with a red ink pen.

"Duncan Hollow, here we come," I declared, putting the car in reverse and easing it out of the garage.

Ten minutes later we were on the interstate, heading to Tennessee.

***

I was surprised at how calm my dad was about letting me drive his car. I figured he'd be a nervous wreck, constantly making comments about how careful I needed to be, but he never said a word. He just sat there staring out the window, seeming to enjoy the ride.

"Do you mind if I put on some music?" I asked, reaching out for the knob of the radio.

"Go right ahead," he said.

I turned the knob until it clicked. The speakers started blaring out a heavy metal guitar riff.

"Sorry," I quickly apologized, reaching out for the tuning dial, "I'll see if there's anything else on."

Even though I liked what I was hearing, I didn't think my dad wanted to listen to that kind of music.

"Don't bother," he said, "That radio won't play anything else."

I ignored him and began turning the dial, looking for something else to listen to, but the music never changed. No matter how far to the left or right I moved the tuner, the music remained the same.

"Is it broken?" I asked.

"Nope," he shook his head, "She just has a very specific taste in music." He patted the dashboard as he spoke.

The engine suddenly revved loudly as the car lurched forward, but I hadn't pressed my foot down on the gas.

My dad made an amused sound in his throat when he saw me looking down at my feet, trying to see if I had accidentally done something wrong to cause the car to react that way.

"What's so funny?" I cast a quick look in his direction, not wanting to take my eyes off the road.

"You've got a lot to learn about this car," was his cryptic reply.

"It wasn't funny," I snapped at him, "I could've lost control."

The smirk that appeared on my father's face annoyed me. I was trying to be serious while he was acting like it was all a joke.

"You were never in danger of losing control," he said.

"I wouldn't be so sure of that." I tightened my trembling fingers on the steering wheel.

When the car lurched forward, there was a moment of panic where I almost jerked the wheel to the side, thinking we were about to drive off the road.

"I'm serious," he said, "Watch this."

Before I could react, my father reached over and grabbed the steering wheel, yanking it as hard as he could in his direction.

I freaked out and raised my arms in front of my face, thinking we were about to crash. But the car only swerved slightly in the direction he pulled the wheel before returning to its original position in the lane. I was jostled a little. That was all that happened.

"You asshole!" I yelled at him, lightly punching him on the shoulder before returning my hand to the steering wheel. My heart was beating so hard that I could feel the beats in my fingertips. "Are you trying to kill us?"

"She's a smart car," he said with a smile, amused at my overreaction, "If she thinks you're about to lose control, she'll take over and keep you on the road."

"It has an ADS?" I asked. That was the acronym for the automated driving system. "When did you install that?" I wondered, thinking it had to have been expensive.

The more I thought about how much it had to cost, the more it pissed me off. If he could afford an ADS for the car, he could've gotten me the new PlayStation I wanted for Christmas.

"It came with the car," was his reply.

I knew he was lying. Cars built in the 70s didn't come with automated driving systems. ADS technology was still being developed at the time and it certainly wasn't as sophisticated as I'd just seen. I figured it was just his way of telling me to drop it, so I did.

I considered asking him if he'd added any other upgrades to the car, but I decided against it. He seemed to enjoy my surprise at discovering what the car could do and wasn't likely to reveal anything else until he felt it appropriate.

Sensing my thoughts, my dad turned to me and said, "Let's just enjoy the ride."

So that's what I did. I leaned back in the seat, turned up the music, and drove toward our destination.

***

"We're in Tennessee," I declared a couple of hours later, pointing at the large blue sign that welcomed us as we crossed the state line.

My dad, who'd fallen asleep, cracked his eyes open and looked around.

"That was fast," he yawned.

"Are you going to tell me where we're going so that I know which exit to take?" I turned and looked at him briefly.

"The car knows," my dad said.

As if on cue, the right-turn blinker came on. I looked down at the dashboard, wondering why it had come on and knowing that I hadn't touched it.

"Take this next exit," my dad pointed.

I quickly changed lanes and took the indicated exit, curving back around toward the overpass we'd just driven under.

"Which way now?" I asked as I approached the light.

Before my dad could respond, the left-turn blinker came on.

"Left it is," I declared. Once we were heading in the right direction, I asked, "How is the car doing this? Is it part of the ADS or is it some kind of GPS?" I assumed it was the latter and that my dad had already programmed our destination into it.

My dad took a deep breath and let it with a sigh, "It's neither," he said, "It's the car."

I was about to call him out for being vague and not wanting to tell me anything about the car and the modifications he'd made to it, but he stopped me with a raised hand.

"It really is the car," he insisted, "And before I hand her over to you, there are some things you need to know about her."

"You're giving me the car?" I gasped. Even though I was hoping he'd give me the car for my 18th birthday, I was still surprised to hear him say that. A part of me thought that he'd never part with the car.

"That's the plan," he said, "But it all depends on how this trip goes."

"Where are we going?" I assumed he'd had this entire trip planned out before I even walked into the garage this morning.

"To see your grandfather," my dad replied.

"Grandpa Ben? I thought he lived in Texas."

Grandpa Ben was my grandfather on my mother's side.

"Grandpa Max," my dad corrected.

"Grandpa Max." I was shocked to hear that name, "I thought you said he was dead."

I hadn't seen Grandpa Max since I was 5 or 6 years old and didn't remember much about him. All I remember is that he stopped coming around one day and when I asked where he was, my parents told me he was dead. I wasn't very attached to the old man at the time, but I was still sad to hear that he was gone.

"He up and left us without a word," my dad explained, "For all intents and purposes, he was dead to us."

"Why'd he leave?"

My dad gave me a somber look before replying, "I can't answer that without telling you about the car first," he sighed.

I got the impression that he was carrying a great weight upon his shoulders and he was about to unburden himself. That thought made me uncomfortable because my dad was never forthcoming about anything. I wasn't sure I wanted to hear what he had to say, especially after having such a great morning so far.

"What about the car?" I asked.

Was it stolen? Involved in an accident that killed someone?

Those were the first two thoughts that ran through my mind when my dad told me he needed to talk to me about the car first. Why else would he say that if there wasn't some sort of stigma attached to it? Whatever it was, it apparently involved my grandfather, and if that's why he disappeared, it couldn't be good.

"This car has been in our family for a long time," my dad said.

"Fifty years," I blurted out, knowing the car was given to him by my grandfather, who I figured had bought the car the day it rolled off the assembly line.

"She's been in the family a lot longer than that," he replied.

I turned and looked at him, wondering how that was possible. As far as I knew, the car was a 1973 Ford Falcon. That would make it fifty years old.

"What do you mean?" I asked him to clarify.

The car blinker came on and my dad waited for me to take the indicated turn before answering.

"She's not a Ford Falcon," he said.

"What?" I was shocked to hear him say that. Especially since he's been telling me and everywhere else who's asked that it was a Ford Falcon.

My dad reached into his back pocket to retrieve his wallet, opened it, and pulled out a folded photograph. He unfolded the photo and showed it to me. It was a picture of my grandfather leaning up against a 1957 Chevy Corvette Super Sport. I'd seen the photo before.

"That's the car Grandpa sold to buy this one, right?" That's the story he'd told me when I first asked about the car over a decade ago.

"He didn't sell it," my dad shook his head, "It's the same car."

His comment confused me.

"I'm not following," I said.

"The car in this photo," he tapped his finger on the Corvette, "Is the same car you're driving right now."

I opened my mouth to tell him that I didn't understand how that was possible, but he cut me off with a raised hand.

"I know that doesn't make any sense," my dad said, "But it's the truth. This car isn't a…" He paused as he tried to think of the right word to say, "…it isn't a real car. It's something else."

I didn't know how to respond to that, so I just stared at him.

"I had the same reaction when your grandfather told me about the car," he said, "I didn't believe him either…not at first."

"What do you mean it's something else?" I asked.

"It's alive." I could tell from the way he was looking at me that he seriously believed that.

"That's impossible," I scoffed at the idea.

"I know it's hard to believe, but it's true. You'll see," he said.

"Why are you telling me all of this now?"

"Because when you turn eighteen tomorrow, the car will be yours," he said, "But first, you have to prove that you're fit to be her driver."

"Is that what this trip is about?" I asked, "To see how well I drive?"

"In a way," my dad confirmed, "I'll explain the rest when we get to your grandfather's house."

"Why can't you just explain it to me now?" I didn't like how cryptic he was being.

The car engine revved loudly, interrupting us.

"Because she doesn't want me to," my dad replied, "Not yet."

I assumed that was the end of the conversation for now and turned my eyes to the passing scenery, trying to focus on something other than all the questions running through my mind.

***

"Five more miles," my dad declared, pointing at the sign on the side of the road. It was the first thing he'd said in almost an hour.

I got a sinking feeling in the pit of my stomach and gripped the steering wheel a little bit tighter. The prospect of seeing my grandfather for the first time in over twelve years was making me feel anxious.

"What's he like?" I asked.

"Who?" My dad was momentarily confused by the question.

"Grandpa Max," I clarified.

"Oh, him," he replied, "He's old." I couldn't tell if it was meant as a joke or an insult.

I considered asking him to elaborate, but decided against it. If he felt like reminiscing about my grandfather, he would've had more to say about him.

Ten minutes later, the car blinker came on. At first, I thought it was a mistake, but then I saw the entrance to a dirt road and figured that must be where I was supposed to go.

I turned onto the road, drove a couple hundred feet, and then had to stop.

"Now what?" I asked, gesturing at the locked gate that was blocking our path.

"Give me a second," my dad said as he started to get out of the car.

Once outside, he came around to my side of the car and tapped on the glass.

"Come here," he motioned for me to get out, "I want to show you something."

I got out and walked to the back of the car where he was waiting for me.

"If you ever find yourself in a situation where you need a tool, all you have to do is open the trunk," he explained.

"Do you need me to pop it open?" I asked while gesturing at it.

"No need." He reached out and rapped his knuckle on the outside of the trunk. A moment later, it popped open on its own.

When I looked inside, the trunk was completely empty except for a pair of bolt cutters lying in the center of the mat. My dad picked up the bolt cutters and then walked over to the gate and cut the lock off. When he was done, he pulled the gate open and then returned to the back of the car where I was waiting.

"I take it Grandpa Max doesn't know we're coming," I said.

"Not exactly," my dad replied as he tossed the bolt cutters back into the trunk and shut it, "Let's get going before he figures it out." He nodded for me to get back into the car.

I followed the dirt road until we came to another locked gate that was adorned with crucifixes of various shapes and sizes, from plain to garishly ornate.

"What's with all of the crosses?" I gestured at the gate. As I did so, I noticed that crosses had also been nailed to the trees on either side of the dirt road for as far as I could see. "Is Grandpa Max some kind of religious nut?"

"Hell no," my dad scoffed at the thought, "This is just some lame attempt to keep us out." He flicked his hand at the gate.

"Keep us out?" I was confused, "Why would he want to keep us out?"

"Because he thinks the car is evil," he replied as he got out of the car.

"Is it evil?" I asked.

"Hold tight," he said, ignoring my question, "I'll get the gate open." He shut the door and walked to the back of the car to retrieve the bolt cutters.

I watched from the car as he cut the chain locking the gate and pushed it open before returning the bolt cutters to the trunk.

"Alright, let's go," he motioned for me to start driving.

I eased the car through the gate, heading straight for the house.

"Stop here," my dad instructed.

"Now what?" I asked after we were parked.

"Now, we wait," my dad said while keeping his eyes on the front door of the old house.

We didn't have to wait long. A moment later, the front door of the house was thrown open and an old man, who I assumed to be my Grandpa Max, came storming out with a shotgun in his hands.

Grandpa Max cocked the shotgun and pointed it at my dad. "What're you doing here, Rus?" he called out.

"Stay in the car," my dad said to me before stepping outside. Once he was out of the car, he stood behind the open door, leaning on it while he talked to my grandfather.

Grandpa Max kept the gun trained on my dad the entire time.

"You know why I'm here," my dad called back.

"It's too soon, I've still got a year," Grandpa Max said.

I had no idea what they were talking about, but it was obvious that whatever it was had been set into motion a long time ago.

"Actually, you don't," my dad replied, "Josh's 18th birthday is tomorrow."

I didn't like that I was being dragged into whatever was going on between the two of them.

"You son of a bitch!" Grandpa Max yelled, "You lied to me!" Then he fired the shotgun at my dad.

Fearing for my life, I yelped and ducked down behind the wheel.

My dad must have been expecting the violent reaction because he jumped back into the car and shut the door right before Grandpa Max pulled the trigger.

"He's shooting at us!" I gasped, thinking we were going to die.

"Don't worry," my dad didn't sound upset about being shot at, "He can't hurt us in here."

Outside, Grandpa Max continued his litany of insults directed at my dad, punctuating each one with a blast from his shotgun.

Surprisingly, at least to me, the car seemed to be unharmed. I expected the windshield to burst apart at any moment, showering us with glass, but that never happened.

"Why is he so mad?" I asked between shotgun blasts.

"Because he thought you were turning 17 this year," my dad replied without looking at me.

"Why is he upset about that?"

My dad ignored me, keeping his eyes on Grandpa Max.

"Dad?" I tried to get his attention.

"The gun's empty," he suddenly declared, rushing out of the car.

I sat there dumbfounded as I watched my dad run across the yard and tackle my grandfather. The two of them struggled for a few minutes until my dad was able to pin Grandpa Max to the ground.

"Josh!" my dad yelled for me. I rolled down the window so I could hear him better. "Get the rope from the trunk."

"What rope?" I hollered back. I hadn't seen any rope in the trunk when my dad opened it to get the bolt cutters.

"It's there," my dad grunted as he fought to keep my grandfather pinned to the ground, "Open the trunk and you'll see it."

"Don't do it, Josh!" Grandpa Max cried out.

I got out and walked to the back of the car, finding the trunk already open. When I looked inside, I expected to see the bolt cutters and nothing else. But the bolt cutters were gone. Now the only thing in the trunk was a length of coiled rope.

"You really are alive, aren't you?" As insane as that sounded, I was starting to believe all the crazy shit my dad had told me about the car.

The car honked twice in reply, confirming the thought.

I carried the rope over to my dad, then stood back and watched as he hogtied Grandpa Max. Before he finished, he pulled an old handkerchief out of my grandfather's coveralls and shoved it into his mouth to quiet him.

"You know the rules, old man," my dad said to Grandpa Max as he got to his feet and dusted himself off.

I had no idea what that meant, but it was easy to see it wasn't a good thing.

"What're you going to do with him?" I asked.

"I'm not going to do anything," my dad said, walking over and handing me the end of the rope, "You are."

"What?"

I didn't want to be an active participant in whatever was going to happen, it was bad enough having to witness it.

"This is the true test to see if you're worthy to drive the car," my dad declared. "He had to do it." He gestured at Grandpa Max, "I had to do it," he gestured at himself, "And now you have to do it." He gestured at me.

"Do what?" I had to force the question out.

My dad held my gaze for a moment before answering, "You have to feed your grandfather to the car." He pointed at the Ford Falcon which was slowly driving itself across the yard towards us.

"What?!" That was insane. I wasn't going to feed Grandpa Max to the car. "I can't do that." I dropped the rope and shook my head.

"If you don't," my dad warned, "It's you who will be fed to the car." When he saw the look of shock on my face, he spread his arms and said, "I didn't make the rules, son, I just follow them."

I looked down at my grandfather, struggling on the ground to free himself. When he saw me looking at him, he tried to speak, but I couldn't understand him because of the gag my dad had put in his mouth.

"Don't feel sorry for him," my dad said, "He did the same thing to his grandfather, and he also had no problem helping me feed my grandfather to the car."

Behind me, the car's engine revved as she lurched forward. When I looked back, her hood was open, allowing me to see the engine compartment, but there was no engine inside. Instead, there was a mass of gears all grinding together like metal teeth.

"Just pick him up and put him inside," my dad instructed, "The car will do the rest."

When I didn't make a move to comply, he walked up to me and placed his hand on my shoulder.

"One of you has to go," he said, "And I'd much rather it be him," he nodded at Grandpa Max.

I believed him and since I didn't want to be the one ground to a pulp by the car, I picked up the rope and used it to drag Grandpa Max closer to the car.

Once I had him in position, I pulled him to his feet and held him upright. He struggled the entire time, but, given how old and frail he was, he wasn't that hard to keep hold of.

"I'm sorry, Grandpa," I whispered. Then I pushed him into the engine compartment where he was quickly pulled into the waiting gears, spraying me with blood and bits of flesh before the car hood slammed shut.

"I knew you could do it!" my dad sounded proud.

"I think I'm going to be sick," I gagged as I tried to shake off the bloody pieces of my grandfather that were clinging to me.

"Let's go inside and get you cleaned up," my dad gestured at the house.

✱✱✱

"Feeling better?" my dad asked after I'd walked out of the bathroom, freshly showered, and wearing some of my grandfather's clothes.

"No, I'm not," I said, "I don't ever want to do anything like that ever again."

"Sorry, kiddo," my dad replied, "But that was just the beginning."

"What?"

"The car needs to eat," he said, "But don't worry, she won't make you kill anyone else you know. And you only have to feed her twice a year."

"What if I can't?"

"You will," he insisted, "I know because I felt the same way you're feeling right now."

"How did you get over it?" I asked, feeling a tremendous amount of guilt weighing upon my shoulders.

"Come on," he motioned for me to follow him outside, "I'll show you."

He took me out to the car where he opened the passenger door and stepped aside.

"Open the glove compartment," he pointed.

I did as he instructed, gasping when I saw the stack of bills inside.

"If you provide for her, she'll provide for you," he smiled.

✱✱✱

"And the rest, as they say, is history," I said to my son, "Does that make you feel any better?"

"A little," he replied.

He was feeling down after having to throw his grandfather, my dad, into the engine compartment of the car, so I told him the story about how my dad and I fed my grandfather to the car.

"Is that why you never told him about me, so he wouldn't know we were coming?" my son asked, "And is that why you stayed away from Mom and me for so long?"

"It is," I nodded.

211

I knew that staying away from him and hiding his existence from my parents meant I'd miss watching him grow up, but I did it to ensure that he had a future. One where I didn't have to feed him to the car.

"I figured your grandfather would run if he knew his time was up," I explained, "And I couldn't risk him finding a way to escape the car."

"What're you going to do when it's your turn?" my son asked.

I shrugged, "I'm sure I'll try and run too, but I've got plenty of time to worry about that later."

TRANSDIMENSIONAL SPACE

"How much further is this place?" my boyfriend, Bryan, asked.

The two of us were on our way to my parent's cabin for a weekend getaway. I was driving for two reasons. The first was because I knew how to get there without having to consult a map app. The second was because Bryan didn't want to bring his precious sports car out into the woods.

When he told me that, I told him that he loved his car more than me. He laughed at the idea and said it wasn't true. But it was true, he did love that car more than he loved me. I was okay with that though. He poured a lot of time and money into keeping it looking like it'd just come off the assembly line and I wasn't going to fault him for having pride in that, even if it was a bit excessive.

"About fifteen more miles," I said, "See that mountain right there," I pointed through the windshield, "The cabin is just on the other side of it."

"There's nothing out here," he complained, "Are you sure I'm going to be able to watch the game on Sunday night?" He looked at his phone, "I don't have any reception."

Bryan was a huge sports fan. The only way I was able to convince him to come away with me for the weekend was to promise him that he'd be able to watch the game from the cabin. That and lots of sex.

I'm not ashamed to admit that I use my body to get Bryan to agree to things he wouldn't otherwise agree to. He's easy like that and it doesn't require much effort on my part.

"Stop worrying," I replied, "The cabin has satellite TV."

"Are you sure it works?" he asked, "You said you haven't been out here since you were 13 years old."

"It works," I assured him, "I have a contract with a rental company. They take care of the place for me and lease it out occasionally. Therefore, it has all the modern amenities."

I'd inherited a few rental properties from my parents when they passed away. They were the reason I didn't have to have a 9-5 job.

"That doesn't sound like a cabin," he said, "It just sounds like a house in the woods."

Bryan wasn't that bright sometimes.

"That's essentially what a cabin is," I explained, "What did you think it was going to be like?"

"I figured it'd be like those movies we watched," Bryan said, "Old and dirty."

He was referring to the *Evil Dead* movie marathon I forced him to watch with me on Halloween.

"Have you ever been out of the city?" I asked. His comment about the cabin made me think he'd been living a very sheltered life.

"You know I have," he sounded annoyed, "You were with me when I went to that car show up north."

"That's not what I meant. I meant out of the city and into nature," I clarified, "Like camping, fishing, hunting, or hiking. Anything like that?"

"Fuck no," he sneered, "Do I look like a redneck to you?" he gestured at himself.

Bryan was the opposite of a redneck. If I had to come up with a term to describe him, it would be *metrosexual*. He cared more about his appearance than I did about mine. Which I was perfectly fine with. Ours was a relationship based solely on appearances. He liked the way I looked, and I liked the way he looked.

"You don't have to be a redneck to enjoy those things," I looked over at him, "But I can see your point."

It wasn't rednecks he was knocking. It was the clothing normally associated with outdoor activities that he was putting down. He considered anyone who dressed like that a redneck.

We drove the rest of the way in silence. I used the time to enjoy the scenery of the mountain drive while Bryan messed around on his phone.

***

"We're here," I declared, slowing down so I could turn onto the winding drive that led up to the cabin.

"Holy shit," Bryan gasped, "That's your cabin?" He was amazed at the size of the place.

When I told him about the cabin, I was intentionally vague about its size, which is why he assumed it would be nothing more than a shack in the woods. I wanted to surprise him and, judging by his reaction, it worked.

"That's it," I replied with a smile, pulling to the side of the cabin, and parking the car.

The cabin was a 2500 square foot, all-wood, A-frame structure with 3 bedrooms and a wide deck that ran around the perimeter of it.

"That's a lot of windows," Bryan remarked as he got out of the car.

He was referring to the fact that the entire front of the house was nothing more than a dozen panes of tinted glass. It was designed that way so you could sit anywhere in the cabin and have a great view of the wooded mountainside. I didn't bother explaining that to Bryan because it wasn't something he cared about.

"Just wait until you see the hot tub," I said. That was something I knew he'd be interested in.

"There's a hot tub?"

I nodded, "It's in the back."

"I didn't bring any shorts," was his reply.

"We're in the middle of nowhere," I gestured with both hands at the mountainous terrain surrounding the cabin, "Why do you need shorts?"

It took him a minute to figure out what I was implying. Once he did, he started grinning.

"Come on," I said, "Let's grab our stuff and go inside."

***

Once we got settled, I made us a late dinner, which we ate out on the deck behind the cabin. While we ate, I listened to him talk about an upcoming car show he was going to be exhibiting at. I couldn't care less about the show, but I acted interested, asking a question here and there to make him think I was engaged in the conversation.

"Want to see something cool?" I asked Bryan after we'd both finished our meals and he'd finally stopped talking about the car show.

"Depends on what it is?" he replied with a sly smile on his face. It wasn't hard to guess what he was thinking about.

"It's way cooler than that," I replied.

"I don't know if there's anything cooler than that." He looked me up and down, undressing me with his eyes.

"Come on," I ignored his comment and walked to the steps that lead from the deck down into the woods.

"Isn't it too late to go walking in the woods?" he asked, "Maybe we should make it an early night and head up to bed. You can show me in the morning."

"It has to be tonight," I insisted.

I started walking down the steps before he could protest again.

"This better be worth it," he complained, hurrying to catch up to me.

We didn't get fifteen down the trail before Bryan started to whine.

"How much further is it?" He stopped with his hands on his hips, "These shoes weren't meant for hiking."

"It's just around this ridge," I gestured up the trail and kept walking, knowing he didn't want to be left behind, alone in the woods.

He sighed heavily and muttered, "It better be," and started walking again, although his pace was much slower than before.

Ten minutes later, I stepped into a circular clearing at the bottom of the valley.

"We're here," I declared, spreading my arms wide and turning in a circle.

"Seriously," Bryan growled, "This is what you wanted to show me, a patch of dirt?"

"No, not this," I said, reaching into my pocket and pulling out a small metallic disc, "This." I held the disc out so Bryan could see it.

"What's so great about that?"

"This is a beacon," I explained, "When I run my finger around the edge of it like this," I ran my finger along the edge of the disc as I spoke, "It emits a signal, broadcasting my location."

"I still don't see what's so great about that?" Bryan sneered.

"It was given to me when I was fourteen," I continued, ignoring his question, "And this is the first and last time I will ever use it."

"I don't care about your stupid little toy and whatever it does. You could've showed me it back at the cabin." He turned and started to walk back toward the trail, "I'm going back."

"Wait," I called out.

He stopped but didn't turn around.

"Don't you want to know who gave it to me?"

"Not really." He continued walking.

Before he could make it back to the trail, the clearing was suddenly illuminated by a bright light.

"You're going to find out whether you want to or not," I smiled as the light intensified, making it impossible for us to see one another.

***

"Where am I?" Bryan groaned.

He was completely naked and covered by a form-fitting membrane that kept him bound to the floating metal table he was lying on.

I, also naked, was sitting on the table next to him when he woke up.

"Why can't I move?" he struggled to sit up.

"The answer to your first question is that you're on a spaceship," I answered, "Cool, right? The answer to your second question is you are bound to one of the exam tables in the ship's medical bay."

Bryan turned his head to look at me.

"Get me out of here," he tried to push against the membrane, "This isn't funny."

"Of course it isn't funny. This isn't a joke," I said, "This is the end of your privileged life as you know it."

I hopped off the table I was on and approached his.

"Remember when I told you that you were the one I wanted to spend the rest of my life with?"

Even though he was confused by the question, he still nodded his head.

"I wasn't really talking about you, I was talking about your body," I cupped his membrane-covered crotch with my hand.

Behind me, a door appeared on the wall, allowing three short gray aliens with bulbous heads and big eyes to enter the room.

"What the fuck are those?" Bryan began to whimper.

"They're my friends," I replied, "They're the ones who gave me the beacon. They promised to help me when I found the right host."

"Host? What host?" Bryan asked, "What the hell does that even mean?"

"Have you ever felt like a stranger in your own body?" I said, circling the table as I talked, "Of course, you haven't," I answered for him, "I've never seen anyone more in love with themself than you are. I can't say the same for myself," I gestured at my breasts and the tuft of hair between my legs, "I've known from an early age that I was in the wrong body.", "These aren't the parts I'm supposed to have." I pointed at him, "I was supposed to be like you."

"I don't understand," Bryan said.

Of course, you don't, you pea-brained idiot. I thought to myself.

"This cover girl image you love so much," I made a circular motion around my face with my hand, "It was all just an act and I hated every second of it. The only reason I did it was so that I could have what you have. What you take for granted."

"You're insane," he spat the words out.

The tallest of the three gray aliens came over and placed his hand on the side of my head. That was how they communicated with me.

Urgency!

The alien didn't say a word but instead filled my mind with images relating to the need for them to hurry. They could only stay in the atmosphere for a limited amount of time without risking being exposed.

I first met the aliens when I went for a hike through the woods when I was fourteen years old. They took me up to their ship, examined me, and became intrigued by my plight when I told them I was a girl trapped in a boy's body. They offered to "change" me, but I declined when they explained that the changes would only be cosmetic.

"I want to be a real boy," I remember saying to them.

The three aliens stepped aside and seemed to confer with one another without speaking, before returning their attention to me.

There is a way. The tallest one showed me images of how the procedure would be done.

I readily agreed and returned home with a new purpose in life. To find the perfect male host for my consciousness.

Ten years later, I'd found that male specimen and was ready to become the man I'd always dreamed of, Minus all his negative personality traits, of course.

The process was a simple one. The aliens were going to transfer my consciousness into his body and his consciousness into my body like in that old movie *Freaky Friday*. Only this time, the swap would be permanent.

"It's time to say goodbye," I said to Bryan, climbing back up on the empty table and lying down.

"Let me go!" Bryan demanded, renewing his efforts to free himself, "You can't do this!"

"They can and they will. But don't worry," I said, "It won't hurt and you won't remember any of this."

That was the truth. After Bryan was moved into my body, the aliens were going to give him a permanent case of amnesia. Then I would set about taking over Bryan's life. I would be a much better friend than he ever was, a better son, and when the time was right, a better boyfriend.

Meanwhile, he would get to know what it was like being stuck in a body that didn't feel right.

CONVENIENCE

Todd took his hand off the steering wheel and placed it on my thigh, giving it a less-than-gentle squeeze.

"You thinking what I'm thinking?" he asked, moving his hand up my leg and pushing my skirt up along with it.

You didn't have to be a mind reader to know what was on his mind.

"No, I'm not!" I pulled my leg away and moved as close to the passenger door as my seat belt would allow, "The only thing I'm thinking about is getting home and going to bed."

Todd had offered to drive me home from a party we were both at when Tanya, the person I was supposed to be getting a ride with, left with her new boyfriend to go hook up at his house.

"Don't be like that," Todd pouted, "I heard about what you did for Brad when he gave you a ride home last week."

"Brad?" I scoffed, "I've never gotten a ride with Brad anywhere and I never will."

Brad was your typical jock asshole who thought all the girls in school wanted to be him. I thought Todd wasn't like that, but apparently, I was wrong.

"That's not what he's telling everyone," Todd said, reaching his hand out to touch me again.

Not wanting to be continuously pawed at, I grabbed his hand and pushed it away while snapping at him to stop. In the process, I accidentally bent his pinky finger back.

"You fucking idiot!" he hissed at me, "That hurt!"

"Sorry," I apologized.

I didn't mean to hurt him. I just wanted him to stop touching me.

Todd suddenly pulled the car over to the side of the road and parked. When I looked out the window, all I could see were trees, which meant we were still a few miles away from town.

"I think you owe me more than an apology," he said, unbuckling his seatbelt.

"Uh…No, I don't." I quickly unbuckled my seatbelt and started to get out of the car. I didn't care that we were out in the middle of nowhere. I just knew that I had to get as far away from Todd as possible.

"Where are you going?" he lunged across the seat and grabbed my arm, yanking me back into the car before I could get away.

"Stop!" I cried out, trying to pull my arm free, "That hurts!"

Todd ignored me and kept trying to drag me over to his side of the car.

"Let go of me!" I snarled.

When he didn't release me, I spun in my seat, pulled my knees up to my chest, and then kicked out at him. One of my feet connected with his nose, knocking his head back in the process.

The action had the desired result. He released me.

I dragged myself backward out of the car, tumbling to the rocky ground, scraping my elbows in the process.

"YOU FUCKING BITCH!" Todd yelled, "I THINK YOU BROKE MY NOSE." His voice sounded garbled like he was talking with his mouth full.

"You deserved it," I spat at him.

Saying that was a mistake. It only made him madder.

"YOU'RE FUCKING DEAD." He sounded like an animal.

I pulled myself to my feet and ran into the woods, trying to get as far away from him as possible. Behind me, I heard Todd get out of the car and retrieve something from the trunk before following behind me.

He must've thought I wouldn't be able to get very far ahead of him because he didn't seem to be in a hurry to catch up to me. That allowed me to gain a significant head start, but it also meant I was getting further and further away from the road into a heavily wooded area that I was unfamiliar with.

I kept running, never slowing down until I stepped on a loose rock and twisted my ankle. I tried to catch myself before I fell, but all I succeeded in doing was throwing my center of balance off, sending me crashing to the ground anyway.

As I lay there on my back, trying to catch my breath, I scanned the woods behind me, looking for Todd. He wasn't very hard to find. I could see the beam of his flashlight bobbing through the woods several hundred feet away from where I lay.

"YOU CAN RUN BUT YOU CAN'T HIDE, BITCH," Todd called out, "I'LL FIND YOU EVENTUALLY AND WHEN I DO YOU'RE DEAD."

That's when I realized I'd left an easy trail of footprints and broken branches in my wake as I fled. With his flashlight, it was easy for Todd to follow behind me without having to hurry.

I pulled myself to my feet and leaned against a nearby tree, trying to be as quiet as I could as I weighed my options. I could keep running deeper into the woods and hope Todd gave up or I could double back to the road and try to flag someone down.

I looked further into the woods to see what lay before me. I couldn't see much, but I did see a light in the distance. It was too far away to see what the light belonged to, but that didn't matter to me. A light meant that there might be a road or a house nearby.

Heading toward the light seemed like my best option so that's what I did, only this time I didn't run, I walked as quickly and quietly as I could, trying to disturb the ground and surrounding brush as little as possible.

***

It took me about fifteen minutes to make it to the light and, when I did, I started regretting my decision to follow it.

"This doesn't make sense," I said to myself, stepping out of the woods and into the asphalt parking area in front of the convenience store whose exterior light had lured me in.

It didn't make sense because there were no roads leading to the convenience store or away from it. It was just sitting there in the middle of the woods.

"Self Mart," I read the name of the store that was painted on the awning outside, "Helping you help yourself." That last part was printed in smaller letters beneath the store's name. I assumed that was their slogan.

I approached the entrance doors and peered inside. The place had all the fixtures of a convenience store, but none of the products. I got the impression that it had been abandoned, but it didn't look old or run down like you'd expect it to be.

When I turned and looked toward the checkout area, I saw a middle-aged man standing behind the counter, dressed in a white button-up shirt with a patch on the breast that featured the Self-Mart logo. Below the logo was the name Chance.

Seeing him standing there in the otherwise empty building startled me.

He smiled when he saw my reaction and motioned for me to enter the store.

I turned around and looked back at the woods.

"I KNOW YOU'RE OUT HERE SOMEWHERE," Todd Taunted, "AND I WON'T STOP UNTIL I FIND YOU." He sounded a lot closer than he was the last time I stopped.

"Fuck it," I sighed, pushing my way into the store, hoping I wasn't going from one bad situation into another.

"Welcome to Self-Mart," Chance greeted me. I assumed that was his name since it was embroidered on his patch.

"What is this place?" I asked, looking from him to the empty shelves and then back again.

"This is Self Mart," Chance declared, spreading his arms, "The one-stop shop for those in need."

"Do you have a phone I can use?" When I fled from Todd, I left my purse sitting on the floorboard of his car, inside which was my phone. Otherwise, I would've already called the police.

"I'm afraid not," he replied, "Even if I did, help wouldn't arrive soon enough to save you. You're going to have to stop Todd yourself if you want to survive."

"What?" His comment shocked me, "How did you know Todd was chasing me?"

Chance gestured at a small TV bolted to the ceiling in the corner behind him, "I've been watching you." As he spoke, the television screen came to life and started showing a video of Todd and me driving away from the party. The view was from inside the car.

"How did you get that?" I pointed at the screen and backed away from the counter toward the doors.

The only way he could have recorded that video was if he'd placed a camera in Todd's car and that meant he must know Todd.

"The how isn't as important as the why," he replied.

"Fine, then tell me why you have it," I jabbed my finger at the TV as I took another step back toward the doors.

"To help you," he said, "Didn't you see our slogan on the sign outside?" Chance gestured, "Helping you help yourself."

"If you really wanted to help me," I said, "You'd call the cops."

"That's not what we do here at Self-Mart," Chance explained, "There are rules I must follow as an employee of the company."

"There's a guy out there who wants to kill me," I jerked my thumb over my shoulder, "And you're telling me that there's nothing you can do to stop him."

After I said that, I wondered why Todd hadn't stumbled upon the convenience store yet. He wasn't that far behind me.

"He won't find you here," he said when he saw me looking through the glass doors at the woods outside, "This Self-Mart location is here for you, not him. As long as you're inside, you're safe."

"If that's true, then I can just stay here with you until morning." It wasn't the best option, but it was better than taking my chances with Todd out in the woods.

"You can stay for about twenty more minutes," Chance replied, "Then I have to close up the shop and head home."

"If you're leaving, you can take me with you," I said, "You can drop me off in town and then I can call someone to come pick me up."

"I can't," he sighed, "As I've already told you, there are rules I must follow. One of those rules, the most important one, is that I cannot take any kind of action on your behalf. I can only inform you of your fate and tell you what you need to do to change it."

"What kind of crazy bullshit is that?" I snapped at him. "What kind of man refuses to help someone in need?"

Chance's face hardened, prompting me to take a step back, "I never said I was a man," he said.

I opened my mouth to reply, but the cold look in his eyes stopped me.

"Watch," he commanded, raising his finger to point at the TV screen.

It was clear that he was starting to lose patience with me.

I lifted my head and looked at the screen, watching as it showed a montage of scenes of Todd killing me in a variety of different ways.

"That's not real," I said. It couldn't be. I was standing right there, alive and well.

"Not yet, it's not," Chance said, "But that is what's supposed to happen to you tonight. At least, it was until you walked into the Self-Mart."

"What are you?" I knew something was off the moment I saw the convenience store, but I was willing to go with it because it offered me hope. Now, I wasn't sure I had made the right choice.

"I'm a chance to save yourself," he tapped the name on his patch, smiling at his play on words.

"By helping me help myself, right?" I muttered the store's slogan, knowing that would be his answer if I asked him how he was going to help me save myself.

"Now you're getting it," Chance's friendly demeanor had returned.

"Was I really supposed to die tonight?" I was still having a hard time accepting everything even though I'd been presented with plenty of evidence that what Chance was telling me was likely the truth.

"You were," he confirmed, "Until it was decided that you would be given a chance to change your fate." He smiled and gestured at himself, "I am that chance."

"Who decided that?"

"That information is well above my paygrade," Chance replied, "I don't know who makes those decisions, all I know is that when someone is given a chance, I am the one they send."

"What am I supposed to do?" I walked up to the counter and leaned on it, "How do I keep myself from dying?"

"Hand me one of those maps," Chance gestured behind me.

"What maps?" When I entered the convenience store, all the shelves were empty. I assumed they would still be empty when I turned around, but they weren't. Every available shelf was suddenly filled with stacks of folded maps.

I grabbed one of the maps from the nearest stack and set it on the counter between us. Chance unfolded it and then used the palms of his hands to smooth it out and get it to lie flat.

"This is the highway you were traveling on," Chance placed his finger on the map and then moved it along one of the black lines. "And this is where you stopped." He tapped his finger. "From there, you ran into the woods here." He moved his finger away from the road a couple of inches and then stopped, "And this is where you are now."

I'd gotten a lot further away from the road than I thought I had.

"If you want to survive," Chance continued, "You need to make it here before Todd catches you." He slid his finger to the side a couple of inches.

"Why there?" I asked.

"Because that's where you'll find an old abandoned cabin," he replied, "Your only chance at survival lies within it."

"So, all I have to do is make it to the cabin and I'll survive?" That didn't sound too impossible.

"That's not what I said," Chance shook his head, "Getting to the cabin increases your chance of survival, but it doesn't guarantee it."

"Oh," I said, "Well, what…," I was going to ask him what I had to do to guarantee my survival, but Chance anticipated the question and cut me off.

"There are no guarantees," he said, "And I've told you everything I can. The rest is up to you."

"How many people have you helped like this?"

Chance shrugged, "I don't really know. I haven't been keeping count."

"How many of them have been able to change their fate?"

The expression on his face changed, becoming downcast, "Far less than I'd like," he replied softly.

Before I could say anything else, a buzzer sounded, filling the store with its annoying clamor.

"Thank you for shopping at Self-Mart," Chance said, the smile returning to his face, "It's been a pleasure helping you."

When he finished speaking, there was a rush of air followed by a loud whooshing sound. I closed my eyes for a second and when I opened them, the store was gone and I was lying on my back in the same place where I had fallen before I saw the light of the convenience store.

It was incredibly disorienting.

I got up and looked around, wondering if I had hit my head, and imagined everything.

The beam of a flashlight swept over me briefly then returned, shining directly into my eyes.

"Found you!" Todd cried out triumphantly. He was standing about two hundred feet behind me.

I quickly got my bearings and took off running in the direction Chance said the cabin was.

Please be real! I silently begged.

Todd chased after me.

***

Holy shit! It is real!

I gasped when I saw the cabin nestled on the hillside. If Todd's flashlight hadn't passed over one of the windows, catching its reflection, I never would've seen it.

I changed direction and started running up the hill toward it.

Todd figured out where I was headed and said, "I don't think you're going to find anyone there to help you."

I'd managed to maintain the distance between him and me as I fled through the woods, but I wasn't going to be able to keep it up much longer. I was exhausted. Fear and adrenaline were the only things keeping me going.

Please be unlocked, I thought as I rushed onto the porch of the cabin and over to the door, throwing myself against it.

It didn't budge. I was about to start panicking but stopped myself as a thought popped into my head.

Pull, don't push.

I grabbed the doorknob and yanked on it.

Thank you, thank you, thank you, I sighed in relief when the door creaked open on rusty hinges just far enough for me to squeeze through.

I slipped through the opening and pulled the door closed, immediately turning around and looking for a way to lock it. There wasn't an obvious lock, but there were two metal hooks affixed to the door. It took me a moment to realize I'd seen something similar in a movie once. I needed to find something long enough to put through the hooks to bar the door and keep Todd from getting inside.

I found what I was looking for, conveniently propped up against the wall a few feet away from where I stood, and wasted no time retrieving it.

Todd slammed against the door moments after I slid the length of wood through the hooks, rattling it as he tried to pull it open. The sudden violent action startled me.

"Knock, knock," Todd said after giving up on opening the door, "Anyone home?" he laughed to himself.

I could hear his footsteps on the porch as he started to walk to the side of the cabin, looking for another way in. That was when I turned around and finally took in my surroundings, wanting to make sure there wasn't another way into the cabin.

There wasn't. Beside the door, there were two windows and a fireplace. The fireplace was much too narrow for anyone to get in that way, and the windows were shuttered and barred from the inside.

Confident that I was safe for the moment, I began to walk around the cabin, looking for anything I could use as a weapon to defend myself. That was when I found the skeleton. It was lying on the floor behind a table.

The skeleton belonged to a man. At least I assumed it did, based on the tattered remains of clothing it was wearing.

Behind me, one of the windows shattered. Todd was trying his luck with the shutters, but like the door, he was unable to open them.

That set me back on task.

There has to be something here I can use.

I scanned the interior of the cabin, resuming my search for a weapon. The only thing I saw that might work was a rusty cast-iron skillet that was sitting on a grate in the fireplace, but when I tried to pick it up, I found it to be far too heavy for me to wield.

I turned back and looked at the skeleton.

"How could you live out here without a knife or a gun?" I asked the pile of bones. "I guess you couldn't," I sighed in frustration, "That's probably why you're dead."

The sound of wood splintering drew my eyes to the door.

"Little pig, little pig, let me in!" Todd grunted out the words as he pried at the hinges holding the door in place.

"Shit!" I cursed.

When I looked back at the skeleton, I could see the knobby end of a femur poking through a hole in its jeans.

I could use that as a club.

It looked like it could do some serious damage if I swung it hard enough.

I hurried over to the skeleton and set about freeing the leg bone from the pants.

Behind me, Todd continued working on getting the door open.

"Sorry, not sorry," I grimaced as I shook the bone free from the hip joint. As I did that, a stack of Polaroid photos slipped out of the back pocket of the jeans the skeleton was wearing.

I didn't pick up the photos. I didn't need to. Even though most of them were stained and stuck together, I could see enough of the images to know I didn't want to touch them.

"You sick fuck," I hissed, staring at the naked and bound ladies in the pictures, "I'm glad you're dead."

I pulled my leg back and kicked the skeleton, watching it clatter across the floor. When I looked back at the spot where it had lain, I saw the outline of a square on the floor.

Trapdoor! Maybe this is what I needed to find to increase my chances of survival.

I set the femur down and examined the outline on the floor until I found a notch.

I glanced back at the door and saw that Todd was moments away from breaking in. Out of options, I shoved my fingers into the notch and lifted the trapdoor, revealing a set of wooden steps.

The musty smell of death wafted out of the opening.

Whatever's down there isn't as bad as what's up here, I reminded myself.

I took a deep breath, grabbed the femur, and descended the steps, closing the trapdoor behind me. Up until that point, there was just enough moonlight filtering through the cracks in the roof for me to see by, now I was in absolute darkness.

"You can do this," I whispered, trying to encourage myself to keep going further into the cabin's basement.

There was a loud crash above me as Todd finally managed to break through the door.

I stood in the darkness holding my breath.

"Where'd you go?" I could hear his footsteps on the wooden floor above me as he searched for my hiding place.

He continued to walk around before suddenly stopping.

"What the hell happened to you," he said.

I assumed he'd found the skeleton and was talking to him.

He resumed his pacing a moment later, stopping directly above where I stood below the trapdoor.

"What the hell?" The beam of his flashlight filtered through the cracks of the floor as he shined it on something.

The pictures!

I had left them lying on the floor where they had fallen. That had to be what he had found.

I started to back away from the trapdoor, taking slow, easy steps until I was no longer standing in the pool of light shining through the floor. As I did so, I stumbled into something, making it jangle.

I whirled around.

When I saw what I had bumped into, I clapped a hand over my mouth to stop myself from crying out.

Handcuffed to a post were the skeletal remains of a woman. I had backed into one of her legs, jostling her body and making the handcuffs jangle.

"Found you!" Todd declared. He'd heard the jangling sound and knew I was in the basement.

He swept his flashlight across the floor, looking for the trapdoor. It didn't take him long to find it.

"Looks like you found a friend," Todd squatted next to the opening, shining his flashlight from the skeleton to me while pointing with the tire iron in his other hand.

I raised the femur, holding it like a baseball bat.

"What do you think you're going to do with that?" Todd chuckled as he descended the steps into the basement.

"Stay away from me," I growled, tightening my grip on the femur.

He continued to advance.

"I mean it." I planted my feet.

"That's not going to happen," he smirked, "Not after this," he gestured at his swollen and bloody face.

Hoping to catch him off guard, I stepped forward, swinging the femur with every ounce of strength left in my body.

Todd raised his arm. The femur connected with his elbow. When it did, there was a loud crack.

At first, I thought I had broken Todd's arm, but that wasn't what had caused the sound. The crack came from the femur breaking in half in my hands.

Todd laughed when he realized what had happened.

"My turn," he snarled, raising the tire iron.

I stumbled backward.

In my haste to get away from Todd, I'd forgotten about the skeleton directly behind me. I tripped over it, falling onto my backside. That caused the skeleton's hands to pull free of the handcuffs, toppling it onto me.

Todd laughed at my distress.

As I tried to push the skeleton off me, something swung in front of my face. It was a necklace, affixed to which was a large Celtic knot in the shape of a cross. The bottom of it tapered to a point.

Like a dagger.

I grabbed hold of the cross and yanked on it. Breaking the chain that was around the skeleton's neck.

This is it, I thought, *This is the chance I've been given to save myself.*

I clutched the cross in my hand, doing my best to keep Todd from seeing it.

He reached down, grabbed the skeleton by the arm, and tossed it to the side.

"You two are about to have a lot in common," He grinned.

"You win," I sighed, feigning defeat, "I won't fight you." I lifted the hem of my skirt far enough for him to see the fabric of my underwear.

Todd stopped and stared at me, weighing the truth of my words.

"Take them off," he shined the flashlight in my face while pointing at my underwear with the tire iron.

I hooked my thumbs into the band and pulled them off. When I'd gotten the underwear down to my ankles, Todd knelt in front of me and pulled them the rest of the way off.

The lecherous look on his face sickened me.

"Don't try anything funny," he warned as he set the flashlight and tire iron on the ground next to him.

"I won't," I said, spreading my legs a little to give him the illusion I was cooperating.

He dropped his pants as fast as he could and leaned over me.

That's when I positioned the cross between my fingers and jabbed it into the side of his neck.

Todd jumped back and touched his throat with his hand, when he pulled it away, it was covered in blood.

"What the fuck did you do?" He put his hand back over the wound. Blood flowed freely through his fingers and down his chest.

"I took a chance and saved myself," I said.

MORE CHILLS FROM VELOX BOOKS